Praise for Judy Nedry's
Emma Golden Mysteries

The Man Who Wasn't There

"An unlikely murder occurs at the most prestigious annual gathering of the Oregon wine industry. Emma Golden, a woman of a certain age with an uncanny ability to solve such crimes, goes to work in this third book of the eponymous series by Judy Nedry. Nedry, a longtime wine writer and resident of the Willamette Valley, brings the Oregon wine world to life in vivid detail as the backdrop for Emma's sleuthing."

-- L. Gault

The Difficult Sister

"Do not judge a book by its set-up. Yes, there's an almond croissant on page two, but The Difficult Sister isn't all bakery shops, teas, and polite, innocent snooping...About two-dozen pages in, when the pair of women drive out to the single-wide trailer on Starvation Lane and start mixing it up with Aurora's last known boyfriend, you start to feel that the PG rating of the first few pages is going to change. And you're right...Stuff, as they say, happens. Bullets fly. People die. Evil happens. There will be mud, "one slow sucking step after another". We are a long way from almond croissants and that gives The Difficult Sister an intriguing, palpable edge."

-- Mark Stevens, Author of the Alison Coil mystery series

An Unholy Alliance

"The first of what is now a trilogy that follows a recovering alcoholic writer, Emma Golden, who is working on a book about the wine industry in Oregon (where the author was also an early vintner). Nedry's main character is an accidental detective chasing down the murderer of a showy new winery owner, who isn't a nice person. Emma is funny, pushy and not afraid to step on toes. Light and entertaining."

-- DK

Get a FREE COPY of Emma's first adventure, An Unholy Alliance! Visit https://judynedry.com and use coupon code: BLACKTHORN during checkout.

In loving memory of
Patrick J. Furrer, Rebecca Gabriel, Andy Whipple

Also by Judy Nedry

FICTION

An Unholy Alliance (Emma Golden Mystery #1)
The Difficult Sister (Emma Golden Mystery #2)
The Man Who Wasn't There (Emma Golden Mystery #3)

NONFICTION

Oregon Wine Country
Washington Wine Country

Blackthorn

A Gothic Thriller

BY JUDY NEDRY

Regions Northwest
Publishing

For information contact :
Judy Nedry via https://judynedry.com

Book and cover design by Aaron C. Yeagle
ISBN : 978-0-9651260-3-8

First Edition: March 2019

10 9 8 7 6 5 4 3 2 1

With blackthorn staff
I draw the bound.
All malice and bane
I thus confound.
-- Unknown

JUDY NEDRY

CHAPTER 1

SEPTEMBER 1965

HOT, DRY, DUSTY, AND WONDERFUL! It was everything Sage Blackthorn had hoped the Pendleton Round-Up would be. The dusty air crackled with excitement. Folks milled and greeted one another on the bleachers below, aromas of horse manure, cigarette smoke, leather, and carnival food drifted up to Sage and her brother Ross as they huddled, heads together like conspirators, eating hotdogs and drinking Coca-Cola. Horses whinnied and steers lowed in the distance, and Hank Williams played on the public address system during the brief time out between events.

Already, the two had seen the Indian village, eaten cotton candy, and watched the parade into the arena, complete with a color guard of local sheriff's deputies, Indians in their traditional ceremonial dress, the rodeo queen and her court, and rodeo queens from other rodeos, each queen and her court resplendent in their satin, sequined, and fringed costumes. The kids had seen bareback riding and calf roping. Sage had wanted to cry, she felt so sorry for the terrified animals, but she'd held back as best she could. If she ruined the day with tears, she might not be able to come next time.

Tiny, red-haired Sage, age ten, and taller, blond-haired Ross, thirteen, whispered and giggled and poked each other in the ribs. Sage was too excited to sit still and acted more like six than ten. Mom's new boyfriend, Grant, had just won the saddle bronc riding event. Flushed from his big win, he'd taken a break from the celebrating to check on the kids and bring them treats while their mother did the work she loved best—competing in the women's barrel racing event. Grant's gesture wasn't lost on Ross. "He's a good one," he said after Grant left them with their food. "Mom should hang on to him."

Most of Mom's boyfriends—and there had been a few—were nowhere near as nice as Grant. When he was eleven, Ross had suffered a broken arm when one boyfriend threw him across a room. Ross never could keep his mouth under control, and he'd made the guy mad. Granny, who was on the premises at the time, had grabbed the shotgun from her office and told the guy to leave. Then she and Mom had one of their huge fights—on the way to the emergency room. "Grown-ups can be pretty screwed up," Ross had told Sage after that scary event. Being three years younger, Sage looked to him for advice. He was handsome and smart and clever, and he didn't miss much. She felt safe when they were together, like now, just hanging out.

"Grant likes kids," Ross told her. "You can tell." Sage nodded, and shoulder- bumped her brother. They each took another bite of hotdog.

Sage looked at the program. The barrel racing event was next, and Mom was favored to win. She had come in second the year before, "But this is the year I'm gonna win," she'd told them. "We can move out and get our own place in town. Then I'll have some privacy and you'll be closer to all your friends."

They had lived with Granny ever since Sage could remember, at Blackthorn Hot Springs a few miles east of Stevenson, Washington, above the Columbia River. It was a nice enough place, except when Mom and Granny argued. And that seemed to be happening a lot more lately. Mom was gone too much during the summer when school was out, and Granny hadn't signed on to raise more kids. Mom didn't help enough around the resort, plus keeping a horse just plain cost too much.

"Blah blah-dy blah," Mom had said behind Granny's back.

Ross jabbed Sage with his elbow, bringing her back to the now. Her eyes roamed the grandstand filled with people eating, drinking, and talking. Most of them, including Sage and Ross, wore cowboy hats. Below, in the dirt, rodeo workers measured distances and set up barrels in the familiar cloverleaf pattern, helped by the ever-present rodeo clowns. "Didn't Mom say she was third on the roster this year?" Ross asked.

Sage nodded. "Yeah, I think so. How much money will she get if she wins?"

Her brother took a judicious sip of his Coke. "I don't know, but Mom says it's a lot. Enough so we can rent a house and live close to school."

"What about Sonny?" Sonny was Mom's quarter horse gelding, nine years old and a great competitor.

"Sonny can stay out on the property. Mom will visit him every day, and practice after she helps Granny with the resort work. But she said we need our own place."

"Granny's bossy."

Ross took another sip of Coke. "Yeah, she is. But I think she means well. She feels responsible. She just rubs Mom the wrong way sometimes."

How did he know this stuff? Sage wondered. He was just so smart. "Maybe everything will feel better if we don't live there," she said. She took her last bite of hotdog and wiped her hands on her napkin. She could see Grant coming up the bleachers toward them. Down below, the workers had finished their task.

Grant scooted in next to Sage on the bleachers and handed each of the kids a PayDay candy bar. "Barrel racing next, you two. When your mom comes out, we're going to make more noise than anybody in the place." He gave them his huge trademark grin, settled against the back rest, and sipped beer from a plastic cup.

Ross squirmed in his seat, barely able to control his excitement. "We're going to be *rich*!" He said it loudly and people turned to look at him.

Grant reached over and tousled his hair. "Settle down, cowboy. She's gotta win first."

"She'll win, she'll win, she'll win!" Sage practically squealed the words, and more people turned around.

"No more sugar for you," Grant said.

Sage stood up and twirled around. "It's *your* fault!"

Grant took her arm and gently sat her down. Sage liked the way he acted like a dad—or how she thought a dad should act. "Pay attention, now," Grant told them. "We don't want to miss anything."

Sage looked down to the arena where the clowns turned cartwheels in the dust. Their padded bellies shifted to their chests when they were upside down. Sage pointed at them. "Why are they down there?" she asked Grant.

"Didn't your mom tell you?"

Sage shook her head.

"Those clowns are out there to help the cowboys," he said. "Especially the bull riders. When the bull tosses a guy, sometimes it'll turn and try to gore the cowboy before he has a chance to get up. The clowns wear rubber barrels with shoulder straps. If a cowboy is on the ground, the clowns the run between the bull and the cowboy to keep him from getting hurt. If the bull turns on the clown, he scrunches up inside the barrel for protection. It's dangerous work."

Sage nodded, serious, as she thought about cowboys and long-horned bulls, and the silly looking men brave enough to get between them.

Grant handed a stopwatch to Ross. "Here. Now, you two use the stopwatch for each barrel racer. That way we can track how she does."

Ross fiddled with the device, and Grant leaned in front of Sage to show him how to reset it. Ross was focused, where a moment ago he'd been all nervous energy. Sage felt settled now too, ready for the first time to watch her mom at work.

Up until now, they'd never attended a rodeo where their mother was competing. Mom liked to travel alone and do the things she enjoyed doing away from her family and what she called "my life as an indentured servant". Granny was a tight-lipped church-going woman who didn't approve of the goings-on at rodeos. While Sage wasn't sure what that meant, but it sounded delicious and fun. And now they were here to bear witness to their mother's accomplishments and the "goings-on" first-hand.

The announcer boomed out the name of the first barrel racing competitor. She burst from the chute on her bay quarter horse and raced to the first barrel. But the approach was too fast, and her horse grazed the barrel on the turn. It knocked the second one over. Although she continued around the third barrel, she'd been disqualified. She rode out of the arena to tepid applause.

"Poor Sandy," said Grant. "She tries so hard." The kids nodded. Both had asked their mom repeatedly to tell them the rules. And she had. "Sonny really gets this," she'd told them. "We're a team." Mom and Sonny never had been disqualified.

The second rider did everything by the book. When Ross showed the time to Grant, he shook his head. "I thought she looked a little slow. She's new, though. She'll improve." It was fun having someone tell them what was going on.

And then from the announcer: "Please welcome our third rider, Susan Blackthorn from Stevenson, Washington. Susan recently won this event at both the Caldwell Night Rodeo in Caldwell and the Snake River Stampede over in Nampa, Idaho." People began cheering as Mom shot out of the gate leaning into Sonny's neck as if they were one. Sage tensed and sucked in her breath. Her mother straightened a little as she and Sonny leaned into the first turn, made it cleanly, and sprinted to the next barrel.

"Go Susan, all the way!" Grant yelled. He and the kids jumped to their feet cheering as Mom and Sonny cleared the second barrel and sped to the third. As they rounded the third, a propane tank in the concession area exploded with a force that rocked the stadium. Sonny shied and lost his footing. He and Mom went down hard in a cloud of dust and confusion. The audience uttered a collective groan. Sage screamed and clapped her hands to her mouth, and Grant reached out and caught her before she pitched forward onto the people in front of her.

The audience went silent. Down on the ground in front of them, Sonny and Mom looked very small. Sonny, covering part of Mom, grunted and rolled and struggled to get to his feet, to no avail. Sage screamed again when she saw the broken bone sticking out of his bleeding foreleg. He let out a long whinny that sounded more like a scream as he flailed helplessly on the ground. Mom lay like a rag doll.

Sheriff's deputies from the rodeo color guard ran onto the field. One drew his gun and shot Sonny in the head before Grant could turn Sage away. "Oh, no," he groaned. And then, "You kids stay here."

"No!" Sage screamed. "Sonny! Mom! No!" She grabbed her brother's arm, crying and screaming.

Her sobbing was the only sound in the stadium. Everything was silent around them as the audience watched in horror. Clinging to Ross, Sage looked up to him. His face had turned the color of ash. Below them, the gory scene played out. Several men attempted to drag Mom from under Sonny while others tried without success to move the dead horse.

Mom lay before them, small and limp. One leg rested behind her at an incongruous angle. "Those dumb shits," Ross muttered under his breath. He started down the bleacher stairs at a run. Still sobbing, Sage hurried after him. She tripped and nearly fell in her rush to catch up with him.

An ambulance, always on hand for rodeo emergencies, pulled into the arena, its siren bleating. The rodeo clowns in their ridiculous gear scurried toward the mayhem. There was Grant, running up to Mom and Sonny, as a group closed around them.

Ross reached the bottom of the bleacher steps ahead of Sage and vaulted athletically over the fence into the arena. Sage clambered to the top of the fence, dropped onto the ground, jamming her ankles painfully. She ran behind him, trying to catch up. When Ross reached the gathering, a man tried to stop him. Ross slugged him in his ample gut and plowed into the group. Panting, Sage ducked under and between the men. She barely managed, but she kept up.

Ross shoved his way to the center. Sage pushed from behind. "You can't be here, kid," a man said. More men closed around them.

"You can't stop me," Ross screamed. "She's my mother!"

And then, all eyes were on him, and Sage, who by now was hanging onto his belt. She saw it all. Sonny, the blood and bone. Mom, her eyes staring at the sky, a trickle of blood running from her open mouth. One of the sheriff's deputies walked up to them and leaned close so no one else could hear him. He put a hand on Ross's shoulder. "You can't do anything to help your mother, son. I'm sorry. She's dead."

Twenty feet away, Susan's white felt cowboy hat with its silver sequin band lay in the dust.

Chapter 2

July 1985

ROSS BLACKTHORN JERKED AWAKE. The full moon had turned his room an eerie bluish-white. He sweated heavily, and his mouth was dry. Something had wakened him. The night sweats again. He rarely slept through the night anymore.

He looked at his watch. Nearly three a.m. Sounds wafted across the broad lawn beneath his window. They came from the boathouse. Normally when they were down there, he didn't hear them. Tonight was different. Someone screamed, then cried out in Spanish. It was a man. He howled out again, obviously in pain. Ross thought he heard another voice, lower, threatening. He rose slowly from his sweat-soaked sheets and moved gingerly toward the window. His head spun, and he thought he might throw up. He was still very drunk.

Outside the trees and shrubbery cast long shadows toward the house. It was quiet. Had he imagined the screams? Were they part of some drunkard's dream? Beyond the boathouse, the river looked smooth and still as a sheet of glass. Across it, on the Oregon side, the occasional headlights signaled movement on Interstate 5. It still amazed Ross how sounds carried in the night, especially during summer. Had the sound come from somewhere else? He thought he heard a freight train. He realized it could be his brain. And then a sickening thunk, followed by another scream, pierced the night. His guts lurched. He quickly turned and grabbed a tee shirt from the floor. He vomited into it.

Panic gripped him, turning him sober in an instant. Carefully he carried the tee-shirt through the living room and into the bathroom. He swished it into the toilet, getting as much of the puke out as he could. He wrung it out and draped it over the bathtub rim, to be dealt with in the morning, and then flushed the toilet.

Presence of mind. Focus. *Normal, normal, normal. Keep it normal, man.* Using the walls for support, he made his way back to his bedroom one slow step at a time. A little voice said, *There's nothing normal about this, man.* He fought down the voice. His brain was trying to drive him crazy.

Back at the window he looked out toward the boathouse. It was quiet again. Nothing. He told himself it was nothing. He'd imagined it. Hallucinated. Whatever. But something had happened. The boat was tied up at the dock, large and sleek, menacing.

He watched the boathouse for several minutes, listening, feeling the soft night air against his bare skin. There was movement. Two men hauled something from the boathouse. It could have been a person wrapped in something, but Ross wasn't sure. They tossed it into the cabin cruiser, and it landed with a solid whump. A long minute later, someone stirred in the shadows. Ross pulled back from the window so he wouldn't be noticed, barely peeking out to see who it was. That someone walked out of the boathouse's shadow and into the silvery light. Ross relaxed a little. He recognized the gait. The figure looked up to his window and Ross allowed himself to be seen. The figure raised his hand to the window, and Ross spoke softly. "Hey, Bro." He turned away from the window and made his way back to the bed. He flopped onto his mattress in the hot, stuffy room, and began to weep.

Chapter 3

September 1985

IT WAS A TYPICAL EARLY SATURDAY NIGHT at the Hoot Owl Bar & Grill. Billy Joel's "Piano Man" was on the juke. An ex-logger named Raymond sat at one end of the bar talking to his beer like it was his recently deceased wife. At the other end, Donald the Pothead scratched his butt with one hand while worrying over a wrinkled piece of paper in the other. A half-full glass of beer sat in front of him. A couple of regulars sat at the bar, and a dozen or so other patrons, mostly men, had positioned themselves randomly around the room. The serious Saturday night crowd hadn't shown up yet.

Andy Murray was wiping down the bar when she walked in. Backlit by the early evening sunshine, her silhouette outlined a small woman with straight hair that touched her shoulders. As she strode across the room, heads turned. Her hair was bright auburn, her eyes hidden by the backlighting. She walked with determination, almost as if she rather than Andy owned the place.

Andy stopped what he was doing and watched as she approached the bar. He took in the flame-red hair, pale green eyes, the long, straight nose, and the arched, dark eyebrows. She wore a denim jacket over an expensive looking sweater, and tight blue jeans. She didn't belong here. Too good for this place.

Andy convinced himself that she needed directions someplace. He leaned toward her so she could hear him over the music. But before he could say anything, she looked him straight in the eye and he saw the fear. She wasn't as composed as she appeared. She was dying for a drink. "What can I get you?" he asked

She sat on the barstool in front of him and laid a ten on the table. Her hand shook. "Black Jack and a Coors."

Andy set her up, took the ten-dollar bill, and brought her the change. "Anything else I can help you with?"

She looked him over, tossed back the shot, and swallowed. She set the shot glass down. "No," she said. "Unless you know anything about what happened to my brother. Ross Blackthorn. Somebody told me you two were friends."

Then he remembered. He'd seen the younger sister at Ross's funeral. She'd looked different then. He had shaken her hand and said a few words to her like folk do at funerals. She had seemed demure in a little black suit with her hair pulled back into a severe bun. She had stood beside her grandmother, who was in a wheel chair. She showed a hardness now that he hadn't noticed two months ago. An edge. It happened sometimes, when people grieved.

"Yeah, we were buddies," he said. It was true. He'd gotten close to Ross Blackthorn over the past two years. He couldn't remember the sister's name. There wasn't much familial resemblance between her and her departed brother. "He was in here a lot. I even eighty-sixed him a couple of times." Andy smiled at her, a smile that offered friendship and nothing more. Maybe she would lighten up a bit.

She half-smiled back at him and took a sip of her beer. The booze had relaxed her a little. "Sage Blackthorn," she said and extended her hand across the bar. "I don't believe we've properly met." As he shook her hand and remembered the firmness of her grip, one of the single men in the room got up from his table and sidled up next to her at the bar. She looked at the man and beamed a smile at him. Andy knew it would be a very long evening.

Chapter 4

SAGE WOKE WITH A START. Was it a sound or the smell of fresh, strong coffee that jarred her from her sleep? For a moment she kept her eyes closed. She was covered with a blanket. But her stomach churned, and her head threatened to explode. She had no idea where she was. Sound of footsteps. Or with whom.

Slowly she opened her eyes. Log walls surrounded her. Through a window paned with wavy glass she noticed the soft dappled light of early morning in the woods. Where the hell was she? Her mind raced through half a dozen scenarios as she desperately tried to remember where she had been the night before. And what she had done. Her body clenched with fear and dread. She couldn't remember a thing. She moaned.

"Good morning, Sage Blackthorn. Can I interest you in a cup of coffee?" It was a male voice. Good God! What *had* she done? And really, where was she? She froze in panic. For a moment she couldn't breathe. She sat up slowly and looked around. She was in a living room on someone's sofa. The man moved into her line of vision. Andy something. The bartender from the night before. Now she remembered going into the bar. She hadn't paid much attention to him after that first drink.

With a wary expression, he handed her coffee in a utilitarian white mug. "You probably don't remember me," he said. "Don't worry. You're okay. I only brought you home because I didn't know what else to do with you."

Great. She accepted the coffee and took a sip, watching him over the rim. "More like butting in where you're not wanted," she muttered. She set the coffee on the table in front of her and arranged herself on the sofa. She pushed the blanket aside. She was fully dressed except for her shoes. She took another sip.

Andy shrugged. He was handsome, with dark, almond-shaped eyes, straight black hair pulled back into a ponytail, and brown skin. His tee-shirt fitted him snugly. Nice abs. He grinned at her. His teeth were small and very white. The sharp eye teeth gave him a slightly feral look. "Suit yourself." He sat down in an old, shabby-looking armchair across the room from her. The chair was upholstered in faded plaid fabric and looked like something her grandmother might have owned. He studied her for a moment, then said, "Believe me when I tell you that you needed someone to butt in last night. You were about to hook up with a very bad man."

Sage made every effort to not wince while Andy took a sip of his coffee and watched her, his expression pleasantly bland. No, she really couldn't remember a thing. Terrifying. But here she was, drinking coffee with this stranger who, apparently, had not taken advantage of her situation. Remarkable. Maybe it *was* all right. At least as good as it could be under the circumstances.

Too soon to tell. He seemed decent enough. But what had she done to end up here? Still a blank. An uncomfortable, guilt-ridden blank of missing time, even more alarming since it had happened so many times before.

"You're Andy." She had to remember something, even if it was just his first name. Talking just made her head pound harder. This was no way to start a new life. Particularly after three miserable weeks of abstinence.

"Yep. Andy Murray. Nice start. What else do you remember?"

She looked around the room. Big fireplace, book cases, and a beautiful Indian blanket hanging on one wall. Vintage Pendleton by the look of it. Despite the gringo name, Andy looked like an Indian. She looked down at her hands, and then out the window, but not at him. She noticed the vine maples, which had turned glorious shades of gold and bright red-orange in anticipation of autumn. "You're the bartender."

"Close. Nice job. I'm the owner of the Hoot Owl. Do you remember dropping in there last night?"

Sage froze for a second, wondering where this was going. Nowhere good. "Sure, I remember stopping by." That was the easy part, before she'd lost track of things. So far, she'd avoided the admission that she had been in a blackout, but the thought was never far from her consciousness.

"And do you remember walking up to the bar and ordering your first drink?"

What was this, twenty questions? "Of course." That much she could remember.

Andy set his mug on the coffee table between them. His expression hadn't changed. Still bland and friendly. A good poker player. "Yes," he said. "But then you started flirting with some of the *real* men who hang out at my place, and the ones who will try to pick you up when you're too drunk to see are the meanest bastards in the house. Do you want to hear the rest?"

She felt her mood changing, the anger welling up inside her. And the fear. He mentioned more than one bastard. It appeared that Andy was going to make it his personal crusade to humiliate her as best he could. "No thank you," she said. "Obviously, I was not at my best."

"Do you want to hear the rest?"

She took another sip of coffee and treated him to what she hoped was her coldest look. "Oh sure. Why not? You're going to tell me anyway."

"Well, you ordered a Black Jack with a beer chaser. By

the fourth one, you'd attracted quite an audience, and you were telling them your life story, and what a big deal you are in New York City. The gentlemen were buying, but at number six I cut you off. Then you told me to go piss up a rope. About that time, the fellow, fresh out of charm school, offered you a ride home. And he had friends. By then everyone in the place knew where you were staying."

"Thank you, Andy. I think I get the picture." With great effort, Sage set down her coffee mug. Her hands shook, and she tried without success to hold them steady. She stood up. "I'll just be leaving now."

"Right," he said. "Home to Blackthorn to take care of your grandmother."

Granny. She was the reason Sage had stopped for a drink at the Hoot Owl—a drink she clearly didn't need since she hadn't had one for nearly a month. It was to put off seeing dear old Granny.

She located her handbag on the floor next to the sofa, grabbed it, and stood up. As she headed for the front door, her legs wobbled beneath her. She opened the door and walked out onto a covered porch. Her stomach lurched. She gulped hard and took a deep breath of pristine, cool air.

Andy followed her out onto the porch. It was a beautiful morning. The log house stood in a clearing surrounded by Douglas firs that towered over the vine maple and sprawling rhododendron. A shiny black Ford pick-up was parked in front of the house. There was no sign of Sage's rental car. Panic stopped her in her tracks. Had she wrecked it? What part of the story had Andy not told her? Desperately she looked back to the door.

Andy stood right behind her, a full head taller than she. "All right, where's my car?" she said. She tried to sound tough, but another wave of nausea hit her like a slug in the gut. She clapped a hand over her mouth and dashed off the porch and toward the foliage, where she heaved into a small rhododendron bush. *Nice job, dipshit.*

"It's at the bar," Andy called after her. "I wasn't about to let you drive. So, if you're going anywhere, I'll have to take you there. Now come on inside and get your bearings. I'll make us some breakfast."

Chapter 5

AN HOUR LATER, SAGE WAS BEHIND THE WHEEL of her rental, a late model red Toyota something, and headed toward home. Or what she used to call home. From the Hoot Owl parking lot, it was an easy two-mile drive. If she had just kept going the previous night, and not stopped at the Hoot Owl for a burger—which she never got around to ordering anyway—she would be just fine now. She wouldn't be sick. Her head wouldn't be pounding. And she wouldn't have disgraced herself in front of God-knows-how-many people. Dr. Lewis, her therapist, had always told her that when she had an impulsive notion, to "play the tape all the way through to the end". But for some reason, Sage often got distracted or the cassette player jammed.

Truth be told, there was another reason she had stopped at the bar instead of going straight home from the airport. Granny. All five feet of her, a hundred pounds dripping wet. When Sage saw her in July, she had been reminded of her duties. Granny told Sage she needed her to keep the resort going now that Ross was gone. His death had hit her hard. Drunk or sober, Ross had been Granny's rock for more than two years. She had depended on him for everything.

The way Sage saw it, Granny had never liked her much on the best of days. Granny said Sage reminded her of her mother Susan. As for the so-called resort? The hotel had been closed for years. Ross somehow had managed to keep the bath house portion of the business open for soaks in the clawfoot tubs fed by the nearby mountain's sulfur springs, and for massages. Ross had taken care of Granny, cooked for her, nursed her and cleaned for her, made certain she was never alone. Sage shook her head at the thought of it. No wonder her poor brother had relapsed!

She turned off the two-lane highway and onto Columbia Street, a smaller blacktop, pothole-pocked road that ran gently downhill toward the Columbia River. The river shimmered before her. Fifty yards offshore, a small boat bobbed on the water. Two people in the boat seemed to be fishing. Her mind dismissed them. She turned left at the sign announcing Blackthorn Hot Springs and onto the aptly named Hot Springs Road.

Nice name, Blackthorn. Sage snorted out loud. It had been a nice place once, probably before she was born. It was okay maybe twenty years ago when Granny and Mom were able to run it properly. Now it was a dump. But it was her dump or would be soon. She would inherit it all once Granny died. From the looks of Granny the last time Sage had seen her, she didn't think it would be long.

As Sage bounced along Hot Springs Road, her head threatened to explode. She didn't want to inherit the rundown old heap. Her life was in New York now. There was nothing here for her, and never had been. But, in addition to taking some time off work to regroup after what had happened to her in New York, she needed to figure out what had happened to Ross, how and where he had died, and why. She wasn't buying the party line from the sheriff's department. She also had to find a place where Granny could go to live out her days in safety and relative peace. Ross wasn't around to run the place, what was left of it, anymore. Those two women who worked here were past their pull dates. And Granny needed care. A couple months before he died, Ross had alluded to medical issues with the old woman, but Sage couldn't remember what they were.

As she neared the hotel, Sage envisioned a nice little apartment in Stevenson where Granny could walk to things. She might be eighty-four, but she could still get around pretty well, couldn't she? with a walker? A housekeeper, perhaps. Someone to help her with cleaning and meals and medications, if there were any. It would be tasteful, lovely, and carefree. She'd even make friends with the neighbors.

And then Sage thought again. Granny had no use for

towns, didn't like them. And she did not make friends with neighbors. At least she hadn't during Sage's lifetime. Granny wasn't accustomed to neighbors. The last time Sage had seen her, at the funeral, Granny was in a wheelchair. But nice try.

Well, something would work out, she told herself as she pulled up to the side of the old hotel and parked next to a pair of ancient looking Japanese-made sedans. She got out of the car and felt the sun on her shoulders. The air smelled so fresh. And then she thought again of her grandmother. Granny would have to see the sense of whatever Sage's plan turned out to be. She would listen to reason, because she couldn't stay here. Sage wouldn't say anything until she had found somewhere Granny could move to and everything was in place. Perhaps she'd find a residential care facility in Stevenson.

Sage's looked up at the peeling remains of Blackthorn Hotel, Est. 1910. The place not only wasn't nice any more, it wasn't even really a business. But while the hotel part had been closed for several years, the baths were still in operation. The old-fashioned bath house, with its clawfoot tubs and modesty screens, offered hot mineral water soaks, wraps, and massages. The dining room opened for lunch, although Sage very much doubted if anyone was desperate enough to eat there—especially since a new, full-service resort had opened five miles up the road that previous spring. The same bath attendants still worked the spa — women Sage had known since childhood—plus an on-call massage therapist or two. People were sentimental, as Ross had told her in one of their few late-night telephone conversations. "They still like to come here, Sis. They have fond memories."

"More likely, they're cheap," she'd retorted. "The ones who still come here. And it's funky. A throwback. Some people are into that shit. Old hippies that come out from under their rocks every five years." She'd been tired of the place since she was ten years old. She'd always wanted something more. She'd gone away, and she'd found it. But now she was back with her tail between her legs. She had to turn her life around, and she didn't have any other place to go. There was nowhere else she *wanted* to go. To go somewhere else required too much effort. Here she could just *be*.

She walked around to the front of the hotel to have a better look at the white, three and a half-story, false-front building. While the words still showed, stenciled neatly on the front of the building, and a pretty floral basket hung by the entrance, the paint was peeling on the clapboard here too, and the old, gray boards showed through. *But it's clear grain cedar, mind you.* Sage could almost hear Granny's voice in her ear. As if anyone gave a rip.

A fire escape hung from the third story window to the roof covering the front veranda. Sage walked past the entrance and explored the other side. The sides of the building went up, up. She noted with surprise an open window on the third floor, next to another dangling fire escape. Who even went up to the third floor these days?

Above it was a row of smaller windows. The attic. The roofline came almost to the tops of its windows.

She entered the building through the front door, and was greeted by musty odors, stale cooking smells, the scent of mildew. Now that was attractive. That would have customers packing in here for lunch. She inspected the photos on the walls surrounding the reception area—images that bespoke earlier days. Antique cars with smiling drivers and their passengers, women in hats and old-fashioned dresses. Then she pounded the little metal domed bell at the reception desk. Damn, it felt good to pound something! But no one came out to greet her.

Unable to rouse a soul, Sage headed through the empty dining room across wide plank floors. Underneath that film of grime, they would be shiny, golden, but full of divots— what her interior designer in New York called "distressed". She'd covet those floors. "Distressed" got big bucks in the City. Here? Not so much. She remembered running across those floors barefoot as a little girl, their smooth surfaces cool to her feet. She shuddered a little as memory after memory flooded through her. The place was full of memories.

A few tables were set up in the center of the room, as if someone expected them to be occupied, but most of the tables were shoved to the room's perimeter. An old refrigerator stood, its door slightly ajar, against one wall next to the Coke machine that hadn't worked since Sage had graduated high school. She sighed and walked into the kitchen through double saloon doors which moved stiffly on their hinges.

A loaf of sliced bread sat on the counter near the sink, beside a colander filled with freshly washed greens. There was no sign of Janice, one-half of the so-called resort's staff. Sage navigated around the large, round, oak dining table in the middle of the floor, past the ancient, empty commercial refrigerator and an old avocado green household refrigerator, passed through a small mud room, and went out the back door of the kitchen.

As expected, it was there she found signs of life. Across a graveled area, two late-middle-age women stood smoking beside a couple of raised beds filled with salad greens and vegetables. For this they were getting paid rather well, considering the market. Granny sat with her back to the hotel. Ever the Queen of the Nile. Her chair, a large and ugly upholstered number with carved wooden arms, featured a back so tall that all Sage could see of her was the white hair on top of her head. "Good morning, ladies."

The women stopped talking and jumped to attention. "Sage, honey," the older one, Betty said, pinching the ash off her cigarette and stowing the unsmoked part in her apron pocket. "We wasn't expecting you 'til tonight."

"Well, here I am. I got in early and decided to just hotfoot it up here." It amazed Sage how her old way of speaking returned the moment she was back on the West Coast. The lying was about the same as always.

Betty was in her late fifties but looked older. Her face

was deeply furrowed from years of heavy smoking, and her long gray hair draped limply onto her rounded shoulders. She had worked at the Blackthorn since she was in high school, and still ran the baths when there were customers.

Janice, the cook, finished her smoke and dropped it onto the ground, where she mashed it out with her foot. She was a bit younger than Betty, but not much, with a pale, wrinkled complexion. Her brittle dyed brown hair was teased in the front to a pompadour affect, the rest trailed down her back. She was tall and scrawny, a contrast to Betty's general roundness, and like Betty wore jeans and a tee shirt under an apron. Unlike Betty, she wore black eye shadow that rose nearly to her eyebrows. Even though she had seen it before, Sage's first reaction was disbelief. She stared at Janice until she picked up her cigarette butt and put it in her pocket. "Hi Sage, it's good to see you. Your room's not ready yet," Janice said. Her voice was flat. Unlike Betty, she had never exuded a motherly warmth.

Sage shrugged and walked toward them, stopping at her grandmother's chair. "Hey, that's okay. I'll take care of my room. You just do what you need to do around here." She turned to face the old lady and kneeled to make eye contact.

Granny looked at Sage for a long moment, trying to register who she was. Those lively blue eyes had dulled in the two months since Ross's death. She looked hollowed out. Food stains adorned the front of her dress. She wore an old, badly pilled cardigan sweater. Her long white hair looked uncombed. Not a pretty sight. She sucked at her cheeks before speaking. "Susan," she said. "It's about time you got here."

Sage stood up, taken aback. The old woman thought she was her daughter, not her granddaughter. Granny's heavy-lidded eyes blinked. "Susan?" This time she sounded querulous, confused.

Sage reached out and took her grandmother's hands into her own. She could feel Betty and Janice watching. "No, Granny. It's Sage. I came home for a visit."

Janice and Betty continued to stare. Granny looked bewildered. Finally, Betty spoke. "Mary Margaret has been having a hard time since Ross passed. Her mind has been wandering a lot." She turned her attention to Granny. "Mary Margaret, this is your granddaughter, Sage. You know Sage. She was just here in July and she's come back to stay with you for a while." Granny focused her attention on Betty but didn't speak.

Janice chimed in. "She's not eating much neither. Glad you're here, Miss Sage. You'll perk her up, won't she, Mary Margaret?"

Granny glared at them. "I'm eating plenty, you stupid cows. And my mind doesn't wander. Get back to work. There's vegetables to be picked."

Sage stood there mortified. She'd never heard Granny talk to anyone like that—except for her mother, herself, and Ross, that is. Janice shrugged like it was no big deal, picked up a basket, and commenced picking green beans.

"What's going on with the baths?" Sage said to nobody

in particular. "Anything today?"

Betty answered. "A foursome at eleven for the soak and massage. They may stay for lunch. They wasn't sure."

Picking up on Janice's look, Sage said, "What do we have to feed them, should they decide to stay? And when does Granny eat?"

This time Janice answered. "I make lunch for Mary Margaret at eleven. She likes her cottage cheese and some nice sliced tomatoes. I can do some chef's salads or sandwiches if the guests stay for lunch."

Sage nodded. "Okay," she said. "I don't want to interrupt anything. I'll just unload the car and make myself at home. Maybe it's time to get Mary Margaret out of the sun." The scalp showing through her thin white hair glowed pink. Janice set down her basket and she and Betty began bustling about Granny to get her inside.

Sage treated them to what she hoped was a cheery smile before walking back through the kitchen. Her mouth tasted like the stench from the New York subways smelled, and she was afraid she would puke again. She headed for the women's restroom near reception. On the way she noticed that the small sitting room for hotel guests had been repurposed into a bedroom. She paused to look inside.

The room was bright with ambient light, painted a fresh, pale yellow. The windows opened to let in the fresh September air. A neatly made twin bed stood to one side of the room, with a little vase of flowers on the night stand. There were two worn but comfortable looking upholstered chairs, a small writing desk. The wood floor was covered with the same old Oriental rug that had been there as long as Sage could remember. Everything looked tidy and clean. Sage wondered how long Granny had been sleeping in this room. Perhaps since before July. She really had no idea. More important, who had fixed up the room? It didn't look like a Betty-Janice job. That left her late brother Ross. Still, she made a mental note that someone was keeping the room fresh and pleasant for her grandmother.

The restroom surprised her too. While it was mostly the same, a shower kit filled one corner of the room, with towels and wash cloths draped on a little wooden drying rack next to it. The sinking feeling Sage had driving up to the hotel was still with her, but its focus had changed. The bedroom and bathroom had been turned into appealing yet purposeful spaces that perfectly served Granny's diminished state. Ross had always been good with his hands, and he'd had a good eye.

She didn't puke after all. She went out the front entrance, hauled three large suitcases into the reception area, then picked up the smallest one and headed up the front stairway toward the guest rooms. The runner down the upstairs hall matched the worn one on the stairs. Up here the floor boards were narrower and painted an ugly brown.

She peeked into the nearest of the long-vacant guest rooms. It was fitted with twin beds with metal frames. The mattresses, under old chenille bedspreads, looked thin and lumpy. A small chest of drawers stood against one wall; a night stand holding a small lamp crowded between the beds. Overhead lighting came from a bulb hanging from the ceiling. The room was tidy, but a film of dust covered everything.

She closed the door and walked down the hall, past the remaining eight guest rooms, the men's and women's toilets, and the shower room. It was a different era now. These days, guests expected *en suite* bathrooms.

At the end of the hall, Sage tried the five-panel wooden door on her right, the door to the family living area. As expected, it was unlocked. There hadn't been a reason to lock it since the hotel closed. A wave of nostalgia washed over her as she remembered how much fun it had been, back when she was little, to hide from Ross and their friends by running up the back staircase that ran from the kitchen to the family's private rooms, cut through that door that should have been locked at all times (Granny's orders), and then hide in one of the vacant guest rooms. That was when Mom was alive, of course, and Granny was busy doing other things. After Mom died, rules became more rigid and there wasn't a lot of play.

The Blackthorns never had been very good at locking things, but it hardly mattered. They'd never had money, or anything someone would want to steal. Even twenty years ago the hotel part of the operation hadn't been particularly busy. Sage wondered how long it had been since someone had stayed here.

She entered the family quarters and dropped her bag on the floor of what had been the living room when she was growing up. It was a large, overfilled open space onto which bedrooms and a bathroom door opened. It was as she remembered it, only shabbier—a common space filled with an overstuffed sofa and five big and little chairs, some of which had side tables. There was a heavy, dark wood coffee table, some old lamps, and a television. A writing desk exactly like the one downstairs in the former guest lounge sat against the wall between two of the bedroom doors. It all looked worn, beat-up, and dusty.

Sage peeked into her own bedroom first and gasped. Again, she was hit by the feeling that she had entered another era. It looked like a museum for the 1970s, even to the same posters she had put on the walls when she was in high school. She hadn't opened the door to her room in July, after Ross died. She couldn't remember if she even had come upstairs. She'd been too numb to think straight. It had been enough to deal with the fact that he was dead.

Foremost in her mind were the circumstances of her brother's death. After the funeral, she'd learned from the autopsy report that he had not drowned as she had previously been told. Ross somehow had gotten himself into the Columbia River and floated two—or was it three—miles downstream after he died. It was disturbing news then, even more so now that she was two months removed and had had time to think about it. What had happened? How did he die? He'd been an excellent swimmer. His body was in bad shape when it was discovered a week after he disappeared. Maybe that's why information was lacking. But something didn't add up.

Sage pondered the few facts she knew as she closed the door to her bedroom. It was, after all, just another room, the room of a girl who no longer existed, who had left this world for New York City more than ten years ago. She'd stayed at a hotel in Portland when she came out in July for the funeral, choosing to drive the nearly fifty miles from the city every day on I-84, across the Bridge of the Gods, and through Stevenson to the Blackthorn. Avoiding memories. Avoiding Granny. She hadn't wanted to deal with those things then, and she didn't want to now. But this time was different. She was here for a while, and there was work to be done. She dug into the suitcase for her cosmetic bag, then proceeded to the family bathroom where she washed her face and brushed her teeth.

After two trips downstairs and struggling trips up again with her heavy bags, Sage collapsed onto the lumpy sofa in the living room. Her head throbbed with pain, and she knew that a drink, just a small one, would take the edge off. It wouldn't cure her, but at least she'd be able to function. She could go back to being sober tomorrow. She wondered vaguely if there was any booze on the premises. Probably not. Granny didn't drink and never had. Any time Ross got his hands on alcohol he drank it all. Still....

She stood up, walked to the room next to her own—Ross's bedroom—and opened the door. Everything looked exactly as if he was still living there. A rumpled bed. Dirty clothes on the floor. The stale smell of socks left unwashed.

It was as if he had never left them. She opened the drawers in his bureau and felt around in his clothing. It was creepy somehow, what she did, but she did it anyway. He may have stashed something. If nobody had been into the room—and that certainly looked like the case—who knew what she might find?

She searched, methodically, until her organized explorations degraded into frantic pawing. There had to be a bottle somewhere! She pulled her brother's hanging clothes apart in the closet and dug behind shoes and dirty socks piled on the closet floor. Nothing. She felt herself sweating with frustration and the anxiety of withdrawal. She tore out of the room and back into the family bathroom where she dug through the linen cabinet, flinging clean, worn-thin towels onto the floor.

Finally, back in Ross's room, she found it—far under the bed, hidden by a pile of dirty tee shirts. Dewar's. *Thank God!* She held the bottle upright and looked at it. Since when had Ross started drinking Dewar's? There was only a bit left, about an inch in the bottom of the bottle, but it was enough. It would take the edge off. And then she could relax, unpack, and get on with the day.

Still on her knees, she unscrewed the cap and sniffed the bottle. As advertised, there was actual scotch in it. She took a swig. It scalded the back of her throat and she felt its promising heat all the way down to her gut. And then the magic happened, as it always did, and the warmth of the alcohol flowed over and through her. She felt her heart expand, her chest warmed, and the sweet promise of relief traveled down her arms and legs and into her groin and upward into her brain. There on the floor, on her knees, in her dead brother's bedroom, she felt real again. Lighter. Her body gave a little involuntary shudder and relaxed. She took another gulp, and then slowly rose to her feet. She screwed the cap back onto the empty bottle and held it to her chest. Smiled.

She walked over to Ross's bedroom window, and opened it, letting fresh morning air riffle into the stale room. She looked south, out over the broad former lawn—now a field of tall, dried grass, Queen Anne's Lace, and towering thistle—toward the boathouse. Beyond it the Columbia River glimmered in the yellow autumn light, its bland smoothness belying the strong current underneath. The Oregon side was steep with basalt cliffs and green deciduous trees. A freight train that looked no larger than a toy moved slowly eastward.

Chapter 6

BY LUNCHTIME, SAGE HAD UNPACKED her bags and changed the bedding in her old bedroom. She'd located the vacuum in the upstairs hall closet. It still worked well. She'd vacuumed the entire family living quarters and was nearly finished cleaning the squalid bathroom when hunger overcame her. She wandered down the back staircase and into the kitchen. Janice was at the long counter putting together a sandwich and muttering to herself.

"Any customers yet?" Sage asked.

Janice's back was to her. She jumped and turned around quickly. "Scared the shit out of me," she said. She looked uncomfortable, almost furtive. With her pale face and the dark eye makeup, Janice looked like a skull with holes where the eyes should be. The sight was unnerving. "Where'd you come from?"

"Down the back way," Sage said, collecting herself. "Any chance of getting some lunch?"

Janice looked longingly at the sandwich, then said, "Here. You can have mine."

Sage waved her off. "I don't want yours. Just tell me where things are. I can help myself."

Janice turned back to the counter. "We may have some folks stopping in for lunch," she said, and put the finishing touches on her sandwich. She cut it in half with a large chef's knife, placed it on a plate, and carried it to the table. "I was just going to grab a bite while they finish getting massaged. Everything is in the fridge."

Sage advanced to the avocado green refrigerator that she remembered so well from her childhood and opened the door. Inside she saw a few condiments and a chunk of deli turkey breast. She grabbed the meat and mayonnaise and closed the door. "Bread's over there," said Janice, and pointed to the half-loaf on the counter. A basket of ripe tomatoes also graced the counter.

Sage began slicing turkey for her sandwich. "Where's Granny?"

Now, her back was turned to Janice, but Sage could hear her scrunching around in her seat. "I gave her lunch, and she's having her nap. She'll be in there 'til about three. Then she'll want to eat again," Janice said.

"How long has she been like this?" Sage said.

"Like what?"

"Not recognizing people. That vacant look. She thought I was Mom earlier. I'm shocked at the change in her." Sage turned around to watch Janice's response.

Janice looked at the untouched sandwich on her plate and took a drink of milk. "She's been in and out for some time, I guess. But mostly we've noticed it since your brother passed. She'll be fine one minute and gone to la-la land the next. I think she was into such a routine with him that we didn't notice. The last two months have been hard on her."

"On all of us," Sage acknowledged. "What about the place? Do we get many customers?"

"Nah, hardly any since that new resort went in. They come here 'cause the massages are cheaper. But they don't eat here no more. I've quit makin' pies. It's not worth the hassle."

Sage spoke with an excitement she didn't feel, "Janice, you can't quit making pies. You just have to make me a pie!"

Janice grinned, revealing the gap behind her right incisor. "Your grandma loves my pies. And Ross, too. He had some of my blueberry pie the day before he disappeared," she said. "Mary Margaret ate a great big piece, and your brother ate the rest of it." She chuckled at the memory.

Sage sliced a tomato and added it to the sandwich—and remembered. Ross had needed a place to live after his second stint in rehab, so he had come home. Granny needed him as much as he needed her, and she had put him right to work. For the next eighteen months, Granny supervised him from that godawful armchair Ross had moved into the kitchen.

Ross, Janice, and Betty did what Granny told them to do.

It had worked just fine until Ross relapsed. Again. She shook her head at the memory. The phone conversations with her grandmother, who had been addled and distraught. The telephone calls to Ross, who assured her it was just a one-time slip. "I can't bail you out again," she'd told him. "Your last try at rehab used up most of my savings. And Granny can't do it again either. You know she's barely getting by now."

"Chill, Sis. It's good," he'd told her. But it wasn't good. Ross returned to his drinking and drugging. As his work became increasingly sporadic, it showed, and what business they'd had dropped to almost nothing. Based on Sage's conversations with their attorney and long-time family friend Thomas Kitt in July, the flow of massage customers barely kept the lights on. Tommy was Ross's executor, and he kept the bills paid and Janice's and Betty's paychecks flowing. He'd offered to help after Ross died, and Sage had gratefully taken him up on it. They got paid extra now, for taking care of Granny. She still had all that to sort out, sooner rather than later.

She slapped the top onto her sandwich and brought herself back to the present. "Ross loved a good pie," she said, more to herself than to Janice, as she joined her at the table.

Janice looked at her, ill at ease despite the pie chatter. "What's it like coming back here after all that time in New York?" she asked.

Sage paused at the question, and what it suggested. "I

don't know yet," she said. Too soon, too soon.

Janice looked her straight in the eye. "Are you going to stay here?"

What was this? Twenty questions? "I'll be here for a while. But long-term, no. I'm going to get things figured out here and then go back to New York. I didn't quit my job, just took a leave."

"Just curious if you're going to keep the Blackthorn open, is all," Janice said. "It's not making any money, in case you're wonderin'. But Betty and I appreciate havin' a job."

Sage pushed her sandwich around on its plate. "Oh, I know that," she said. "But I've been away a long time, and now I'm in charge. I'll have to look at the books and talk to some folks, see what makes sense. I must think about Granny. She can't be here by herself anymore. She needs to be closer to medical care. I'll have to make some hard decisions in the next few weeks."

Janice still hadn't touched her sandwich. "Well, I'm going home after these customers leave," she said. "Unless you got something for me to do."

Sage shook her head. "Go whenever you'd like. No reason for you to wait around to see if anyone wants to stay for lunch. I can make somebody a sandwich if they come in. I grew up making sandwiches for people."

Janice looked relieved. She cleared her place, wrapped her sandwich in plastic film, pushed it into her purse, and left through the open kitchen door.

Sage took another tentative bite of her sandwich. Her

stomach still churned from the previous night's drinking. She knew she'd feel better after she ate. She rose from the table, crossed to the refrigerator, and opened it, looking for a beer. Of course, there weren't any. Ross couldn't keep alcohol around. If it was there, he drank it. He'd been gone for a while, and she was on the wagon again, anyway, wasn't she?

She ran herself a glass of water and sat back down at the table. Ross had been a hot mess, but she reckoned she wasn't any better if all she could think about was drinking. She finished eating and carried her plate to the sink. Then she walked out the kitchen door and into the sunshine.

The raised beds were overflowing with vegetables. Sage noticed the ripening tomatoes first, sparkling from under their leaves like gems—red, yellow, orange, green. She reached out and touched a reddish one. It felt warm and alive. She leaned down and breathed in the smell of the tomato plants. Heaven. This was what home smelled like.

When she was small, her mother had been patient, but Granny did not appreciate small girls underfoot. Granny would hand her a salt shaker from the kitchen table and say, "Here. If you can salt the bird's tail, you can catch it." Sage spent much of her earliest summers with the salt shaker, chasing birds around the garden. It dawned on her that perhaps she always had been a teeny bit naïve. She probably still was. Despite her successes in New York, she'd screwed up badly in life, often by believing fairy tales, by believing someday her prince would come. She'd prowled a lot of bars over the last ten years. So far, no prince.

She picked a couple zucchini squash and cradled them in her shirt tail. The plants were almost done, the leaves covered with powdery mildew. Back in the kitchen, she set the squash on the counter and then walked through the dining room to peek into Granny's room. The curtains were drawn, and Granny snored contentedly.

She walked out the front door just as Betty emerged from the bath house pulling a laundry cart filled with towels and body wraps. A cigarette dangled from her lips. She looked at least seventy, but Sage knew she was younger, just shy of sixty. She walked across the parking lot toward Betty. "Need some help?"

Betty looked up and pulled her hand across her forehead. "Sure, honey. I gotta get this stuff in the laundry."

"How did it go?"

"Well, I couldn't talk 'em into stayin' for lunch, if that's what you mean." She looked around. "Just as well, since Janice took off." She paused to take a pull on her cigarette, then exhaled a blast of smoke. "They was good tippers."

Sage grabbed the cart from Betty and started hauling it down the driveway toward the laundry room, which had been built underneath the far end of the bath house. "She wanted to leave," she said. "There's not much food in the kitchen, anyway. I'm going in to Portland soon, so I can pick up the things we need."

Betty nodded. "Good, I'll start a list," she said. "We're low on everything."

At the end of the bath house, Sage pulled the cart around the building. Betty took a key from her apron and unlocked the padlocked double door that let them into the dark, cavernous laundry. She flipped on a light, which did little to allay the dungeon-like atmosphere. Sage did a double-take as she saw the huge industrial washer and dryer, the same awful machines in use every day when she was growing up and the resort was busy with paying hotel guests, diners, and day-trippers. As a child, she had been terrified of them. They loomed like huge, gothic monsters in the semi-darkness of the laundry room. Each stood nearly six feet tall. They didn't scare her now; she only registered surprise they still worked.

Betty opened the door of the washer and began throwing damp towels inside. They barely filled half of the oversized machine. It was a huge waste of energy, running the machine with so little in it, but Sage also knew from her visit two months ago that the supply of towels was low. They all needed to be replaced, and she briefly considered picking up some new ones when she went into Portland. But that would be silly, she told herself; they weren't going to be doing this much longer.

Betty was talking a blue streak. Earth to Sage. "…and I told her, you can't just stop making pies. That's what folks want when they come here. They aren't going to get homemade pie at that new place down the road."

Sage tried to focus on the pie sermon, which threatened to continue for some time. Betty had a story to tell, and she'd found an audience. "Maybe she's just tired of making them,"

Sage said. Should she talk to Janice about the pie situation? It probably would bring them a little business, or at least cheer Granny up a little. But what would be the point of it? She sighed inaudibly, she hoped, and touched her pounding head. So much shit to deal with, and all she really wanted to do was lie down and disappear for a week. Or a month. That really was the purpose of the visit, wasn't it? To disappear for a while? And rest? Who cared about cheering Granny up anyway?

"Nah, somethin' else is going on with her. She hasn't made a pie since your brother disappeared."

That made sense. There were plenty of things Sage hadn't done since Ross died. Then she recalled Janice's furtive looks in the kitchen, her jumpiness. Something *was* going on with her, and although Sage could not imagine what the problem was, she doubted it had much, if anything, to do with pie.

Betty threw in a cup of laundry detergent, started the washer, and then said, "There's no sense me wasting your money waiting for this load to finish. Can you put it in the dryer when it's done washing?" She said "warshing" just like she always had. The sound of her speech patterns felt homey and familiar.

"Sure," Sage said. She only hoped she could remember how to run the dryer. They started up the gravel drive together.

Chapter 7

THROUGHOUT THE WARM, QUIET AFTERNOON, Granny slept. Sage tried to return to her tasks upstairs, but a restlessness consumed her. Downstairs, she looked in the refrigerator. Turkey breast and a bit of cheese. Condiments. The tomatoes on the counter. A couple zucchinis. Half a loaf of bread. There was basil in the raised beds. She walked outside to check on the supply. Something white caught her eye, nestled at the base of one of the basil plants. As she walked closer, she realized it was Janice's barely touched sandwich wrapped in plastic film.

"What the hell?" Sage bent, picked up the sandwich, and turned it over in her hand. It was thick with meat. A large apple was tucked underneath it in the shade of the large, bushy plant. She stood there for a moment, puzzling over the possibilities. Did Janice leave offerings to invisible people? Aliens? The gods? Did she have a secret friend? She carefully replaced the food and made her way back into the house. Whatever was going on, she wasn't going to deal with it now. Restlessness gnawed at her. She had to get to Stevenson and pick up some groceries. Something to cook that Granny would like. And some wine for dinner. Otherwise she'd never get to sleep tonight. *No! No wine. You're done with that.*

She grabbed her handbag and car keys, checked on Granny, who was snoring, then went outside and fired up the rental car to drive the seven miles to town. She had passed through the short street that was Stevenson last night, before stopping at Andy's tavern. She could have stopped and bought groceries then, but at the time she was in a hurry to get to the home place, such as it was. Or was she more in a hurry to get that drink? Maybe she felt safer now that she was in Washington? Maybe she thought it would be fun, like it once was even back just a few months ago. It had been an unfortunate detour, even though the repercussions had been relatively minor, thanks to Andy. She hadn't been so lucky her last big drunk in New York.

The day was warm, a delightful late September day. Sage drove with the windows down, enjoying the fresh, dry heat so different from New York in late summer. The highway curved past timber that rose steeply to the highway's right. On the left, small acreages with golden brown fields sloped down toward the Columbia. Across the river basalt cliffs carved by the Bretz Floods of the Ice Age towered over thick standing evergreens along Interstate 5. The sky held the faint golden tinge of early fall. The day continued windless.

Stevenson wasn't much of a town, but it did have a decent little grocery store where Sage purchased milk, juice, eggs, butter, and breakfast cereal. She also bought a whole chicken, intending to roast it for supper. She stood in the wine aisle for several long minutes, staring at labels until she felt a little dizzy. Her body ached for alcohol. *I've done this before,* she told herself, while her brain screamed another, opposite message: *buy the fucking wine!* Her hands sweated, but she kept them on the grocery cart. She made herself think about toilet paper as she pushed the cart down the aisle and away from the alcohol. And yet, that clawing, empty ache for the drug continued.

The rest could wait until her trip into Portland. Back in the car, she arranged the groceries in the trunk and started back toward the Blackthorn, where, she promised herself, she would prepare a delicious, healthy supper.

On the north side of the road, she saw the Hoot Owl Bar & Grill again, perched invitingly overlooking the river. No cars in the parking lot. People weren't off work yet. Without thinking about it, she veered across the oncoming lane and into the parking lot and turned off the engine. She cracked the windows, locked the car, and walked onto the wide covered porch of the old cedar-shingled building. At the door she hesitated. Did she really want to do this?

Inside, it was cool and dark. Andy sat at the bar with his

back to her. He appeared to be absorbed reading a newspaper. A sad country song played on the juke box. The place was empty. Sage walked quietly across the floor and stood behind him. "Who do I have to fuck to get a drink around here?"

Andy jumped in his seat and jerked around. "My God, you scared me!"

She stepped back, suddenly feeling foolish. But she laughed, anyway. "Yeah, I'm sorry," she said. "I stopped to apologize for last night. And this morning."

Andy stood up, turned around, and looked her over. "I'm not going to let you get drunk here again tonight," he said.

"Yeah. Like I said, I'm sorry. That was completely out of character for me." Pants-on-fire lie, but it sounded good. "I can't stay long anyway. I'm going home to cook dinner for my grandmother. But I do apologize for what I put you through. And thanks for taking me to your home. Sometimes I realize that I'm not as big a deal as I think I am."

Andy held her gaze for a moment, as if to see if she told the truth. He didn't believe her, which for some reason was very important at that moment. He saw people like her every day of his life. He probably was sick of them. Sage certainly would be. She pulled out a bar stool and sat down. He shrugged, then walked behind the bar where he picked up a glass and held it to the light. Satisfied, he pulled a draft Coca-Cola, squeezed a lemon wedge into it, and set it on a napkin in front of her.

Sage took a delicate sip, set the glass down, and said,

"Can I buy you one?"

Andy looked at the clock on the wall. It was just past four. "Sure," he said, and grinned. The small white teeth, the beautiful smile. "It's five o'clock somewhere." He grabbed a glass, filled it with Coke, and squeezed a wedge of lemon into it. He took a sip and stood in front of her. "How's it going at the Blackthorn?"

She took another sip of the Coke and then took a deep breath. It felt weird to be talking to this unknown person without a drink in her hand. "It's strange," she said. "I don't know if it's home anymore."

Andy again seemed to consider what she said. "I knew your brother well," he said, after a brief pause. "He was a good man."

Sage sighed with relief. A good man. A good-hearted man. Andy knew Ross, and he got who her brother was. "He was a drunk," she said. Her words tasted bitter. "I paid for one of his stays in rehab."

"Sage, he was a good man with a bad disease," Andy continued, looking at her. "When he relapsed, it was a horrible shame. It was awful to watch him come apart. I tried to help him, and I couldn't. He knew what to do, but he just couldn't seem to do it. It's like he gave up."

Sage felt her eyes begin to fill. This was not the time. She finished her Coke in a couple of large gulps, then stood up. "Thanks. I miss him," she said. "I'm going home now."

Andy nodded at her and raised his glass. "To good men," he said. "Any time you want to talk, you can usually find me here. And it was an honor to help you out last night." She gave a curt nod and turned to walk out of the tavern. "He didn't have to die," Andy said to her back.

The car was stifling from being closed. Sage flopped behind the steering wheel, turned on the ignition, and opened all the windows. She turned on the air-conditioning, took a deep breath and tried to exhale, but it came out a sob. She rested her arms and forehead on the steering wheel and cried like she had the day she learned Ross had died. She stopped abruptly when a car pulled up next to her. She wiped her eyes, put the car in reverse, and drove out of the parking lot.

Back at the Blackthorn, she hauled the groceries into the kitchen. She put away everything but the chicken. Then she remembered. Granny. Oh, God!

She found Granny sitting up in bed, her hands fussing nervously with the edge of her blanket. When Sage walked into her room, Granny looked at her in dismay—like she'd been caught with her hand in the cookie jar. A tear had trickled down amid the wrinkles on her cheek. "I wet myself, Susan," she said. "I don't know what to do."

Jesus! Sage managed a fake smile and nodded. "It will be okay," she said. "Don't worry. We can fix this in no time." Why had nobody *told* her about this little problem? Well, she should have known. She walked into the restroom-turned-Granny's bathroom and opened the cabinets. Toilet paper, cleaning products, *no adult diapers!* What the hell!

She walked into Granny's room feeling shaky. "Let's get

you into some clean clothes," she said. Hopefully she sounded matter-of-fact. And why was she shaking! Because caregiving was a pain in the rear? Because she needed a drink?

Granny nodded at her. "Thank you, Susan. I'm sorry I'm a bother."

Since when had Granny ever been sorry for anything? "I'm not Susan!" It came out snappish and Granny recoiled as if she'd been slapped. Sage felt horrible. "I'm so sorry, Granny," she said, her voice gentle now. "I'm Sage. You remember, don't you? I'm your granddaughter. I'm Sage."

Granny looked at her. Whether she understood or not was anybody's guess, but slowly her features relaxed and she said, "Oh, yes, Sage. Hello. Where did *you* come from?"

"I came from New York. I'm going to stay with you for a while."

Granny's face clouded with worry. Then she said, "Well, don't eat too much. My money doesn't grow on trees."

Right. "I'm here to help you Granny," she said. "I'll buy the groceries. Let's get you changed and you'll feel better."

Sage dug around in a chest of drawers for clean underwear and a nightgown. Then she gritted her teeth. She did *not* want to see her grandmother naked, but nobody else was here to do it, so she turned around to do what she had to do.

It could have been worse. Really, it could have, Sage thought as she stripped the bed, and checked around for other dirty clothes, and found a full basket in the closet. She walked Granny into the kitchen, sat her at the table, and poured her a glass of milk.

Granny sat at the table nodding. Sage walked to the sink and filled herself a glass of the cool well water. She looked out the window at the garden area where the sandwich had been. It was gone. Had someone or some*thing* taken it? She needed a glass of wine. *Now!* She almost slammed the water glass on the counter.

She forced herself to focus and brought herself back into the room. "Granny, are you okay? Here, have a drink of milk." Granny looked up at her as she leaned down to help her with the glass. She pursed her thin, wrinkled lips. "You smell like wine, Susan. You know I don't like that."

"I don't smell like wine," said Sage. "There's no wine in the bloody house!" Enough with the lecture. "Can you just sit here for a minute while I go start a load of laundry?" Granny didn't answer. Sage left the kitchen and walked straight to the basil out back. The sandwich and the apple were gone. Who was Janice feeding? And why? She checked the spot again to be certain the offering had disappeared. Yes, it truly had been taken.

She found the laundry cart right outside the bath house, where they'd left it. She threw Granny's dirty laundry into the bottom of it and lugged it down the driveway to the laundry room. When she unlocked and opened the double doors, she felt like she was entering a dungeon. She pulled the cart in behind her. It was cool inside, and quiet until something scurried in the corner of the room. Sage jumped.

Rats? She shuddered, moved the morning's wet towels from the washer, placed them in the dryer, and pushed the "on" button. The thing started with such a roar that she jumped again. Her heart pounded as she loaded up the washer, set the dials, added soap, and started the cycle.

Back in the kitchen, Granny showed signs of restlessness, picking at her hands and tugging at her bathrobe. Sage helped her move from the table to her old, beat-up chair where she'd be more comfortable. She pulled open cabinet doors and drawers to locate the cooking equipment needed. While disorder reigned everywhere, she was able to find the items necessary for preparing the meal.

She turned on the oven and buttered the bottom of a heavy metal baking pan, then removed the chicken from its wrapper, rinsed it in cold water, and patted it dry. She set it gently in the pan and slid pats of butter under the skin. It felt good to be banging around in the kitchen again.

Outside in the raised beds Sage located and picked thyme and rosemary and pulled a shallot from the ground. She took the herbs inside, chopped them, and stuffed them into the chicken's cavity. Then she liberally salted the bird and placed it into the heated oven. Thank God she had learned how to cook! She wiped her hands on her jeans and looked around.

Granny dozed in her chair. It was now or never! Sage grabbed her handbag and ran for the rental car. With Granny fast asleep, she could make it to Stevenson and back and never be missed. She revved the engine and peeled out of the driveway. She needed those diapers. And wine. Just one bottle of wine, then she'd be good. It would mellow her out, get rid of the nerves and tension, the gnawing inside her body that made her feel as if she was being eaten from the inside out. She couldn't stand the way she felt. One glass of wine would take reverse that.

When Sage returned to the kitchen nearly an hour later, Granny was still asleep. She quickly poured herself a glass of the wine she'd purchased and stuck the cork back in the bottle. She took a generous sip, and let her mind follow the warmth of it down to her stomach. Another sip. The relief. She set down the wine glass and pulled the chicken from the oven to check it for doneness, then covered it with a sheet of foil. She sliced up some zucchini and threw it in a pan with butter, sliced a plate of tomatoes, and refilled her glass. That would be enough for the evening. She stashed the bottle under the sink with the cleaning products. With any luck, she'd forget where she put it and that would be that. Time to wake Granny.

She touched the old woman's shoulder and she jerked. She opened her eyes and looked around, confused. If this was the new normal, Sage was quickly getting used to it. "Let's go to the bathroom, Granny," she said. "Then it's time for dinner."

"You smell like wine, Susan. The Lord abhors a drunk."

"Yeah, yeah," Sage said as they shuffled across the dining room and down the hall to the restroom, where she assisted Granny with her ablutions. At least she hadn't wet herself again. Even in her haste to get the wine, Sage had remembered to grab a box of disposable adult diapers. She managed to get one on Granny without an argument.

At the kitchen table, Granny sat and stared at the backs of her hands. When Sage located the silver candle holder and lit a candle on the table, Granny cast a gimlet eye on the tarnished item before receding back into her world. She said nothing, but when Sage set a plate of chicken and vegetables in front of her, she grabbed her fork and attacked. So much for the myth that Granny had become a picky eater. She may be little and scrawny, but the woman could eat.

Sage took another sip from the quickly diminishing wine in her glass. Around them, the family had gathered at the round table. It was 1960 again. Granny sat in her usual spot; Mom at Granny's right; Sage and Ross completed the circle. Ross, who was about nine at the time of this vivid memory, sat nearest their grandmother, squirming in his seat. Granny picked up her teaspoon and popped him a good one on top of his head. "Waaah! No fair," he screeched as tears sprang from his eyes and ran down his face.

"Sit still, little man," Granny had intoned at the time. Then she calmly had picked up her fork and resumed eating.

Mom had glared at Granny but said nothing while Sage cowered in her seat. That's the way it was. Their grandmother had her standards, and this was her place, as she reminded them constantly. Sage had both revered and hated her. Not only did her grandmother scare her, but also, she ran the place with an iron fist.

Mom and Granny had existed under an uneasy truce

since Mom returned to the home of her upbringing with two children in tow and no husband to help support them. Mom had been a professional barrel racer. She was good, and during the rodeo season she made a lot of money. Somehow that never translated to a better lifestyle for her and her kids. She always managed to piss it away more quickly than she should have. At least, that had been Granny's assessment of the situation.

And then the arguments would begin. Susan worked long hours at the Blackthorn, cleaning, changing beds, and doing laundry to earn her family's place there as her yearly boom and bust cycle repeated itself. When she wasn't working for the resort, she was working with her beautiful horse, Sonny. Granny cooked. Mom wasn't allowed to touch anything in the kitchen. But over the years Sage watched. And learned. Eventually, she was allowed to help Granny with the food preparation. Granny had taught her a number of life skills over the years, but never with any show of affection.

Sage finished her meal and the wine in her glass. The memories that had joined her were uneasy, bitter, and resentful. Granny had begun playing with her food, but it was better than eating alone. She got up and cleared her place and Granny's, rinsed the dishes, and left them in the sink. Then she pulled up a chair close to Granny. "How are you doing?" she asked.

Granny eyed her warily. "Sage is no name for a girl," she said.

Fuck you, hag, Sage thought, but she allowed herself to smile pleasantly. "Granny, can I get you anything else?" Granny's face slackened, became blank. Everything with her was so transparent now. And it never seemed to make sense. One minute she was there, the next she wasn't. Was she someplace else, or nowhere at all? And yes, her condition was much worse than it had been two months ago. Sage stood, finished tidying up the kitchen, and refrigerated the remaining chicken. She thought of the wine hidden under the sink. Her body burned for more of it. Granny just sat there staring at the spot where her plate had been.

Sage walked out the back door. The temperature had dropped considerably. She wished she'd purchased a pack of cigarettes. A smoke would taste good. It would change the way she felt. She looked at the spot where the sandwich and apple had been. She walked over to the spot and once again searched under the basil leaves. Had Janice purposely left the food for someone, or had she mistakenly left her lunch behind when she headed home? Did an animal get it? If so, what kind? A vision of the gun cabinet flitted through Sage's mind. A bear? Raccoon? Either one of them would eat anything. She decided to put it aside, at least for the moment. It wasn't a big deal really.

In the kitchen, Granny was trying without much success to pull herself up to a standing position. Sage gripped her arm to steady her and steered her toward the dining room. "You're ready for bed, aren't you Granny?" she asked. Granny nodded. She shuffled her feet as Sage helped her through the dining room and into the bathroom. She gave Granny her pills to swallow and helped her brush her teeth. She tucked the old woman in and closed the curtains.

Already Granny had started to doze. Sage thought about her grandmother alone in that old hotel, and asleep every night, unprotected. Why had no one been hired to stay there with her? And then it dawned on her. *She* was the reason Granny had been on her own. Nobody else was going to step in to fill Ross's place, and she hadn't thought about it. She'd been wrapped up in herself, her job, her partying, her, her, *her*. It was nothing short of a miracle that Granny hadn't burned the place down, or wandered off, or God only knew what. Did she sleep through the night? Or did she wake up in the dark, alone and terrified and confused and soaked in her own urine?

Would she sleep through the night? Sage certainly hoped she would. She returned to the kitchen and retrieved the wine from under the sink, wiggled the cork out of the bottle, and filled her empty wine glass. Darkness was complete, and with it the enveloping stillness of the countryside. The only sound came from crickets. Millions of crickets. She walked outside, where she looked across the deceptively calm Columbia and watched the lights of traveling vehicles while she sipped her wine. For a moment, she wanted to be in a fast car headed somewhere, anyplace but here.

But there was work to be done, a lot of it. Once again and for the final time, Sage would clean up after her brother. Who knew what evils awaited her in that office? What had he or hadn't he done? She teared up, then quickly wiped her eyes. Despite her loss, she needed to buck up and somehow keep going, to figure out a plan for Blackthorn that was simple and would bring in enough money to pay off any debts and take care of Granny. Selling the place seemed the most viable option.

She would talk to Tommy—Thomas Kitt—childhood friend and Ross's closest pal since they were in fifth grade. Once the local poor boy, Tommy now was a highly regarded lawyer for people who had large bank accounts and troubles with the IRS. He'd overseen payroll for the Blackthorn staff, such as it was, since before Ross relapsed. He'd done it as a personal favor to the family, and not at his usual hourly rate. All that needed to be sorted out. Sage did not for a minute entertain the notion that he'd been compensated for his efforts. She needed to know where things stood with the Blackthorn aside from the day-to-day things.

She realized that Granny's situation presented the biggest challenge she faced. Granny was old and, since Ross's death, had become very frail. She'd changed visibly in two months. Along with the normal health issues of a person in her eighties, Granny had dementia, or Alzheimer's disease. Sage really didn't know the difference, nor did she care. Bottom line, Granny's mental capacities had failed her, and now she needed full-time care. She needed a place to live where she got the right kind of care. That meant learning the old woman's financial situation—Tommy again, hopefully—and finding a place for her to live based on her ability to pay.

Sage sighed and walked back inside. So much depended upon money. She locked up the hotel, then made her way back to the office and turned on the light. She didn't know what she was going to do there. She was stupid-tired and more than a little tipsy. She walked back to the desk and sat in the chair behind it. Only after she sat there a minute sipping more wine did she notice the pile of unopened mail. She grabbed the large pile of envelopes and began flipping them onto the desk, one after the other, as if she was dealing cards.

Shit! They were bills, a pile of bills. Two months' worth, or more, by the looks of them. She tore open the most recent ones, and indeed, inside the envelopes were the past due notices she dreaded finding. She realized that Blackthorn was grave in danger of losing telephone and electric service, and that these things needed to be dealt with first thing in the morning.

Sage pawed through piles of papers on the desktop, searching for a piece of scratch paper. Once she had something to scribble on, she opened the top drawer of the desk in search of a pen. She found one. Chewed on. Ross liked to chew his pens. *Had liked to.* She printed herself a note that she would put on the kitchen table as a reminder. She had to get those bills paid tomorrow, when she was sober. She'd need to locate the checkbook first. Always something.

Then she looked across the room to the shelves heavy with Susan's barrel racing photos and trophies. A gun cabinet stood next to them. There'd always been guns at Blackthorn.

She'd grown up with them. She gazed at it for a few seconds, and then, on impulse, searched the top desk drawer. She located the key, right where it had always been, and opened the cabinet. The old, familiar shotgun stood on its butt in its usual spot. Granny would fire that off now and then, when she heard something roaming around the place at night. The .22 rifle rested next to it. She wondered how long it had been since the guns had been used.

She reached up to the shelf, trying to remember what was kept there. She felt a box of ammunition, and behind it her hand bumped against something cold and hard. She wrapped her fingers around it and brought it out into the light. It was a compact, very modern looking handgun. Sage cradled it in both hands. It felt heavy and dangerous. Her mind tried to process the meaning of such an object. Why was it here?

The Blackthorns had never owned a pistol. It was a good thing to have a rifle if you lived in the country, in case of emergency or to scare off a wandering bear. Years back, family members had hunted deer and elk, but the hunting rifles were long gone. Sage had never until this moment touched a handgun. In New York, where she lived, handguns meant one thing. They were used to shoot other people. Quickly but carefully, she returned the gun to its shelf. She wiped her hands on her jeans.

Back in the kitchen, she placed her note on the table where she'd see it in the morning. She poured the rest of the wine into her glass and sat at the table staring at nothing in particular. Listening to the crickets. She finished the wine. She didn't remember going upstairs to her bedroom.

Chapter 8

SHE HAD BEEN SLEEPING SOUNDLY, and all at once she found herself wide awake. Where was she? She lay there, head spinning, trying to place herself, her body tensed and unmoving. The purr of an engine somewhere in the distance. She took a deep breath. It was dark, but she'd forgotten to draw the curtains, and in the ambient light from outside she remembered where she was. Home. The Blackthorn. Her body relaxed against the soft clean sheets.

And then she realized something was not right. It was the sound of boat motor, probably inboard, that reached her through the open window. It sounded very close, so close that in her mind there was a whiff of gasoline, that familiar aroma that always came when Mom started the old outboard. The promise of an adventure on the river.

Sage glanced at the clock, two-thirty. Who was it that had said, "Good things don't happen at two in the morning."? She sat up in bed, and familiar waves of nausea washed over her. Her stomach clenched, head pounded, and her mouth felt like it was filled with sawdust. But there was that infernal noise. Who the hell was out on the river this time of night?

Slowly, with great care lest she fall, she got out of bed and crept to the window. To the west, the moon was high and bright, and the river glimmered. Down at water's edge, a man stood on the shore. A good-sized cabin cruiser idled at the dock, and a man on the boathouse dock held a rope to contain it. The man glanced toward the buildings and Sage withdrew from the window to avoid being seen. Then he turned his attention back to the idling boat. When the pilot killed the engine, he pulled the boat closer to the dock and hitched it at one of the metal loops. He grabbed the side of the boat and slowly eased it parallel to the dock and secured the rear of the craft to another loop.

Two people came out of the boathouse—*her boathouse!*—carrying packages the size of a breadbox. Their movements were furtive, they didn't speak. As she watched, they scurried ant-like, loading packages out of the boathouse and onto the waiting boat. The guy on the shore turned and looked in her direction, and again she ducked back into the darkness. What on earth was going on?

Sage felt herself in a dream. The eerie night lit only by a crescent moon, the dark, furtive characters moving in and out of shadows at the edge of her property. Taking things out of her boathouse. It was unknown and crazy. Surreal.

She watched their clandestine movements with dread, not knowing what to think or do. Drugs? It had to be drugs. And if so, why here? No, it couldn't be. Drugs were a dangerous business.

Suddenly her stomach revolted. She rushed from her bedroom to the bathroom and made it just in time. It only took a few moments to pull herself together, but by the time she returned to her room the boat was gone. Indeed, except for small waves from the wake lapping at the shore, the night was peaceful and undisturbed.

She stood in the window and looked hard at the boathouse. Nothing. No men, no boat, no noise. But the shadow of a wake trailed into the darkness, and little ripples of water made gentle slapping sounds against the boathouse. Where had they gone so quickly? And how? It was as if a phantom had been there. The wake melded with the current and the river rolled by undisturbed. Her mind raced. Across the river she again noticed the occasional lights of vehicles passing soundlessly in the dead of night. It almost seemed that she had dreamed the entire thing.

No, it was too real. The motorboat had woken her, and she had stood and watched at this very window. She had seen them down there moving about, trespassing on her property. Her first thought was to put on some clothes and go down and see what was going on. *And then what, dumbbell? What if someone is still there? Or what if it was nothing?* Should she call the sheriff? And what then? Unless the visitors had left some evidence of their presence, she'd be out there explaining a phantom.

There was a good explanation. There had to be. She just didn't know what it was yet. She tip-toed down the stairs and made her way through the darkened hotel to Granny's room. The old lady was her back, mouth wide open, snoring loudly. She sounded like a bull elk! At least that part of the picture was probably normal.

Upstairs, she stood at the window staring at the boathouse. Her stomach churned, and her mind refused to settle. She thought about the packages. About the size of a breadbox. Or a Thanksgiving turkey. She glanced at the clock. It was nearly three-thirty in the morning. Maybe some tribal members had rented the boathouse and were storing their fishing gear in the boathouse. Gillnets, stuff like that. It was almost time for the fall salmon run. Those things didn't look like fishing gear. Maybe those men—they were most certainly men—were friends of Betty. Or Janice. Maybe this had something to do with the person who may or may not have taken the sandwich from the garden—if there was, indeed, such a person. But why in the middle of the night? *Because it's drug dealers, you idiot.* No, not that. There was a better explanation. One she'd like. There had to be.

Sage shook her head as if to clear it, and only succeeded in making herself more nauseated. She crawled back into bed and pulled the blanket up to her chin. She lay there staring at the ceiling. Her stomach began to settle and her head slowly quit spinning. She heard a creak above her and gasped. It sounded like a footstep. She listened for several minutes, barely breathing waiting for another. Other sounds came to her, and she realized they were the sounds of the hotel settling its bones for the night. She would check everything out in the morning. It made sense to wait, to check on things in daylight. Now, she felt completely insane. And then, at last, she began to breathe deeply and slowly, in and out, in and out.

Sage awoke to a room flooded with sunlight. Again, it took her several seconds to place herself in Washington, at the Blackthorn, in the moment. And then she remembered. Last night. Was it a dream or was it real?

She glanced at the clock. It was nearly nine. She hadn't managed to sleep so late for ages, but as she had been awake for a long while the night before, she probably needed it. She sat up too quickly and her head pounded. It was time to get things done. She tied up her hair and padded through the living room to the bathroom, where she took a very quick shower. She dressed in jeans and a camp shirt and headed downstairs. And then, to the reception desk. During the last two months, she had learned Thomas Kitt's phone number by heart.

"Law offices." The receptionist sounded chilly.

"Thomas Kitt, please."

"May I say who's calling?"

"Sage Blackthorn."

"May I tell him what this is regarding?"

"He'll *know* what this is regarding!" *Jesus!* The receptionist put her on hold. She should have had a cup of coffee before attempting this.

And then his voice. "Sage." Warm and comforting, smooth as butter. "You're back. When can I see you?"

It felt so much better to talk to someone she knew, someone she could trust. "As soon as you're available, Tommy."

Thomas chuckled. "I knew you'd get right on it. How have you been? I know the last couple months have been especially rough."

There it was again, that horrible, desperate feeling that washed over her like a tsunami leaving her mind in chaos. "Oh, Tommy. You have no idea."

There was a brief pause, then Thomas said, "I think I do, Sage. It'll take time, believe me. Grief always does, and this has been particularly hard. But you're here and you're mobile, so hey. Let's get together. We have a lot to talk about. I'll buy you lunch on Monday. We can get caught up and go over some of Ross's estate stuff, too. Meet me at the office about noon."

"That would be great, Tommy. Count me in."

She hung up the phone and smiled. Tommy had said all the right words. Over the years, he had learned that, and it hadn't been easy for him. As a scruffy, scrawny kid, Thomas Kitt had been a fixture in the Blackthorns' lives since childhood. He had been Ross's best friend, almost a second brother to Sage. He'd helped her get her feet on the ground in the days after Ross's body was found. He watched out for her.

She walked back to the kitchen and checked the coffee pot. Empty. She started another pot. Surely, her so-called employees would need a break by now, after the strain of all their cigarette smoking out in the garden. She fried a couple eggs and toasted a piece of bread.

Janice walked into the kitchen just as Sage sat down to eat. She carried several ripe tomatoes and set them on the counter. Sage looked up from her meal. "Good morning, Janice. What are you up to this morning?"

Janice set the tomatoes on the counter and washed her hands. "Just the usual, Miss Sage."

"Find anything out there by the basil?" Janice's head gave a quick jerk. And then she dried her hands, her back still to Sage. *Got her!*

Betty quickly followed her into the kitchen, unwittingly giving Janice a moment to recover. "Good morning, Sage." She smiled. Sage nodded. She smelled the cigarette smoke on both of them.

"What have we got today, ladies? Any wraps or massage bookings?"

They both shook their heads. "Nope," said Betty. "It's a pretty quiet day."

"What's going on with my grandmother?" Granny was their primary responsibility these days.

Janice piped up, "She had her breakfast early and told me she wanted to rest. I'm about to go give her a shower."

"Great," said Sage. "What about the boathouse?"

The two women looked at her as if she'd grown two heads. "What about it?" Betty said.

Sage calmly took a sip of her coffee. "Have you seen anybody down there lately?"

Betty shrugged. "There's nothing in there," she said. "There haven't been no boats and such for a long time." Janice had turned her back to them again, her attention focused on something in the sink. An errant fork, perhaps? She turned the water on, then off.

"Janice, have you seen anyone going in or out of the boathouse?"

Janice turned around, her face pale as a death mask setting off garish black eyelids. "No, ma'am, I ain't seen nothin'. It's been pretty quiet 'round her since your brother passed."

Sage shook her head. "It's a shame it's just sitting down there empty. It occurred to me Ross maybe rented it out to one of the folks around here who fishes. Or someone from the city. It was just a thought." She took a bite of toast.

Betty and Janice looked at each other, then back at her. Betty said, "If he did, he never said nothin' to us about it. We never seen anybody there, did we, Janice?"

Janice just stared at Sage, eyes wide. Then she seemed to collect herself. She wiped her hands on her apron. "I'm going to go check on Mary Margaret," she said, and left the room.

Betty went to the sink and ran herself a glass of water. "She's sure been on the peck lately," she said.

Sage chose not to remark on Janice's odd behavior. Whatever was going on, she'd have to figure it out. But now was not the time. Later, when she was alone. "I'm going in to Portland in a few days," she said. "I want you two to put together that list, anything you think we'll need out here for the next month or so. And, since we're not busy today you can both go home at noon. I'll handle Granny for the rest of the day."

Betty nodded. "I'll just go down to the laundry and pick up the warsh."

Sage finished her breakfast and washed her dishes while she made a few mental notes. Her main task: get that office sorted out. It seemed that Granny had everything she needed. Shower, time in the kitchen with people, lunch, nap. Meanwhile, Sage needed some aspirin for the headache. No drinking today. *You were sober for nearly a month. You can do this.* Every drink she took further removed her from what she needed to do. There was a lot of sorting, cleaning out, and bookkeeping to do, plus decisions to be made.

She lumbered up the back stairs to the bathroom, where she downed three aspirin. In her room, she dug from her luggage the book she'd wanted to read for the past six months. Maybe this afternoon, after her work was done, she'd be able to start it. Back in the city, she reminded herself, it was deadline crunch time. Her piece on the Greek islands would run in the November issue. Christmas in Vienna was scheduled for December. The next two issues, January and February, were someone else's problem. While she wasn't exactly on vacation, she felt a little lighter realizing that she was free from the pressure, and the rat race that also was the most important thing in her life, for a while.

Correction, she had *thought* being travel editor at one of the nation's leading fashion magazines was the most important thing in her life. And then Ross died. They had been so close at one time. Inseparable. They had loved each other across the miles, even when he groveled, even when she raged, even when they didn't speak because of his inability to get control of his life. Well, she was a fine one to be talking about control, wasn't she?

And there were questions. Sage had a lot of questions about her brother's death. When did he die? What really happened? Those were just for starters. She knew she wouldn't rest until she answered them. Finding answers required a clear head.

Downstairs, Sage went outside and made a quick assessment of the garden, amazed by how much she remembered from her growing up years. The zucchinis were struggling with powdery mildew. She rustled between their leaves for anything she may have missed the day before, including that damned sandwich, truth be told. Could she have imagined it? Not likely, particularly given Janice's weird behavior. The tomatoes required some aggressive pinching back. No use for the plants to set fruit in late September. The ones already on the vine might not have time to ripen. The beans needed harvesting, and there was enough basil for a large batch of pesto. But who would eat it? She picked a bunch and pulled up a head of garlic—pesto for a couple of meals. Granny would love it. She wondered why Janice and Betty had—oh, right. Ross would have planted the garden back in the spring, not Janice and Betty. He was alive then. He'd always loved to garden. They both did. When Mom was alive. A big, sad lump formed in her throat. Janice and Betty had kept it going, enjoying the bounty.

Inside, she listened to the shuffle as Janice brought Granny into the kitchen and helped her settle into the dreadful chair. That awful, cosmic joke of a chair. "There you go, Mary Margaret. Just take it easy. There!" Janice's sharp voice grated on Sage's nerves as she rinsed the basil and patted it dry with a towel. Granny muttered ominously, but nothing coming out of her mouth made any sense.

"Did you help her brush her teeth?" Sage asked once Janice had settled Granny.

"Of course I did." Janice sounded offended. "I been doin' this for a while, you know."

Sage crossed the room and kneeled to get eye level with her grandmother. "Granny, how would you like some pasta with pesto for lunch?"

Granny straightened herself and said, "That would be wonderful, Susan. About time you learned to cook." Sage drew back just in time to see Janice roll her eyes. Well, it was an eye-roll moment, no doubt about it. And so nice to be appreciated, Granny. Thanks very much.

"That's what we'll have then," she said with an enthusiasm she didn't feel. "Do we have Parmesan, Janice?"

"Nope." Janice was still fuming about the tooth brushing question.

"Okay," said Sage. "I need to get some for the pesto. I'm going to run to Stevenson and pick up a few things." *And get out of here for a while.* "Can you think of anything else we need? Anything Granny might need?"

"Maybe some more milk," said Janice. "And graham crackers. Mary Margaret likes her graham crackers."

Sage grabbed her handbag and made a beeline for the rental car. She nearly bumped into Betty as she bolted out the door.

"Where are you going in such a rush?" Betty asked after Sage's hasty apology.

"I need to pick up some items at the store before you leave," said Sage. "Can you think of anything we need?"

Betty shook her head, and Sage practically bolted to the car. Once inside, she revved the motor and peeled out of the parking lot. She felt suffocated. Her skin crawled. It was all she could do to stay at the speed limit as she drove to Stevenson. Once there, she parked, dashed into the grocery store, and headed straight for the wine section.

She selected two bottles of California cabernet sauvignon. It calmed her somehow just to have them in her basket. She needed to be calm. She felt her life was spiraling out of control, and she realized how shaken she was from the events of the previous night. She moved through the aisles, picking up items and inspecting them carefully. Parmesan and walnuts for the pesto, a new toothbrush for Granny, and some Pepperidge Farms Milano cookies. She remembered how Granny had loved them in the past. Screw the graham crackers.

Why did she even care about the old bag? Good question. On her best days, Granny had been difficult to live with—imperious, self-centered, and stingy with praise. She had raised two children she didn't particularly want. She had given them every advantage of which she was capable. She sent them to college. She was a tough old bird, and smart. She had worked hard for everything she had.

In a moment of grocery store clarity, Sage realized that she respected her grandmother. Even when she didn't agree with her, or even like her much. The old woman had done what she could for Sage and Ross; in fact, even when she was hard on him, Ross had been the love of her life. She had seen how scarred he was. She had taken him in again, that final time when he got out of rehab and had nowhere to go. They had made it work for a while. Feelings flooded Sage. She felt the tears welling up again in her eyes so unused to them. Her mother was gone, her brother was gone. She didn't even know who her father was. Granny, she realized, was her last connection to family, and she realized that she owed her a great deal.

Driving back to Blackthorn, Sage forgot about family and thought about the wine. She would go home—imagine that! The Blackthorn. Home. She would make the pesto, get rid of the useless employees for the day, and have a glass of wine. Just enough to take the edge off. After lunch, Granny would take her nap. Sage would tackle the office. And then in the evening, well, one would just have to wait and see.

Chapter 9

CRISP MORNING MERGED INTO A LAZILY warm afternoon. A glass of cabernet with the pasta with pesto and leftover chicken worked its soporific magic on Sage. She'd brought Granny out by the garden to enjoy the early fall weather, and the old woman had talked for more than ten minutes, nonstop, about the past. She was clear and animated about her wedding, how tiny her waist had been more than sixty years ago, and the people who came from miles around and filled the hotel for the occasion.

Sage listened with interest. It was a story she hadn't heard before. There had been one sister and two brothers. Yes, Sage had seen their graves in the family cemetery next to her great grandparents, who had built the hotel. But she'd never known much about them. "They were drunks," Granny said of her brothers, as she expanded her story. "On my special day, my brothers got drunk. They brought a baby pig to the wedding and turned it loose. It ran around squealing and pooping on everything. The guests were scandalized!"

Sage found herself laughing out loud. That was enough to jolt Granny was back into the present with all its attendant issues. "Why were you gone so long, Susan?" she asked. And, "Are you going to leave me again, Susan?" And, "The Lord abhors a drunk." Clearly, nap time had arrived. They shuffled inside, and through the kitchen and dining room, and made a stop at the toilet. Sage closed the bedroom curtains, gave her grandmother a drink of water, and tucked her into bed. Then she warmed herself a cup of coffee and made her way to the office.

The dreaded office.

The bills were where she left them. Sage located the hotel checkbook in the desk's bottom drawer. Underneath it, she noticed a fat manila envelope. She seized it and undid the clasp, and out poured a pile of cash, all fifty and one-hundred-dollar bills. "Holy shit!" She said it out loud, then looked around the room as if someone was there to notice, to judge her. To take the money from her? Her eyes rested on the large, framed photo of her mother on the shelf across the room. It showed Susan at her best—in her rodeo outfit— all satin, sequins, and fringe with tight bell-bottom pants. Beside her, Sonny head-bumped her arm. Sage's reaction was sudden and visceral. Tears sprang from her eyes. "Mom?" she wailed.

She closed her eyes and took a deep breath. When she opened them, she slowly counted the money, wondering why. Why this? More proof of drug dealing? Was Ross involved in something that was over his head? It certainly was starting to look that way. If that were true, it would mean he had become someone else. Not her emotionally fragile, gentle brother. And whose money was this, anyway? She counted the bills out into piles of ten and finished with twenty small stacks. Twenty thousand dollars even. She picked up the manila envelope and looked at both sides. No name, no nothing. She slid the money back into the envelope and returned it to the drawer. It was part of what she would call her evidence file.

The Blackthorn account, alas, did not have twenty thousand dollars in it. She looked in the stack of mail for bank statements and found them for July and August. The account balance was low and showed no deposits after July tenth. Ross had disappeared on the thirteenth. Somewhere in the hotel was two months' worth of payments from spa customers, plus credit card receipts. She thought about the money she'd found in the drawer. This could be several months of cash from massages. But that didn't wash. Most people didn't pay in hundred-dollar bills. It probably wasn't much. Deposits into the checkbook averaged around a thousand a month. Tommy had been paying the staff from an account he'd set up after Ross's relapse.

She sorted through the bills, wrote checks for the utilities, and called their billing offices to let them know payment was on the way. Then, she tackled the desk drawers.

There were no more envelopes filled with cash, nor could she locate personal checkbooks for her brother or her grandmother. She riffled through all the desk drawers twice, just to be certain she hadn't missed anything.

Sitting with her hands on the desk, Sage looked across the room to the gun cabinet. The handgun. What a weird surprise that had been. Had Ross been prepared to use that gun? Had he used it? She opened the desk drawer and located the key, crossed the room, and opened the cabinet. Her hand reached the shelf and searched for the lump of cold metal. Nothing. It wasn't there. Her search became an obsessive patting. When she realized she couldn't reach the back of the cabinet, she grabbed the old captain's chair from against the wall, pulled it to the cabinet, and stood on it. Nothing. *Nothing!* Was she truly, madly, off-the-deep-end crazy?

It was there last night. *Yes, but you, dipshit, drank all that wine.* She had drunk half a bottle of wine before she came into the office. In her world, that wasn't very much. *Okay? And that proves what? You saw a boat last night, too. You were drunk. You threw up. And then it wasn't there.*

Sage felt for the gun one last time. There was no handgun. She stepped down off the chair and returned it to its place. She knew she hadn't imagined it. She couldn't have. She looked into the open gun cabinet. The shotgun and the .22 were there, no handgun. She carefully locked the cabinet and took the key back to the desk. As she opened the desk drawer, she had a thought. She took the key upstairs to her bathroom and dropped it into her makeup bag.

There! Nobody would be messing with the gun cabinet unless they broke it open. As she returned to the office, Sage thought about the handgun. She saw herself turning it over in her hands, felt the cold heft of it. It was real. She was certain it was real. It had been there and now it wasn't. Which led to one conclusion: someone had taken it. She sat behind the desk and stared into the room for a very long time. Betty? Janice? Did it belong to one of them? Why would they have left it here?

As she drew papers methodically out of drawers and crannies, looked them over, and either returned them to their places or threw them into the wastebasket to be burned, Sage grew restless and agitated. The thirst stirred in her. She looked at her watch. It was after four, and time to get Granny up for her evening activities. She left her work in progress on the desk, turned out the lights, and gently closed the office door. She was tempted to lock it. That would mean locating the office key. Not a bad idea, but not now.

She found Granny stirring in the bed. When Sage opened the curtains, the old woman's eyes popped open. She smiled. "Susan."

Sage bent down, the better to be seen. "No, Granny. It's Sage. Susan isn't here." She reached for Granny's glasses and slipped them onto her face.

Granny looked at her, blank, confused. "Susan said she'd

be here when I woke up."

Sage attempted a laugh. "No, Granny. That was me." *Ha ha*. She helped Granny to a sitting position and slid slippers onto her feet. "Are you ready?" Granny stood, and Sage steered her into the bathroom.

Once in the kitchen and ensconced in her chair, Granny became petulant. "I want chocolate," she said.

It looked like the beginning of a long evening. "We don't have any," said Sage. "How

about a glass of wine?" She pulled the cork out of the cabernet and poured herself a glass. She took a sip.

Granny recoiled as if from a rattlesnake. "The Lord abhors a drunk," she screeched. "You're a drunk, Susan, just like your uncles." She started to cry. "I don't want to find you in the river like your uncle Blaine."

Sage set the glass down. Blaine. He'd been found in the river? What the hell? Was history repeating itself? Was this a family curse? Suddenly, she felt mean. She wanted to scream and kick something. She didn't want to be cruel to someone who had lost her ability to think clearly, her only living relative, but she needed that glass of wine. She walked over to her grandmother and put a hand on her shoulder. She dabbed her grandmother's face with a kitchen towel. "It's okay, Granny. What would you like for dinner?"

Granny gazed off into space, her normally blank look replaced by one of profound sadness. Sage sighed as she pulled leftover pesto pasta and chicken from the refrigerator and turned on the oven. After placing it in a casserole to reheat, she popped it in the oven and went outside to pick enough beans for supper. She took her glass of wine with her.

The beans were abundant. In a couple of minutes, she picked enough for the two of them. And then she saw it, peeking out from under the basil same as yesterday. Another goddamn sandwich! She walked over to it and looked down. Another apple, too. She slugged down some wine. Tonight, she'd be ready for him. Her. Whomever.

By five o'clock, they were eating. At five-thirty, Sage had nearly finished the kitchen cleanup. Granny dozed in her chair. This had been her brother's life—well, maybe not quite this bad—for his last two years on earth? How had he stood it? How had he filled the time? Cooking and caring for this old woman, dealing with Janice and Betty, puttering around the place doing chores, building the raised beds, planting the garden. It was lonely. It was slow and tedious. It was just fucking awful. Even with his commitment to Granny, this was hell on earth. No wonder Ross relapsed. She looked at the Cabernet bottle. Only about two inches of wine remained. She wondered if there was anything stronger in the house. She knew better.

And then it was Granny's bedtime. The interminable shuffle to the bathroom. Instructing Granny on how to brush her teeth. The diaper. The curtains. The final tuck-in and goodnight. At last it was over. She returned to the kitchen and filled her glass with the last of the wine, never forgetting that another bottle awaited her should she need it. Then she walked into the office. It was time to confront more piles of paper.

She approached the desk in the private room that had served as Granny's office during the hotel's heyday and turned on the banker's light. Then she walked behind the desk and sat firmly in the big oak swivel chair. She placed her hands on the desk with grave deliberateness. She was Granny in this chair. She was Ross. What had he done while sitting here?

Facing her on the desk was a small framed photo of the two of them grinning, laughing like wild things. She remembered that day. It was the day Ross was released from his first rehab nearly nine years ago. He was twenty-four and floating on a clean and sober pink cloud. She'd driven up from Eugene to help celebrate. They had screamed and laughed and gone out to dinner together. Who had snapped the picture? She remembered. Tommy. He'd just started at Northwestern School of Law at Lewis & Clark College. He'd joined them for dinner. Just kids back then, and beautiful. The last time she'd seen Ross it wasn't beautiful.

The old Royal typewriter rested on the desk amid seemingly random stacks of paper. Sage picked a couple of the piles up and then set them down. Why couldn't her mind keep up with her actions? Among the papers were random notes and lists in Ross's handwriting. Her eyes stopped at a plastic-covered binder. She lifted it and opened it. Inside were several pages of neatly typed poems. She read the beginnings of a couple poems, but the words jumbled in her mind. She realized they had been written by her brother, but they made no sense. She wanted more of the warmth of the red wine in the kitchen. Poetry could wait. She put the file back on the desk, left the office, and turned out the light.

She peeked in to Granny's bedroom to make certain she was asleep, then walked to the kitchen. She opened the second bottle and filled her glass with more wine, walked outside, and looked downhill to the river.

The boathouse and distant trees cast long shadows in the lowering light. The grass glowed golden. Sage could not remember noticing the beauty of this location growing up. She remembered little but the discomfort of being raised under her grandmother's critical reign. There had been little room for error or enjoyment. Granny ran a tight ship. But she did keep Sage and Ross fed and clothed. She sent them to college. Looking back, Sage couldn't imagine how her grandmother had managed the expense of all that child rearing. Until this moment, she only remembered that at age eighteen she had run screaming from the Blackthorn, hoping never to return. Except for brief visits, she never really had come back. Until now.

She took a sip of wine and began walking toward the boathouse. The place was basically hers now. She would own it outright when her grandmother died. It was a dinosaur. She hoped that Ross hadn't run it into too much debt. There seemed to be no end to the surprises around here.

She looked back at the hotel and bath house, the derelict barn and the outbuilding behind them. Lots of lumber and plaster and old rooms and, for the most part, bad memories.

Then she looked to the river and beyond. Riverfront property should be worth something these days. Tommy would be able to place a ballpark value on the place. She'd sell the Blackthorn and go back to New York.

She stopped herself with a shudder. Back to what? New York hadn't been working very well for her lately. *And why was that? Because you fucked up and did stupid things.* Life had gotten out of hand. Her personal life was a disaster. Work? Only less so. She still had managed to hold it together at work. But only barely. And she still had her apartment, sublet to a work associate for the couple months while she straightened things out here. Since she needed to be away from the city, Sage felt fortunate she'd had a place to come to. Here she could have the time she needed to get sober again. She would figure it out. She would take the time she needed to process Ross's death and grieve without acting out, without doing self-destructive things. Here she would learn soon enough what she had to do to turn her life around. She'd find the answer here because, let's face it girl, aside from Granny, there just wasn't that much else to do. Except figure out what happened to Ross.

Sage reached the boathouse. It wasn't anything fancy. There had been a boat of some sort years ago. She tried to remember it. Years ago, when they were small, Mom sometimes took Ross out in it and he tried to catch a fish while Mom drank beer. Sage didn't like to fish. And she hadn't thought much about the beer back then. It had just been there every day, part of life as she knew it.

She stepped onto the dock and walked to the boathouse door. It was padlocked, and the lock looked new. Strange. She peered into one window and then walked around to the other side and looked through the other. It was dark in there. Old fishing rods hung on the far wall. And below them on the narrow wooden walkway around the boat moorage rested a neatly folded stack of empty burlap bags. Who had padlocked the thing, and why? Even when they had the boat, they'd never locked the boathouse. The Blackthorns had rarely locked anything. There had been no need.

Up close, she noticed the windows which had been rotting in their frames the last time she'd paid attention had been replaced. The entire structure was in better shape than she remembered. Probably another of Ross's projects before he relapsed. She took a sip of wine and thought about it for a moment. So many changes. She'd look in the office and see if she could find that padlock key.

Sage stepped back onto dry land and began to walk back across the upward-sloping field toward the buildings. She thought she saw something move near the garden area and stopped. Someone was in the garden! It was the sandwich snatcher! Had to be. Tall and gangly with loose-fitting clothing that flapped around him when he moved.

"Hey," she yelled. "What are you doing?" He looked toward her, momentarily paralyzed.

She walked quickly toward him, picking up her pace to a jog. She would put a stop to this immediately. Her foot caught on something. She tripped and landed hard on the ground. She screamed in pain as her ankle buckled underneath her. Beside her, the wine glass lay shattered. Her hand was cut and bleeding, she noticed, but it wasn't that bad. A simple cut. The ankle? That could be a problem. Stupid to be wandering around in a field half drunk. *Stupid, stupid, stupid!* She looked up toward the hotel. The man was gone.

Whimpering, she rolled over to inspect the damaged left ankle. *Stupid!* Was it broken? She sat there a moment, breathing deeply into the pain. Then she pulled herself to her feet and tried to put weight on her left foot. Searing pain shot up her leg. She had to get back to the house. She lurched through the tall grass toward the back door. How was she going to deal with this? What if she'd broken something?

She walked slowly now, watching where she stepped, feeling the stab of pain each time she put weight on her left foot. It seemed like forever, but at last she arrived at the back door. She stepped into the cool kitchen and ran a glass of water at the sink. Then she limped, one miserable step at a time, to the reception area and picked up the telephone.

A drawer in the reception desk contained the phone numbers she needed. Betty was at the top of the list. "Please, please, please," Sage moaned as she dialed the number. She let it ring six times. No one picked up. She tried again. Nobody home. She felt shaky. The pain was maddening. Was she in shock? She dialed Janice's number next. Nothing. Where the hell was everyone? The bingo parlor? Finally, she called information and wrote down the number she did not want to dial. It was her only choice. She dialed the number and waited.

"Hoot Owl. This is Andy." She could hear music and voices in the background.

"Andy, this is Sage. I need help." Speaking out loud, she realized how shaky her voice sounded. She inhaled sharply.

Slight pause. "What's going on, Sage? What's wrong?"

"I fell, and I may have broken my ankle. I don't know. It just hurts so bad. I need to go to emergency." She stopped, realizing that shaky was only the half of it. She realized that she was slurring her words. "And make sure I didn't do any real damage."

Except for the background noise, it was quiet.

Into the vacuum at the other end of the line, she said, "I'm scared. I don't think I can drive." Still nothing. "I'm not sure where the nearest hospital is."

She heard a sigh. "The closest one is Vancouver, remember? Just stay put. I can come and get you, but I need to find someone to tend bar here, so it might take a few minutes. Are you okay with that?"

She'd have to be. She let out a long breath. "Oh, thank you so much. Yes."

"Then sit down and take it easy. Elevate the foot if you can." He hung up before she could say any more. Her ankle throbbed. Pain ripped through her. And fear. She felt so very scared. And alone. She wanted to scream. She returned to the kitchen and sat at the table. She propped her left foot onto another kitchen chair. Andy had told her to elevate it. Why was she so confused?

The sun had set. Time crept. Sitting alone with her pain, Sage noticed that the kitchen door was still open. A big moth flew in and flapped around the light above the table. She was faintly aware of the soft night air closing down the day. She could hear crickets. It was a comforting sound, but her mind was in turmoil. At the hospital they'd know she was drunk. She didn't want them to know. Andy would know she was drunk, and that wasn't good either. She'd already messed up badly with him because of alcohol. This was as bad as New York. Same shit, different day. Different place, too, but that hadn't helped, had it?

The endless quiet. The absence of human noise. That part was not like New York. Here it was vast, but quiet. Except for the crickets. She heard tires on gravel, saw the light from headlights as Andy pulled up near the back door.

Andy got out of the pickup and slammed the door. His face registered concern as he walked into the kitchen toward her. He even looked a bit fierce, eyebrows drawn together. "What have you done to yourself?" His voice was stern, no nonsense.

"I fell out in the field," she said. A tear rolled down her cheek and she wiped it away as he knelt by the chair to examine her ankle. This was no time to cry. "Down by the boathouse. Somebody was in the garden and I started to run up the hill and tripped."

Andy started to lift her foot. "Do you mind?" he asked.

Sage shook her head. He sat down and rested her foot in his lap. He moved it slightly back and forth, and she gasped.

His fingers firmly but gently prodded the entire area. Yes, it hurt like hell, but she wasn't going to die. He poked, grunted, and asked her a couple of questions. Then he got up and set her foot back on the chair.

"Look, nothing's broken," he said. "I can fix this. We won't need to go the hospital."

Sage let go a huge sigh. "Thank God," she said.

"I'll go get my kit," Andy said. "How much have you had to drink?"

"I beg your pardon?"

"You've been drinking. How much?"

"It's none of your business."

"If I'm going to show up at your place and patch you up after you fell down drunk, I think it is my business," he said. "I called in my other bartender so I could come over here. Is this going to be a pattern?"

No trauma. No drama. Just the facts. Sage narrowed her eyes at him. She wanted to argue, but in her inebriated state she knew she was guilty. "Look, I drink," she said. "I enjoy drinking, and I've been under considerable stress. Just keeping it together has been very difficult since Ross died. I had some wine tonight. Probably more than I should have. But I don't always drink like this."

Andy held her gaze for several long seconds, then turned and headed for his pickup. As he walked out the door, he said something under his breath that she couldn't hear. She leaned her head back and closed her eyes. It didn't matter. She didn't give a shit what he thought about her. She didn't.

Screw him.

He re-entered the kitchen carrying a leather tote. He set it on the floor, settled himself with her foot in his lap, opened the bag, and began rummaging. He set several items on the table, then began with more poking and prodding. "Does this hurt?"

Gasp!

"Does that hurt?"

"Yes, dammit!"

He rubbed some balm all over her ankle and foot, then chose two cloth bandages from an assortment of wrapping materials. "What was that stuff?" Sage asked as the balm dried on her foot and ankle.

Andy began wrapping her foot with a soft, stretchy bandage. "Arnica montana. It's an herb with analgesic and anti-inflammatory properties. People have used it for centuries."

Sage focused on him, absorbing what she could. "So, that means…?"

He used a small metal clip to secure the wrapping, then picked up a second bandage, this one heavier, and wrapped some more. "It will make you feel better. I also recommend you take some ibuprofen if you have it."

"How do you know all this?"

"Medic. Vietnam. 1972-'74. Honorably discharged in 1974, rank lieutenant. Any other questions?"

Sage shrugged. She'd forgotten about the pain. "I didn't know the Army used herbs."

Andy tugged on the bandage and stuck his finger under it. "They don't. My mother used them. She was a member of the Chinook tribe, and a healer. Does this feel tight?"

"I think it's okay. You were young then."

"I was young." Andy placed her foot on the chair. "Now, let me see your hand." He cleaned and dressed the cuts on her hand, wrapped it lightly in gauze, and left a tube of antiseptic salve on the table. "Tell me about this guy in the garden," he said. "Who was it?" His dark eyes flashed at her.

Sage thrummed her fingers on the table. "I don't know. Someone is hanging around here and Janice is feeding him. She leaves sandwiches and apples under the basil plants. I have no idea what's going on."

Andy grunted. He seemed about to say something but stopped himself. He stood up and walked to the refrigerator, where he took a tray of ice cubes from the freezer. "Where are your plastic bags?"

Sage directed him to a stash in the entry. He grabbed one and dumped the ice cubes into it, tied it closed, and wrapped it in a dish towel. He returned to the table and laid the ice on her swollen ankle. "I'm going to look into this," he said. "It could be a guy named Phil. He's another Vietnam vet, has PTSD. Ross let him sleep in the barn last winter, so he may have come back to find a place to stay dry."

"That's all I need," said Sage. "Another person to take care of around here."

"I won't say for sure he's harmless, but if it's him I can find him and talk to him. Don't worry about it now. Just keep off the foot, elevate it and use the ice pack. Take ibuprofen as directed. I'll come back tomorrow, and I better not find you drunk."

Sage felt a stab of guilt, followed by resentment. She only said, "Yeah. I owe you dinner. Or something."

He nodded. He'd seen the anger in her eyes. "You know where to find me. Good night." Then he was out the door, closing it gently behind him.

She waited several minutes, until the pickup was gone, until it was quiet again and the crickets outside felt safe enough to resume their chorus. How could she have made such a mess of things? She began to cry. As waves of shame and desperation rushed through her, the sobbing escalated. She pounded her good fist on the table. She was a drunk, just like her mother. And Ross. Just like Ross. She couldn't control it and she couldn't stop.

And Ross, dying out here all alone? She snorted and shuddered and continued to blubber. Truth was, she didn't even know where Ross had died. His body had been found washed up along the river halfway to Stevenson. A final sob came out, another shudder.

She grabbed a paper napkin from the holder on the table, patted her eyes, and blew her nose. She felt almost sober, but knew she wasn't. She looked at her watch. Two hours since she'd fallen and cut herself and messed up her ankle. And Ross was dead. All the crying in the world wouldn't bring him back.

Finally, she stood up and hobbled to Granny's room to

check on her. There was nothing left to do after that, so she made her way scooting on her butt, one step at a time, until she reached the top. She brushed her teeth, took the ibuprofen, and crawled into bed.

Chapter 10

SHE HADN'T MEANT TO SLEEP SO LATE, and in fact, had lain in bed for probably half an hour reflecting on the previous night, feeling the steady dull throb of her ankle. It had been a complete fuck-up, starting with falling and injuring herself. Memo to self: leave the glassware inside where it belongs. Enduring the scrutiny and questions from Andy had only made matters worse. She hadn't really had a choice, she realized. And her own actions had gotten her there. Memo to self: take a day off from alcohol and get yourself back into balance.

Then she remembered the noises that had awakened her the night before her accident. She shut her eyes and could see the furtive figures moving in and out of the boathouse. She could hear the regular purr of the boat's motor. Someone was using the boathouse without her knowledge or permission. Who were they and what were they doing there? Or had she imagined the entire thing? She squeezed her eyes tightly shut and tried to concentrate. She was hungover again and her head pounded, making it hard to think. She had seen them, she had gone into the bathroom, they had vanished.

It was real to her, but she had to ask herself again: had it been a dream? As hard as her mind fought for an answer, she couldn't be certain one way or the other. More than twenty-four hours after the incident, it seemed dubious at best. Ridiculous. She knew how often she mistook reality when she drank. It was one of the things that concerned her. And yet there was that new padlock on the boathouse. Another reason to take a day off alcohol.

By the time Sage crawled out of bed and donned her bathrobe it was nine o'clock. She hobbled down to the kitchen. Her ankle felt better than on the previous night, but it was still very sore and throbbed. There was hot coffee in the coffee maker on the counter. Her spirits lifted a bit until she smelled it. Burnt. She poured herself a cup anyway and looked around the room. She heard voices out back. It was time to do something about those two and their smoke breaks.

She limped outside to find Janice and Betty smoking by the raised beds. No more Miz Nice Girl. "Good morning, ladies."

Something in her crisp tone of voice must have gotten

their attention. They both looked at her as if they'd seen an alien. Betty mashed her cigarette butt into the gravel and then pinched it and put it into her apron pocket. She squinted at Sage. "What happened to your foot, honey?"

Sage had already decided to tell them the bare minimum. None of their business. "I fell down by the boathouse," she said. Betty's pale eyebrows raised into her wrinkled forehead and disappeared under her lank, gray bangs. She looked like one of those dolls with a shriveled apple for a head. And the stringy hair. "It's no big deal," Sage told her.

Now it was Janice's turn to snuff her cigarette and reluctantly pluck it from the gravel in front of her. "That's too bad," she drawled. "Did you patch yourself up or go to emergency?"

"Andy from the Hoot Owl came over," said Sage. And yes, it hurt like a motherfucker, but she'd been hurt worse.

The two women looked at each other, then back at her. "You're not going to be able to do much with your foot that way," said Janice.

No shit, Sherlock. Sage drew herself up. "That's why I am going to ask the two of you to step up. I'd like you to schedule yourselves a ten-minute break every two hours, and half an hour for lunch. You know better than I what needs to be done around here."

Sage felt unreasonably angry. Janice and Betty were just doing what they'd always done. They didn't have as much energy these days. She turned her anger on herself as she limped back into the kitchen. Janice and Betty followed her.

She located the bread and placed two slices in the toaster. They probably thought she was a bitch, half their ages and telling them what to do. Tough noogies! She rummaged in the refrigerator for the butter and refilled her coffee.

She looked at Betty. "Do we have any business today?" She couldn't seem to stop herself from sounding angry.

Betty nodded, avoiding eye contact. "We got three massages booked this afternoon."

"Wonderful. That's a bit of money coming in." Then she turned on Janice. "And I want you to quit leaving food out in the garden. I fell running to catch a strange man in the garden last night. Just cut it out. If you must feed someone, do it at your place, not mine!"

Janice pulled herself upright, as if to challenge Sage, but her mouth dropped open. She said nothing. Betty looked at her, complicit and guilty as hell. Great.

Sage nodded. "So, you'll be doing laundry and cleaning in the bath house," she said to Betty. She then turned to Janice. "What's on your agenda?"

Janice looked around, somewhat uncomfortably it seemed, and then shrugged. "Not much, unless folks stop by for lunch."

"I imagine there is a lot to do taking care of my grandmother."

Janice nodded. Her normally grim demeanor had turned into a solid frown. "Yes, that'll take up most of my time."

"Good. So, if anyone asks about lunch, tell them the café is closed today. I'm obviously not going anywhere, so you both can leave after the massages are done and Granny has had her lunch." Janice shot her a sullen look, but she nodded.

Sage grabbed her toast and began buttering the slices. "I don't want to make either of you nervous about your job security, but I am seeing our lawyer when I go into Portland on Friday," she said. "We can't keep limping along like this. During the next few weeks I'm going to have to decide whether to try to make a go of this place or shut it down. Perhaps you two can put your heads together on your breaks and try to come up with ideas as to how or why we should keep the Blackthorn open."

Again, they looked at her, and she couldn't read their expressions. "If neither of you have any questions you can get back to work." As she tucked into her toast she thought she heard one of them mutter "yes, ma'am" under her breath as they left the room. She finished the toast and the bitter coffee. After that, she scooted on her butt up the stairs and swallowed several ibuprofens.

An hour later, cleaned up and dressed, Sage made her way down the back stairway and into the kitchen. Rather than try to get into the shower, she had made do with a sponge bath. She found Janice standing on a chair. Dishes were piled on the counter and Janice was scrubbing the cabinets inside and out. She'd piled her hair up and tied a bandana around it. The effort was a striking contrast to her former demeanor. Granny was dressed and nodded, half asleep, in her chair. Betty was nowhere in sight. A list of needed supplies and food had been left on the table.

Chapter 11

THE NEXT DAY, SAGE TOOK IT EASY. She spent some time in the kitchen, when Granny was awake, and tried to keep her left foot elevated. She worked a bit in the office, and when the old woman went down for her nap, Sage spent most of the afternoon upstairs on her bed reading.

That evening she stood at the sink and looked out the window. She watched as the sun dipped low in the late September sky, casting its long golden shadows across the field. It would be down in a few short minutes. Her eyes searched the landscape and paused at the boathouse. The side where she'd stood the previous evening, where she had seen men moving goods into a boat the night before, was in dark shadow. She gained confidence that she really had seen something when she remembered the new lock.

She wanted to go down to the boathouse and snoop some more. She wanted to find the key that unlocked that padlock, but not tonight. Granny needed her dinner. She could barely stand, let alone walk. By the time she got her grandmother into bed and settled, it would be dark. Still…maybe tomorrow after Janice and Betty showed up. If she felt up to it. Meanwhile, she'd try to locate that key. Or a tool strong enough to cut off the lock.

She scrambled some eggs and made toast for dinner. It was all she could manage, given the pain in her ankle. Granny ate slowly, off in her own little world. Sage thought about the bottle of wine, what remained from last night. There must be half a bottle left. She checked under the sink and then searched the kitchen. Andy. Had he disposed of it? He probably had, she thought angrily. When it came to alcohol, he was as bad as her grandmother.

Half an hour later, with Granny in bed for the night, Sage made another search of the kitchen, to no avail. She heard tires on the gravel outside. She clutched at her throat and took a quick breath. Who could be coming here at this hour? It was dark, and she wasn't expecting anyone.

She flipped on the back porch light and peeked outside to see a familiar pick-up. Shit. The alcohol police. Andy pulled up, opened the door, and slipped from under the steering wheel. He had on a tan cowboy hat, which he tipped at her as he walked toward the back door. It looked good on him. "Howdy."

"Howdy, yourself. What brings you slumming?" She thought her voice sounded snarky.

Andy chuckled. "I wouldn't call it that. I took a break from the bar to check on you. How are you doing after your ordeal last night?"

Sage nodded. "I should be honored." She wasn't particularly, although it was nice, she decided, to have someone give a rip. "I'm still among the living, if that's what you're worried about. And my ankle still hurts like hell." She turned and walked back into the kitchen. "Come on in," she said over her shoulder.

Andy removed the hat and walked inside. "If you don't mind, I could check your ankle and rewrap it," he said. He took a chair at the table.

"That would be great," Sage said. "You seem to be good at it. Can I make you a cup of coffee?" She figured she could at least be polite. The guy had bailed her out twice now.

"Coffee would be nice. And yes, I'm good at it. I patched up a lot of men in Vietnam." His face remained expressionless.

Sage let the information settle, then said, "And then you came home."

"Yes, I did. I went to Clark College for two years and certified as a paramedic. I did that for a couple years, and then my uncle decided to retire. He practically gave me the Hoot-Owl. It was too good to pass up."

Sage nodded. She really didn't know what to say to the man. He could fix her up, get out of here, and leave her alone.

After the coffee. She filled the reservoir with water and poured ground coffee into the brew basket. She turned it on and sat down at the table across from him.

Andy had brought in his tote from the pickup. He scrubbed his hands at the sink, looked over his shoulder and smiled at her. "Are you ready?" He grabbed a kitchen towel and dried his hands.

"Sure, I'm ready. Let's get this over with."

Andy pulled his chair up in front of her and gently placed her foot in his lap. She felt very light as he carefully unwrapped the stretchy bandage. Once everything was removed, they both gazed at her ankle. It was twice its normal size and dark purple. "Disgusting!" said Sage.

Andy gently touched the swollen flesh and Sage gasped. Andy glanced up. "Did I hurt you?"

She shook her head. "It already hurts," she said. "You didn't hurt me more."

He smiled, but his eyes were serious. "It looks pretty angry," he said. He removed the tube of arnica from his bag, squirted a small worm of it onto her ankle, and carefully rubbed it all over the swollen area. "We'll let this dry for a while before I wrap you up again," he said. "What were you doing today that got it so swollen?"

Sage shrugged. "Oh, this and that. Up and down the stairs a couple times."

Andy shook his head. "Too much activity," he said. "That leg needs to be elevated as much as possible. And iced. You must stay still for a couple of days, until the pain goes away and the swelling goes down. Use the ice packs every hour or so. That will help more than anything."

Sage sighed. "Sure, whatever. Are we about done here?" She sounded curt. Maybe she meant to.

Andy seemed unaffected. He rewrapped her ankle gently and competently. "A few more minutes, then I'll leave. But first, the coffee."

Thank God he'd be gone in a few minutes. "The cups are above the coffee maker," she said.

Andy washed his hands again, then rummaged through the cabinet, brought out two mugs, and filled them. He placed a cup in front of her and sat down. He took a sip from his mug and gave a satisfied nod. "Great coffee. How do you feel?"

Sage realized that the pain had abated a little. "I think it's better," she said. "Thank you."

They sat in silence. Sage could think of nothing to say— nothing she wanted to say—and it bothered her. Andy, on the other hand, seemed completely at ease as he drank his coffee and took in the surroundings.

When he finished, he took his cup to the sink and rinsed it, returned to the table and patted her forearm. "Take it easy," he told her. "Take some ibuprofen. Go to bed. Elevate the foot with a pillow when you're in bed. I need to go now." He put on his hat and headed for the back door.

Sage got up to walk him out. Only then did she realize how tired she felt. She limped behind him to the back door. He turned to face her. "Thank you again," she said, hugging herself as cool autumn air blew into the kitchen. It sounded lame. He'd come to help her again, and she'd been a brat.

Andy smiled at her, small white teeth, nicely shaped lips. She couldn't read his dark eyes. "My pleasure," he said. "Somebody's got to take care of you. Consider it a favor to Ross. He was like a brother to me." With that, he got in his pick-up and drove away.

Sage closed the door and locked it. She left the outside lights on, just in case. She wanted any boathouse invaders to be on notice that someone was at the Blackthorn and paying attention. She walked through the dining room and into the office. She checked on Granny. All quiet on that front. She eased her way up the stairs on her butt and crawled into bed without brushing her teeth.

Another boring day passed at the Blackthorn. There were no soaks and massages that day. Grumpy from inactivity, Sage kept to her room, pouting and reading and going downstairs only briefly to see Granny midday. She sent Betty and Janice home at lunchtime, and finished her book while Granny napped. The only reason she stayed still was so that she would feel better on the next day.

And then it arrived, that day she had been waiting for. Sage put a bit of weight on her foot going down the stairs Friday morning. She felt an ebullience she hadn't felt in ages. She was going to Portland to have lunch with Tommy. She would see the city, eat delicious food, and get caught up on things. It all sounded wonderful.

She managed an appearance of calm until ten-thirty, at

which time she got into the rental car. She had dressed carefully in a stylish but understated beige linen jacket and slacks and an emerald tank top. The ensemble showed her hair to great advantage. As far as looks, Sage knew her hair was her best asset. And for some reason she wanted to look especially nice for her meeting with Thomas Kitt. Business-like but stylish. One thing she'd learned working for a fashion magazine in New York was how to dress. Not that she needed to worry about having competition in Portland. Portland women didn't know how to dress.

She started the rental car and put it in gear, grateful that she had ended up with an automatic transmission even though she had asked for manual. She always had enjoyed driving. Automatic never felt like real driving to her, but with her foot so messed up, it had turned out to be a blessing.

The day was bright and crystal clear. She drove out Blackthorn Lane onto Columbia Street, and turned west onto Highway 14. On this day she felt a little brightness in her life, a twinge of anticipation and excitement at the thought of her visit and lunch with Thomas Kitt. She hadn't really visited with him for a very long time. He'd come up in the world.

She needed information—a lot of it. What, for example, was going on with the investigation into Ross's death, if indeed there even was one? How bad, really, were the Blackthorn's finances? One of Tommy's tasks over the last two months had been to sort through that mess. God only knew what Ross had been doing since he relapsed. Sage wanted answers. But she also longed for the companionship of an old and trusted friend, a familiar voice, and maybe even some laughs.

She thought of the mysterious cash in the manila envelope in the office drawer. Would she tell Tommy about it, or wait and see? Maybe it was the cash that had come in from massages and lunches during the past months. She knew she'd be kidding herself if she believed that lie. She paid the toll at Bridge of the Gods and crossed the Columbia River into Oregon. Once on Interstate-5, she hit the gas pedal hard and shot past several lumbering semis. Then, satisfied she'd arrive on time, she settled to a fast and easy drive into Portland.

In downtown Portland, Sage parked in the new parking structure next to Tommy's office. If she had been more mobile, she would have walked through the sunshine, enjoying the bustling streets. Portlanders smiled a lot on sunny days like this one, and she found herself caught up in the general good feelings such a day brought to the city. Almost smiling, she limped into the building and took the elevator to the eighth floor.

Thomas Kitt had joined a prestigious law firm straight out of law school and quickly became one of its rising stars. Although his name did not yet figure prominently on the firm's stationery, when she was escorted into his new office, Sage knew that it was only a matter of time. He sat behind a huge desk of polished walnut. The only thing on it besides a multi-button telephone was a Rubik's cube. Before she locked eyes with her old friend, Sage noticed the lush Oriental rug, the antique sideboard, the expensive art.

"Tommy!" He gave her an electric smile and rose from his seat. As he crossed toward her, she took in the expensive suit well-tailored to his tall, rail-thin body, the shiny black shoes, the expensive watch, the perfect razor-cut dark hair. He looked like a film star. He grabbed her upper arms and planted a kiss on each cheek. A lightning bolt thrill shot through her body.

"Sage, you look beautiful—much better than when I last saw you!"

She stepped back and looked into his warm brown eyes. He was healthily tan, and his teeth gleamed white. "I was in terrible shape two months ago," she admitted. "The only way was up." Pants-on-fire lie, but good enough for now.

Thomas released her and walked back behind his desk. "Have a seat." He gestured to a chair across the desk and she seated herself and rested her handbag on the floor. And then a look of concern darkened his face. "What on earth did you do to your foot?"

Sage glanced ruefully at the injured appendage. "Long story. The short version is that I tripped over a rock." That was all he needed to know.

"Ah, well." Tommy glanced at his showboat watch. "Oops. We can talk at lunch. I've made reservations at the Multnomah Athletic Club. We need to be there in ten."

Sage perked up at mention of the MAC. In fact, she'd never been there. Growing up on the river, she'd never even known anyone who was a member. Indeed, until she was a senior in college, she never knew such places existed. Clubs were for British novels and movies. She had been so naïve, so buried in her little country bumpkin world. "That's a feather in your cap, Tommy," she said.

Thomas took a key from his pocket and locked the top drawer of his desk. He stood and buttoned his suit jacket. "Yes, isn't it," he preened. "My bonus from the firm two years ago."

Sage rose, and they headed out of the office. As they paused at the elevator, Sage marveled again at the new Thomas Kitt. Tommy had not always been the polished lawyer who walked beside her now. He had been the poor kid at Stevenson High—the one whose pants were pegged too tight, who was a bagboy in the local grocery store when everyone else was doing their homework or hanging out, the one with horribly crooked teeth who never ever mentioned his family. He and Ross were best friends, and yet in all the times he'd visited at the Blackthorn, Ross never had been invited to his home. It was a mystery she and her brother had discussed more than once.

Somehow, he'd found time to play baseball in high school, and that was when he and Ross truly became brothers-in-arms, winning state championships in their division four years straight. Thomas Kitt had graduated in the top ten of his class and earned a full-ride baseball scholarship to University of Arizona, where he promptly disappeared for four years. Ross also had won a UA scholarship. He, however, had partied relentlessly, and flunked out of college before he even played his first season.

Sage wandered in her memories as she and Thomas stepped onto the elevator. Her brother had been the most intelligent person she knew. Alcohol, and later drugs, had prevented him from having the life he deserved. In rehab they'd told him he was a good person with a bad disease. She'd always known he was a good person, a thoughtful and kind person. Beautiful. But he'd changed somewhere, sometime when she wasn't paying attention. So perhaps it was true he had a disease. And perhaps the disease had proven fatal.

In the parking garage Thomas's led her to a shiny black Mercedes-Benz and opened the door for her. Sage felt it would be tacky to comment—she'd already said enough about his change in status—but she mouthed a silent wow as she slid into the passenger seat. As he got into the driver's seat she said, "Tommy, you must be Portland's most eligible bachelor."

He turned the key in the ignition and chuckled. Perfect smile in her direction, "Working on it."

At the club, he entered the dining room like he was walking onto the proverbial yacht. The maitre'd promptly seated them at a window. Once settled, Sage perused the menu while Tommy ordered them Tanqueray martinis. "She likes two olives," he told the waiter.

So much for an alcohol-free day. Sage looked up at him. "How did you know about the olives?"

Tommy tapped his temple. "My dear," he said, smoothly, jokingly. "Most-eligible- bachelors are required to remember such things."

They both laughed at that one. And when the drinks arrived, they toasted, and each sipped. Sage felt the immediate, welcome rush of the alcohol into her system and took another sip. It had been two days without alcohol. Two miserable days. She nibbled one of the olives. By the time they'd ordered lunch—halibut for her and a salad for him— her martini, along with the throbbing pain in her ankle, were forgotten. She felt safer and more relaxed than she had in months. Maybe longer.

Their food arrived—along with a second martini for Sage. Tommy was working on his, rather slowly she thought. Once again, they toasted, then Tommy set down his glass and said, "Well, I guess you came here to talk business. And since you've been gone so long, the local gossip won't mean anything to you."

He smiled at her across the table in a way that momentarily made her think of him as more than a friend. She felt warm all over. *Stop it!* It wasn't going to be that way with him. She picked up her fork and said, "Tell me what I need to know."

Tommy took a bite of his salad and nodded. "Well, to begin, Ross's investments, now *your* investments, are doing very well. That's the good news."

Sage nearly dropped her fork in surprise. "What investments? How could he have any investments?"

Tommy shrugged. "Well, he did. As does your grandmother. She had some money socked away, and she gave it to him some time ago, so he could continue running the resort after she became unable."

Sage didn't remember Granny ever having any money, or that the money she didn't know Granny had was put under Ross's control. Ross certainly would have told her. Wouldn't he? He was always complaining about being broke. But as she'd been scratching and clawing her way to become travel editor at the magazine, she could have missed something. She had been busy. Preoccupied. Not as tuned in to family as she might have been. The old woman had money? Who would have guessed? "So, she gave him control over her funds so he could run a property that is bleeding to death financially? What kind of sense does that make?"

Again, Tommy shrugged and offered her his sideways grin. "Well, he was sober for a while and doing well. She must have thought he had a good shot at staying that way. Her mind had started to go, and she's always been in denial about that place. It was her life. Ross understood that, and he stayed there and took care of her up until he died. He made good on that."

Sage took a large sip of her second martini. She bit her lip to keep from saying something she might regret. Tommy sensed her struggling. "There wasn't anything I could do about it," he said. "Ross was determined to do things his own way. And then he relapsed. Not fair. But as President Carter said, 'sometimes life is unfair'."

Sage bit back another sarcastic remark. "So, tell me about this money," she said.

More than two hundred thousand dollars, as it turned out. Of course, the value had increased significantly in three years, since Thomas had guided Ross into some very good investments. "When your grandmother was making the decisions, she squirreled it away out there," he told her. "Literally under mattresses. She had little cash stashes all over the place. Over time, Ross found them and asked me what to do, so I helped him."

Sage shook her head. "There are a lot of mattresses at the Blackthorn," she said. "But I still don't believe it. That's a lot of money." In fact, it didn't seem possible. Granny had never had two nickels to rub together. And yet…. And yet, there may have been something held in reserve. Something Sage had never dreamed existed. Certainly not that much, but it could explain the twenty thousand in the envelope. Mattress money.

"The bad news is Blackthorn." Tommy brought her back into the moment. "It's costing a lot of money each month just to keep it open. I've been covering the bills, including wages for Betty and Janice, from your brother's account, which now becomes yours. You really need to do something about that."

Another sip of the martini. Sage already knew he had been taking care of things until she could decide what to do. "Well, certainly. Send me a bill for your time, and hopefully the account will cover it."

Tommy finished a bite of salad. "The best thing you can do, from a financial standpoint, is close the place. You should sell the property—the buildings are tear-downs without major renovation. The other option would be to fix it up, bring it back to life. It would take the better part of your family's investment accounts, but with the money you have in the bank, you probably could get a loan. People love retro. It's a historic structure. Take care of the deferred maintenance, modernize the rooms, bring things up to standard, and start having overnight guests again. It would be quaint. Like the Columbia Gorge Hotel, only more rustic, and a smaller scale. That might work."

Sage felt her family history tugging at her. She could do it! "Yes, I can see that," she said, suddenly flushed from the martinis, excited. "Yes, it could be very cute, and retro, as you say. We could hire a really good chef in there and make things happen."

"Yes. It's risky and would cost a small fortune, but it would be fun. You'd need to find a professional manager."

"What do you mean?"

Tommy was suddenly Thomas, the attorney. "Are you going to stay in Oregon to manage it? Do you know the hotel business? Blackthorn would need someone on site, someone with experience, vision, and the commitment to move things forward. Otherwise, and I mean no disrespect, but you'd have a bunch of local yokels doing what they do out there now. You'd have spent the money, and it would still be running in the red. Who would be the soul of the place?"

Sage pondered that for a minute. Betty and Janice were only okay at their jobs. No fire in their guts. Thinking about them made her tired. "I already have a job, Tommy. A very good job, and one that I love. My goal is to find a comfortable place for Granny to live and go back to New York City. I don't want to stay here."

Tommy nodded. "How's that halibut? Let me order you another drink."

Sage grinned. She was enjoying herself. "It's excellent. And sure, why not?"

The lunch hour had passed, and Sage felt right at home with her food and her dear friend. The martinis were excellent. Tommy hadn't looked at his watch once, and she felt very comfortable, as if they might make an afternoon of it.

Her third martini arrived, and a double espresso for Tommy. Sage looked around the room at what was left of the lunchtime crowd—mostly wealthy women of a certain age clucking and giggling like old hens. She looked back at Tommy. Why had she never noticed how good looking he was? It was the teeth, she told herself. Finally, he'd had something done about his terrible teeth.

"The reason I'm asking you about the Blackthorn," he said, when the waiter left their table, "is because I'm interested."

For the second time during their lunch, Sage nearly dropped her fork. "Interested in *what?*" she said. "The Blackthorn? You? Why on earth would *you* be interested?"

She was talking more loudly than necessary.

Tommy looked abashed, and for five seconds perhaps, a little less than sure of himself. "Interested in the Blackthorn. Yes. Is there something wrong with that?"

"Well, no. No. Of course not," Sage grasped for words. "But why?"

He shrugged and flashed another perfect grin. "Short term, it would be a place to get away on the weekends. Close enough to Portland, but away, if you hear what I'm saying. Long term? Well, you've got a hundred and sixty acres there, and ten of them are waterfront. It would be a good investment. Someday I might want to turn Blackthorn Hot Springs into a five-star resort myself. Upgrade the hotel and make the spa a real spa. Put in a golf course."

Sage threw back her head and laughed out loud. Several of the ladies who lunch looked at them from across the dining room. Tommy sipped his espresso, then sat back for a moment and watched her. It occurred to Sage that the third martini hadn't been such a great idea. They were talking serious business here, and she felt giddy. She took another sip anyway. It was almost gone. "Well, I'll be dipped in shit," she said.

Tommy chuckled, but not loudly. "I have my dreams, too, you know," he said. "They just happen to be closer to home than yours."

"Seriously. The Blackthorn."

"I'm willing to start talking at two million— "

"You have got to be kidding. For a weekend getaway?

Get real."

"—payable in four installments. Or maybe you want more. We'd get an appraisal, of course. We could even put it on the market. That way, if a better offer comes in I can just up mine. Then you could take the first payment, walk away from the place, and never think of it again. Unless you wanted to come for a visit. Any time, of course."

Sage's mind whirled around her. She tried to catch snippets of thought as they rushed past. So much money, just out of nowhere. How on earth could Tommy afford to make such an offer? She figured the place was probably worth it. But who, today, would pay so much? She guessed they'd find out.

As if reading her addled mind, Tommy said, "Listen, I am not made of money, if that's what you're thinking. I have silent partners, and we're interested in doing something like this. We've been talking about it for some time now. Let's face it. Nobody's making more land. A top-drawer resort close to Portland only makes sense. That new one out there now is just the start. I want to get in on the ground floor and make some serious money in my life. And it's a nice site. It would be fun to do something with a place I often think of as home."

"It sounds as if you already have made some serious money," Sage said.

"Oh, not really. I've made good investments for myself, as well as helping Ross with his," he said. "I had minimal education expense. Hell, the first four years were free. And this job has been very good to me. It's easy to get ahead around here if you're smart. Portland is still just a sleepy little city."

Sage had never thought of it that way. It was always the big city when she was growing up. Then, once she moved to New York, she hadn't thought about Portland much at all. Her life had been all about her career. Visits home for a holiday or to deal with emergencies had been inconvenient. She'd never stayed long. Oh, cancel that. Ross's death had been more than inconvenient. It had been overwhelming— she was so out of touch—and devastating. It still was. Just thinking about the Blackthorn made her tired, and the part of her that wasn't fully drunk knew she was in no shape to make a big decision.

Their waiter appeared at the table again. "Will there be anything else today, sir?"

Sir? Thomas, the rising star attorney, shook his head and was presented with the bill. Sage finished her martini and looked at him. "I guess you're right, Portland might grow some," she said.

Thomas added a tip and signed the bill. "Thank you, sir," the waiter said, and disappeared.

When Sage stood up from the table her feet wobbled under her. A shot of pain rose from her ankle. Tommy was at her side, his hand at her elbow. He supportively guided her out of the dining room and to the parking lot. Once in his car, Sage looked at him and said, "Now, we need to talk about my brother." She might have been slurring her words. She wasn't certain.

Tommy looked at her and fastened his seat belt. "Back at the office."

"I wanna know what happened to Ross. What *really* happened to him." Her voice was rising. She needed to control herself.

"Of course you do." Tommy sounded patient, gentle. "We all do. I've got some notes at the office. We'll talk about it there." He placed a cassette in the tape player and mashed a button. Dire Straits. Mark Knopfler singing about some chick named Juliet. Sage relaxed into the leather and closed her eyes.

Chapter 12

IN THE END, SAGE'S VISIT TO PORTLAND was less than successful. Once in his office, Tommy summoned his secretary and asked her to bring Sage black coffee. Coffee delivered, the door was closed, leaving the two of them. They chatted a bit, and while she drank her coffee, he picked up the Rubik's cube and twisted it. *Click, click, click.* His mind was elsewhere, and he was clearly anxious for her to leave so he could work. It was past two by the time she made her way to the rental car.

She had learned nothing new about Ross's death other than that there had been bruising all over his body when it was found. Tommy remembered someone telling him Ross's body had been in the river three to four days. "But you'll have to check with the Skamania County Sheriff's Office, Sage. They handled the investigation." Sage didn't like the sound of that. He implied the investigation was over. In her opinion, it was just beginning.

She got into the car, exhausted and far from sober. Her ankle throbbed painfully. She hadn't told Tommy about the boat in the night, either. So many things she had meant to go over with him had been forgotten because of the martinis. She sighed. Rather than pick up the supplies, she decided to drive straight home. Before the traffic got bad, she told herself.

The trip back to the Blackthorn was uneventful. Sage drove the familiar highway with little attention. Once at the Blackthorn, she sent Betty and Janice home, then checked on Granny—sound asleep and snoring so hard Sage imagined she saw the curtains moving. Making her way slowly upstairs, she swallowed some ibuprofen and headed for the bedroom. She needed to elevate her foot. Maybe if she took a quick nap she'd feel better.

She noticed a terrible taste in her mouth as she flopped on the bed. She was so tired. the room was warm from the afternoon sun. She thought briefly about unwrapping the dressing on her ankle. Lying down, it throbbed a little less. She closed her eyes, and when she opened them it was six-thirty. She sat bolt upright. *Oh my God! Granny!*

Sage struggled onto her feet, pulled on shoes, and limped down the stairs to the kitchen, through the main rooms, to Granny's bedroom. She still felt drunk. The old woman lay in bed, eyes open, gazing about wildly. From her mouth came a distressed croaking sound, not quite words. "Granny, I'm so sorry. I'm here. It's all right." She moved as quickly as she could to the old woman's side and helped her sit up. "Let's get you sorted out and then have some dinner, okay?"

Granny looked at Sage, and as she focused on Sage's face, her own expression brightened with alertness. Still, what came out of her mouth dripped with malice. "Where have you been, Susan? Which man were you out with this time? You stink of alcohol. The Lord abhors a drunk."

Crap. Not that again! "Give it a rest, Granny," Sage muttered as she helped the old woman to her feet and steered her toward the bathroom.

Once in the kitchen, with Granny in her chair, Sage rummaged in the refrigerator. Time to keep it simple. It was late for Granny; she, herself, was hung over from lunch with Tommy, and certainly not hungry. She quickly scrambled some eggs and toasted bread. Comfort food.

She thought about the conversation with Tommy, about the two million dollars. It seemed astronomical, but then the large property with broad riverfront access and spectacular views would have high value. It made sense, especially with a fancy new resort just down the road, that prices would rise. She made a mental note to check out the new place. Somebody had dropped millions into that operation, she was certain.

After Sage got Granny to the table and spread jam on her toast, she sat and picked at her own food. She considered

Ross. She'd learned very little about his death. Tommy had not been proactive about the investigation, probably because he considered it to be her job. Still, he was able to do more, wasn't he? Across the table, Granny finished her meal. Sage got her up, walked her around the dining room for a couple minutes, and then got her to bed.

As she passed the office on her way back to the kitchen, she thought about the shotgun.

It had always stayed out of sight and out of mind, unless Granny took a notion to shoot at varmints. When it came to moles, Granny could be a madwoman. One time, when Sage was very young, Granny had gone nuts with the shotgun. She remembered Mom making grim allusions to the Gunfight at the OK Corral—something Sage had not understood at the time. The gun had always frightened her a bit—all that wood and steel and power. And noise! Maybe Tommy would come out and help her. Did he know about guns? Most of the men who grew up around here did.

She went into the office and checked the gun safe. Locked, as it should be. She wanted to look inside, but the key was upstairs. She felt lonely and vulnerable. She felt sad about the changes around her, how she'd run out of what was left of her family, or what there had been of it. Granny was lost to her as surely as Ross was. Nothing could be done, but it felt crappy just the same.

She returned to the desk and picked up the folder she'd glanced at the night before. It contained several sheets of poems, each neatly typed and dated with Ross's name in the lower right-hand corner. Now this was interesting. She tucked the folder under her arm and headed for the office door. Before she turned off the lights, she looked back into the room, at the shelves with the familiar array of silver trophies all different sizes. They were so tarnished. She needed to polish them. And, among the other photos, that painfully familiar picture of Mom and Sonny taken that summer twenty years ago, the month before she died. She was grinning like she was on top of the world. The most recent love of her life had been behind the camera. Dusty, next to the photo was her white Stetson hat with the sequin band. The one she'd worn the day she died. Again, feelings of loneliness and loss welled up in her. She turned out the light and left the room, shutting the door hard behind her.

Sage changed into her nightgown, brushed her teeth, and climbed into bed. She placed a pillow under her foot, picked up the folder, and began to sift through the pages of her brother's poetry. She was almost sober now, and she felt more at home at that moment than she had since she returned to the Blackthorn. She felt like an editor, in familiar territory. More important, she felt Ross's presence. She felt herself getting to know the side of him that had eluded her all those years since his troubles had begun. Here was the sweet soul she remembered from childhood, as well as a man with uncanny vision. There was something more, too. In his poems was a sureness and sharpness she didn't recognize. In his poetry, the lost boy was a man.

One poem after another. They were dated until the day

before he probably died. Was anyone certain what day—or night—that was? Sage made a mental note to check in with the sheriff tomorrow to see what she could learn. It had been more than two months, for godssakes. They should know something.

She paused to re-read one of the poems. It was good. The next one? Not so much so, but it was marked "draft". And then another. Excellent. She hadn't realized her brother had such an aptitude. Suddenly she was done. She flipped through to the last page in the notebook, and there, scrawled in Ross's handwriting, she read, "With blackthorn staff I draw the bound. All malice and bane, I thus confound–old verse".

Not her brother's poetry. It was strange, arcane. "All malice and bane"? She shut the notebook and put it on the night stand. Where on earth had those lines come from, and what was he referring to? Or was it just some drunken rambling? Sage turned out the light and snuggled under her blanket. The days might be warm, but in late September the nights cooled down quickly.

Chapter 13

July 1985

ON THIS PARTICULAR NIGHT, SAGE desperately needed to check out—have some drinks, have some laughs, go home, pass out. Ten days before, she had learned her brother was dead. The shock of it—after a mad dash to the West Coast, funeral arrangements, Ross's burial, and realizing she had to figure out what to do with the Blackthorn so-called Resort, and her grandmother—was just beginning to sink in.

P.J. Clarke's had been Sage Blackthorn's favorite watering hole since she arrived in New York nearly ten years ago. It was only a few blocks from the magazine offices, so she often walked there after work. It was a popular hangout for people from the nearby publishing houses and magazine offices, along with young and upwardly mobile professionals, mostly men. And tourists. Always lots of tourists, hoping to glimpse a celebrity. Often those wishes were granted, which only added to the mystique.

Paddy's, as the regulars liked to call it, with its historic mahogany bar and turn-of-the century charm, was like Jake's Famous Crawfish in Portland—only better. It was light years beyond what Jake's ever hoped to be. The drinks were always perfect, plus it was a great place to meet men.

Sage wanted to meet Mr. Right with a desperation that grew as the weeks and months passed. She recently had turned thirty and hadn't met him yet. Not even close. Most of her friends had paired up, even if they hadn't yet tied the knot.

She told herself that her life was fine. She had just purchased her own apartment, she finally made decent money, and she enjoyed her career. But she had other needs too—companionship, a steadying force in her life, and, let's face it, regular sex. Without a man in her life, those needs were not getting met. She had always wanted a partner, a nest, and even, perhaps, children. More often than not, these days, her coupled-up friends excluded her from their social activities. She told herself that she should have found someone by now. And why hadn't she? Was there something wrong with her? The feeling was constant and nagging.

Occasionally she hooked up with a man at Paddy's and it always led to wild sex, either at his place or hers. She wouldn't go with just anyone. He had to meet certain criteria. Sometimes they saw each other afterwards, but usually not. She had been attracted to a lot of the guys she met, and even tried following up with some of them afterward. But things never worked. Smart as she was, Sage hadn't figured out that the man who wanted a one-night stand seldom wanted anything more. So, she continued to put on her best clothes, freshen her makeup after work, go out, and try again. Her prince was out there somewhere. She believed this with every cell in her body. Somehow, she would find him. She almost always went alone to Paddy's or any other bar.

The tectonic plates that were her life had shifted. Her only remaining family was Granny, eighty-five years old with advancing dementia. Sage had some friends, mostly from work, but they weren't close. She felt sad and lost and deeply confused, much as she had when her mother died. But she was older now, her own woman. There was no Granny to step in and do damage control and tell her how it was going to be, how they would go on. She didn't *know* how it was going to be, or *if* she could go on. She felt she didn't even know who she was anymore.

She walked into Paddy's and looked around. It was early, and she'd come straight from work. The place was crowded, and the bar was full. She spotted Stuart Ketchum, the magazine's art director, in the corner nursing what looked like an Old Fashioned. He was a bit of a mystery, aloof, but he'd always been nice to her. Polite. Friendly. She approached his table. He looked up and smiled. And stood up. "Sage, how are you? Here, have a seat. I was so sorry to hear about your brother."

Relieved, Sage sat at the table. She ordered a Tanqueray martini from a passing waiter, then folded her hands on the table. Stuart seemed all attention. "Thanks, Stu," she said. "I'm still in shock, I guess. It's a nightmare."

Stuart took a sip of his drink. He looked at her closely and she could almost see him rearranging her artistically like he would the photos and copy on a dummy page of the magazine. She'd never thought of him as handsome, but he had beautiful eyes. Intent eyes. She watched them, unexpectedly captivated.

"It takes time," he said. "My mom died last year. It was a huge shock. Still is. I used to visit her in Westchester every Sunday, and I still wake up every Sunday morning and think, I'm going up to Westchester today to see Mom." He smiled ruefully. "Not."

Sage didn't know him very well. In fact, this was the first time they'd ever talked outside work. "Wow," she said. "I'm sorry." Her martini appeared on the table in front of her. She smelled it and took that wonderful first sip. Divine. Then, "Do you come here often?"

What he said surprised her. "Probably as often as you do." Again, he was looking straight into her as if he knew her better than she knew him.

His eyes were large, hazel with golden flecks, intense. Sage wasn't certain what he meant. Probably nothing. She blushed. "Yeah," she said, "I'm here fairly often. I like the atmosphere. The activity."

"I meet friends here a lot," Stuart continued. "In fact, I'm meeting some tonight."

Was he trying to get rid of her? Sage looked around. "Well, I certainly won't keep you," she said.

Stuart reached across and patted her hand. "Sit still." That intent smile again. "I'd like you to join us. You'll like my friends, and you look like you could use some company tonight."

She looked around her at the crowded, bustling bar. "I'm grateful for the moment just to have a place to sit," she said. Stuart arched his dark eyebrows. Shit. That sounded rude. "I don't mean," Sage stuttered. "I don't mean that present company isn't more than acceptable. It came out all wrong."

He laughed. She laughed. She finished the martini. Stuart signaled for another round.

Fast forward. Sage was laughing. She leaned across the table and laughed hard at something Stuart had said. Other people were with them, sitting and standing around their table. They were so beautiful, so chic. All the pretty people, all drinking and looking around, wondering who would come in next and would he or she prove to be important enough to join their party. Tonight, Sage was one of those beautiful, hip New Yorkers. This was why she loved the City. The waiter set another drink in front of her. Her brain had stopped yapping about Ross. She didn't hurt any more, and that was enough. And then the screen went blank.

Someone was on top of her. Someone was hurting her.

She opened her eyes and saw a face, distorted with effort, shoving himself into her with brutal force. "You're hurting me," she cried, and he clapped a hand over her mouth. She tried to scream, to get away. He reared back, and she saw his face. Dark eyes, dark hair. Did she know him? Why couldn't she think? He slapped her. Hard. She heard laughter. Male voices. Where was she? He called her a horrible name and hit her again, this time with his fist. Then, grunting, moaning, he came. He rolled off her, and away. Someone applauded. More laughter.

She couldn't feel her body. Her legs and arms would not do her bidding. And then he was on her again and she looked into his face. She saw a blur of skin and pale eyes and hair. It wasn't the same man. His grin was a death mask. She felt something hard enter her vagina and she screamed again. The pain was unbearable. The man held a hand over her mouth. She struggled as much as she could. Nothing helped. Someone grabbed her feet to keep her from moving. The strange animal noises she heard were coming from her own mouth. The man on top of her put his hands around her throat. There was no air. Panicked, she tried again with all her might to shake him off her. Nothing moved. The screen went blank.

Chapter 14

September 1985

SAGE CLAWED AT THE SHEETS as she awoke from a dream where she had tried to scream. She had screamed with all her might, but no sound came out of her. She had dreamed of that night again and again, and the dream always ended with her soundless, helpless scream. Her heart pounded from thrashing about so frantically. Her body shook. It was dark, and she lay there stiff with terror. She had been on the floor of her own apartment. They had nearly killed her. But here she was now, in her own bedroom, in her own bed, alone. She was at the Blackthorn. The men who raped her and nearly killed her weren't here. Conscious, she inhaled and exhaled, trying to slow her heartbeat, trying to feel safe again. It took all of her strength to focus.

Lying there in the dark she wondered, why hadn't they killed her? Fear of getting caught? A tsunami of shame washed over her. There were times when she wished they had. Her life was out of control. She felt dirty all over again, a filth she couldn't wash away. And demeaned. Once again, she felt exactly how they had wanted her to feel. She had been less than human to them, and she didn't know who they were.

She remembered that Saturday, how she had showered, crawled into bed, and lain there in pain. Between throwing up and passing out, she'd wondered how badly she was damaged inside. The pain was nearly unbearable. On Sunday, the second day, she moved around a little. She threw out all the clothes she'd worn that night. Her head had quit throbbing and finally she was able to eat a little, but the pain was worse.

On Monday she called in sick. She had managed to get an appointment with a doctor. Hers was out of town, and his associate, a short, aging Jewish woman with an eastern European accent, had examined her. Wearing the ubiquitous open-back gown, Sage had crawled onto the examination table and put her feet in the stirrups. Dr. Franken commenced her explorations, tutting to herself and uttering small exclamations. After the exam, while washing her hands, she had looked over her shoulder at Sage and said, "You have reported this, dahlink?"

"I'm not going to report anything," Sage had said from her position of disadvantage.

Dr. Franken had returned to the examining table. She took Sage's hand and held it in hers. Her eyes registered concern. "Ve need to report this. You were assaulted very violently, dahlink. It is a crime ve cannot ignore. Other vomen could be hurt as vell, you know."

Sage's eyes had filled with tears. "I can't report it. I don't know who did it."

The doctor had blinked once and nodded. Before Dr. Franken turned away, Sage had seen that the concern in her eyes had turned to pity. Sage did not want anyone's pity. It was her own damn fault, and she'd live with it.

"I see," the doctor said, rummaging in a cabinet. "Vell, then. I need to patch you up some. So, I first must give you a little shot for the numbness, and then ve go to work."

Sage remembered leaving the office an hour later, numb but "patched up some". She carried prescriptions for a strong antibiotic, and a pain medication. She'd stayed home two more days. When she returned to work that Thursday, the first person she'd seen when she walked into the magazine offices was Stuart Ketchum hanging around out front joking with the receptionist. He'd smiled at her, given her a thumbs up, apparently not noticing the unseasonal scarf around her neck and the bruises on her face, which she'd attempted to conceal with makeup. "Lots of fun Friday night," he'd said. She'd smiled back at him—a tight little smile—and walked down the hall to her office. Once inside, she shut her door and threw up in the wastebasket. Friday, she applied for a two month leave of absence. She told them she was needed at home.

Sage stared through the darkness toward the ceiling. Her heart rate had slowed somewhat, but she still felt tense, uneasy. She would never know if Stuart or anyone else at their table that night had been involved in the rape. She'd blacked out. Hours could have passed before she woke up in her apartment being brutalized by those men. She might have left Stuart's group and moved on to another bar. She had no recollection. She didn't even know how many had been in her apartment. Two? Four? And who were they? She'd never be able to identify them. Not in a million years. She could hear Granny yammering away. "It was your fault, Sage. Nice girls don't go out to bars to pick up men. You should have gone with a friend. You shouldn't drink so much. You're just like your mother."

Sage sat up in bed. "Shut the fuck up!" she yelled into the empty room. She burst into tears. "Leave me the fuck alone, will you?" she screeched between sobs. "Go away. You fucking ruined my life." But that wasn't the truth, and she knew it.

She got out of bed, walked down the hall to the bathroom to wash her face, and returned to the bedroom. She walked over to the window and peered out. All was calm. No boats, no strangers. The moon was down. It would be getting light soon. She still felt hungover from yesterday's lunch. The damning evidence against martinis increased every time she drank them. She vowed to herself to quit drinking martinis. She'd stick with wine. It was much easier on her system than gin had proved to be. Wine was slow, easy relief. Wine could get her to a good cruising altitude and let her stay there for a while.

That dirty feeling from the dream stayed with her. Sage knew she'd never get back to sleep. She donned a bathrobe, picked up Ross's poetry file, and headed downstairs to the kitchen. She made a pot of coffee the way she liked it, strong, and sat down at the big, round kitchen table. She found her brother's poems fascinating. The imagery was original. They showed energy, a fresh voice, and, most important, were rich with emotional truth. They were better than many published in her magazine. More significant, she felt they spoke directly to her. And then she had the thought: What if they did? She felt her skin prickle. What. If. They. Did?

Oh my God! She flipped to the back of the file, to the handwritten note. "With blackthorn staff I draw the bound...." What if Ross was declaring himself guardian of his life, his property, his soul? What if he had been on a personal crusade to defeat "malice and bane"? That would put a new spin on everything. The only question was, when was the note written?

She laid the notebook down and took a sip of coffee. His last poem was dated July 11, 1985, the day before he disappeared, and he'd hand-written the little verse on that page. It constituted his last words. She thought of the trespassers at the boathouse. Ross would have known about those people. He was drawing a line in the sand. He was going to fix it. At least that's how it seemed to her.

She stood up and, coffee cup in hand, began pacing around the table ignoring her sore ankle.

Sage walked to the office and flipped on the overhead light. Was there something she'd missed? She sat at the desk and began opening and exploring each drawer. If he was sending her a message, wouldn't there be more? Something that would give her more information? She found nothing that meant anything, nothing she hadn't already seen.

She looked around the office. Next to the bookcase sat a tall file cabinet, gray with chipped paint, so old that it was part of the office landscape. She would have to search there as well. For now, she had the poems. She would read through them more thoroughly this time, searching for clues. She walked to the file cabinet and peeked inside. Folders had been removed and shoved back in randomly. Someone had plowed through those files, just as she planned to do later. But right now, she didn't have the energy. Just that short walk to the office, just standing a little while, caused her ankle to resume its throbbing. She slammed the file drawer shut.

So, who had been into the files? Not Granny. Janice? Betty? Did the sheriff's deputies search the Blackthorn after Ross's death? It seemed unlikely, since his death had been ruled accidental. But still, she thought, better them than someone else. And if it was someone else, then why? Nobody had any business in that office now but her.

Sage turned around as she left the room and looked back at the picture of her mother—a smallish person with coppery hair lighter than Sage's and a white cowboy hat—standing cheek-to-cheek with a beautiful quarter horse. Sonny. Sage's eyes filled momentarily. Her mother had made mistakes, plenty of mistakes, yet Sage never once doubted her love for her children. And Susan Blackthorn had always had more spunk than any six people in the room!

In the kitchen, Sage poured herself another cup of coffee. The sun was up. It was a crisp, beautiful morning. She stepped into a pair of flip-flops by the back door and walked out to look at the garden and the river. She could smell the tomato plants. She loved the pungent green aroma the plants emitted. Growing up, there had always been the garden. Granny canned, of course. That's what women in her era did. It had been a much bigger garden twenty years ago. There had been rows of corn, potatoes, cabbages, and onions, berries on the south side of the old barn, and a smaller kitchen garden where the raised beds now stood. Susan's death had taken a laborer out of the mix. Despite Granny's complaining, Mom had done most of the heavy work around the place. On hot nights in the summer, she would take sleeping bags out on the lawn and she, Ross, and Sage would sleep under the stars. So many fine memories up until that deadly rodeo.

Sage walked back into the hotel. It was time to stop whining and get to work. She decided to take her bath before Janice and Betty arrived at eight, and then get to work on the office. She'd clean in there. That would be her excuse. She knew she could ask Janice to do it, but Janice wasn't on a mission to find something.

Upstairs in the tub, Sage soaked her swollen foot. She decided she could probably rewrap the thing almost as well as Andy had. She allowed her thoughts to ramble, holding to the notion that Ross had something to say to her. The feeling that his small scribbled verse meant something was so strong in her mind that it gave her energy. She couldn't move very fast, but her brain still worked. She'd be careful physically, but relentless. She'd sort through individual pieces of paper until she had looked at everything, until she found what she was looking for. Or not. Maybe there was nothing more to find. But she didn't really have anything better to do.

Dressed and back downstairs, she heated another cup of coffee, scrambled two eggs, and made a piece of toast. She'd been awake for hours, and she devoured the food like a starving dog. She tried to focus her mind away from the horrible nightmare, reminding herself that she was safe here. It couldn't happen here, she told herself. But she knew better. It could have happened that night at the Hoot Owl—if not for Andy. It could happen anywhere she was, unless she took care of herself.

Janice entered the kitchen, apparently deep in thought. She jerked herself when she saw Sage at the table. "Good morning," Sage said brightly. "Nice job on things yesterday."

Janice managed a ghoulish smile. She looked like Morticia in The Addams Family. "Thanks."

Sage continued, "There's coffee but you'll have to warm it up."

Janice nodded. She took off her sweater and hung it on a hook in the entry, along with her handbag. She tied on an apron and moved toward the coffee maker. She poured coffee into a small saucepan and set it on the stove to warm. "You learn anything from that lawyer?"

Sage took a sip of her now-tepid coffee. "Only that we're losing money. We already knew that." She decided not to tell Janice about Thomas's interest in the property. No use to start a rumor. Until she knew what she wanted to do, there really was nothing to say about it. She felt a listless, low-grade depression coming on. "Maybe you can work on the garden today," she suggested. "Once you've taken care of Granny, of course. Those zucchini plants are about done."

Janice filled her mug with the heated coffee and sat down at the table. "It's due for a weedin'," she said.

"Pick whatever is ready out there," Sage said. "You and Betty are welcome to take home whatever you want. We can't eat it all."

Betty entered the kitchen and the apron ritual repeated itself. Janice poured her some of the reheated coffee. Betty announced that they would be busy with soaks and massages most of the day, and wasn't that wonderful? Sage supposed it was. At least the two women would be occupied, and the massage therapists would be earning more than usual. As she made her way back toward the office the phone rang.

Sage answered it on the third ring. "Good morning,

Blackthorn Hot Springs."

"Sage, is that you?" It was Thomas Kitt.

"Hey Tommy, what's up?" Sage had been planning to call him but hadn't summoned the energy. The nightmare had sapped it out of her.

"I was hoping you could join me for dinner Saturday night."

Sage felt unsure, tenuous. If she went to Portland for dinner, she would be looking at a long drive home in the dark. And then there was the alcohol. She couldn't trust herself. Not really. She'd proved it again and again. It was a lot simpler to drink in New York, where she could walk home or catch a cab.

Apparently, Thomas was on the same page, as he said, "We can dine at the new Heathman Hotel. It's been refurbished into a luxury hotel, and they hired a great chef." He paused, but still she said nothing. "You're going to love it. I'll book you a room and you can drive home in the morning."

Sage expelled a great breath. As usual, he'd made it perfect. Effortless. "Oh, that would be lovely. Yes, of course. What's the occasion?"

Thomas cleared his throat. "Nothing, really. I just decided, after seeing you yesterday, that I'd really like to spend more time with you. Not as your attorney, but personally."

Sage felt a flutter in her chest. "Really?"

"Really." Thomas paused. "So, let me make the

arrangements. You can check in Saturday afternoon. I'll come by your room at seven."

When Sage hung up the phone, she turned herself around before walking into the office. A date—a big date—with Portland's most eligible bachelor. Her mental cloud lifted, and she laughed to herself. Who would have thought that little Tommy Kitt with his tight pegged pants and bad teeth would ever be the person he was today? He'd always been cute, in a small-town way, and smart. Very smart. But she never could have imagined that he would have great success in life. Not in a million years. And yes, she did want to know that Thomas Kitt. All the better that they had a history.

In the office, she turned on the banker's light and sat at the desk. She looked around the room. And then she remembered the dream. It flooded over her—the shame, guilt, and fear. More than enough for a lifetime, and all because she hadn't been present. She'd been blackout drunk. She stood up from the desk and gimped out of the room. She had to get out of this place, if even for a few minutes. She left by the front door and hobbled down the driveway, past the barn and turned into the field behind it. And there, at the far side of the field, enclosed in a peeling white picket fence, lay the Blackthorn family cemetery.

Sage let herself in through the sagging gate, making a mental note to have it repaired. She was in charge, after all. Inside the fence, she paused. It felt so weird to be there alone, especially after the mash of people who'd showed up in July to bury Ross. She closed her eyes and saw the crowd. Forty or fifty people. She'd been amazed. Thomas tall and sleek in a beautiful designer suit. Older people, neighbors who'd known her family for years, Granny's acquaintances from her church—the ones who were still alive. Several folks Sage's age who had been schoolmates of hers and Ross's. People who looked like Ross's drinking buddies.

For the most part, she knew who they were. And then there was Andy. Yes, he had been there too. She hadn't remembered him earlier, but she could see him now, standing at the edge of the group, handsome and ill at ease in a gray suit. Alert and watchful. In her mind's eye, he stood out, because he was looking intently at something. She wanted to follow his gaze and see where it ended. Then one of her old high school teachers touched her arm and distracted her, so she never knew. She hadn't remembered him being there until now, but he had told her he was close to Ross. Like brothers, he'd said. She didn't remember him much from high school. A kid who never stood out. So, when had he and Ross gotten so close?

She opened her eyes and looked around. Maybe it had been at Stevenson High School and she'd never noticed? She thought about it. Perhaps. It was possible he was one of those serious, quiet individuals who never had drawn attention to himself. He was part Indian, so he wouldn't have run with the popular kids. He would have been invisible. She had been pretty wrapped up in her own dramas and plans and manipulations back then. She had been popular. And once she graduated, she was gone, baby, gone. She had exploded out of the place and on to college. But no matter where you go, there you are. Who'd said that, anyway? "Huh!" she said aloud.

At the center of the small graveyard stood a tall monument—a concrete monolith topped with a Celtic cross facing east. In front of it stood her grandparents' markers, side by side. Cyril had died in 1950, when her mother was just a child. "Died of the drink," as Granny chose to remember him. Mary Margaret had made it thirty-five years without him and had never remarried. Maybe once was enough. She'd outlived her only child by twenty years already.

It was Sage's great grandparents who had homesteaded the property and years later, in the early 1900s, built the hotel. Great grandmother Margaret had been a school teacher in Vancouver. Sage's great grandfather, a swaggering Canadian from a wealthy entrepreneurial family, had come west after being ousted from his family in Toronto, scooped her up and carried her upriver to the place they called the Blackthorn Farm before it became Blackthorn Resort.

Sage wandered among the grave stones, touching one monument and then another. Less well-known-about relatives were interred here as well—cousins, her great grandmother's sister, people with minor chapters in her family history. She stopped at her mother's grave for a moment and found herself tearing up. Since she'd been home, she had turned into a blubbering mess. "Mom," she said, her voice husky with emotion, "you have to help me here. I don't know what I'm doing." But Susan Blackthorn, "Beloved Mother of Ross and Sage", offered no pearls of wisdom.

Sage wiped her eyes and moved on to the mound left by Ross's recent burial. It would settle soon and become part of the flat plot of land. There was no grave stone yet. That was one of her tasks in the coming weeks, to choose an appropriate stone to mark his place among the Blackthorns. Perhaps she would find something in his poetry that would help to memorialize him.

A strong breeze rose from the west, and Sage looked to the river to see riffles of whitecaps. To the west, menacing pewter-colored clouds gathered. The first serious fall rain was on its way. She turned to walk back to the hotel and noticed a man standing inside the fence. He walked toward her as she dabbed her eyes and focused. Andy. His pickup was parked by the road fifty feet away. He waved, and she lifted her hand in acknowledgement. What the hell was he doing here?

She hobbled to him and tried to manage a smile. "Good morning," Andy said. He wore a tee shirt and jeans, and baseball cap that said Hoot Owl. "You're supposed to be off that foot."

"What are you doing here?" she said. It wasn't meant to sound hostile, but she didn't sound particularly friendly either.

Andy eyed her carefully from under the bill of his cap,

but his mouth smiled. "I like to stop by once in a while to say hey to Ross," he said. "We must be thinking alike today."

Sage shrugged. "Maybe. I need to get a gravestone for him before I return to New York."

Andy lifted his cap and pushed back a stray lank of hair. "When are you going back?"

She walked toward the wobbly gate. "I don't know yet. I've got a lot of things to look after here." Like finding out what happened to Ross.

"Well, good luck on that." Andy fell into step beside her. "How's the foot doing?" he asked.

"Better, thanks."

"I'd be happy to come by tomorrow morning and wrap it for you."

"I'm doing all right," she said. "I took a bath this morning and wrapped the ankle myself. But I'd like to get rid of it. I have a date in Portland Saturday night. What do you think, doc? Can I wear party shoes?"

If Andy was taken aback, he didn't show it. After a short pause he said, "You need to stay conservative where the shoes are concerned. But that's great. You deserve to have some fun. And you're not going to listen to me anyway, are you?" He laughed.

Sage lifted her head toward the wind, and her hair blew back. She smiled. "No, probably not," she said. "But I appreciate your concern."

They reached the sagging gate. Andy opened it for her and she limped through. He stayed at the gate. "I've been meaning to fix this ever since the funeral," he said. "Might as well do it while I'm here."

Sage hoped she didn't appear as startled as she felt. "How kind of you," she said. "Come over for steaks on Sunday?"

Andy shook his head. "I'm working then. Mondays are better."

"Monday, then." With a short wave, Sage turned to walk back to the hotel. It was strange, that encounter. She couldn't determine how she felt about it. When she looked back to the graveyard, Andy was not working on the gate. Rather, he was standing by Ross's grave, looking down at it as if he, like Sage, was looking for answers.

Chapter 15

THAT AFTERNOON, AS HEAVY PEWTER-COLORED clouds moved up the gorge toward the Blackthorn, Sage drove to Stevenson, leaving Janice and Betty with Granny and their respective tasks. She burned for alcohol as if monsters were clawing at her insides. But she couldn't drink. She intended to talk to the Skamania County Sheriff. Luck was with her. Sheriff Terry Thompson was in his office. He was removing something from a file cabinet as she was shown in. He set the file on his desk, walked around it, and shook her hand. "Sage Blackthorn, great to see you."

He gestured for her to sit down and took a seat behind his desk. Thompson was a big, genial-looking man with thinning, sandy hair, and a well-tended beer gut. He wore a wedding band on his pudgy left hand. His office was decorated with amateur photos of himself posing with dead fish, deer, elk, a bear, and even a moose. Sage had seen the office briefly in July, but given her state at the time, she hadn't registered the endearing personal touches of dead animals.

The man she knew well, at least by reputation. In his days at Stevenson High School, Sheriff Thompson had been known as "Terry the Terrible". Even though he was five years her senior, the legend had lived on. When Terry was on the prowl, mothers locked up their daughters. Sage smiled to herself at the memory. Truth be told, Terry hadn't been any worse than the rest of them. He just happened to be the one who got caught! He was the guy who planted the outhouse on the high school lawn at Halloween. He'd gotten his girlfriend pregnant their senior year and married her. As far as Sage knew, they were still together.

As Sage seated herself, Terry Thompson looked up and bestowed a smile on her. "What brings you in here today, young lady?"

Sage smiled across the desk at him. *Young lady, my ass.* "I need to find out what happened to my brother."

Thompson opened the file he'd retrieved from the cabinet. "Cause of death: heroin overdose. Found on the river bank by fishermen three miles west of your property. He'd been in the river several days." He looked up from the file. "We haven't spent a lot of time on this case, to tell you the truth. It appears to be death by misadventure. We've closed the case."

Sage recoiled as if she'd been slapped. "Closed the case? How could you?"

"There's nothing more we can do. Ross Blackthorn overdosed, his body was found several days later. There were no signs of foul play, so that's the end of it. We would like to know where he was getting his drugs, however. We never found any at your place."

Sage tried to conceal her irritation. "You *looked*? When was that? Did you have a warrant?"

"Sage, I told you we were going to look around. Two months ago, you sat in this office and said we could go ahead. Remember?"

Hell, no, she didn't remember. She didn't remember much, truth be told, about that horrible visit home. "Right," she said. "And where did you look?"

Thompson rested his hand on his gut and smiled blandly. "Oh, the usual places. We checked all over the hotel, his room, the office. The boathouse. The barn. Nothing, nada, zilch."

Her mind spun. The money. How could they have missed that big wad of money in the office drawer? She said, "Well, you must have been very tidy about it. It doesn't look as if anything was disturbed."

"I told the guys to go gently. It's not like your brother was dealing or anything."

Really. And how do you know that? "That's right. Just one of us natives," she muttered. "So, you're basically telling me you've set this business of my brother's death aside because you didn't find any drugs? How is that possible, given a heroin overdose? Death by misadventure? Where did he get the heroin? And how in the hell did he end up in the river?"

Thompson sat up straight and folded his hands on the desk. He shot her an annoyed look. "There's not much to do here that I can see. He overdosed and fell in the river."

Sage knew she had to keep her cool. If she lost it with this guy, he'd dig in harder and she'd never get to the bottom of things. "*Fell* in the river? *After* he died of a heroin overdose? Doesn't that seem a little bit unlikely to you? He didn't drown, so we know he was already dead. It looks more likely to me that someone shoved him into the river, hoping he'd never be found!"

Thompson squirmed in his chair. "Has anyone ever told you, young lady, that you catch more flies with honey than you do with vinegar?"

Sage took a breath and counted to ten, then said, "I'm sorry, Terry. I still get emotional about Ross. And no, nobody has ever said anything to me about flies, honey, and vinegar. Pardon me if I don't quite follow how those things relate to your investigation into my brother's death. I hope you're not telling me to forget about it." She *was* losing it, faster than she could stop herself, faster than she thought was possible.

Thompson leaned back in his chair and folded his hands over his gut. "You can take it any way you want," he said. "We went through the hotel, and all over the property. Our efforts didn't point to anything more than an unfortunate mistake on your brother's part. He had a record, in case you didn't know, for drunk and disorderly conduct. I've had him in my jail more than once. And we've been keeping close tabs on some of the people he hung out with. But so far, we haven't found evidence of drug dealing or anything else that might have led to his death. He was a junkie, and the case is closed. Period, end of story."

Sage had to let some of it pass—either that or wage an all-out war she'd lose. She decided to stay calm. "All right, then. I understand. So, who were you keeping tabs on, if I may ask?"

Thompson shook his head. "I can't tell you that. Once again, I offer my sincere condolences to you and your family. As for Ross's death, we can't assume he was dumped into the river or anything else until we find some evidence that points us in that direction. Unfortunately, for now, we have no reason to believe that he was anything more than a small town drunk and drug addict."

The words stung. Sage found herself blinking back tears as Thompson closed the file folder and centered it on the desk in front of him. "And now, unless you have something to tell me that could help us form another conclusion, I'm not sure what else I can do for you. I'm sorry. We're open to any suggestions, of course, and are monitoring the situation. But, currently, there's nothing new to go on. If you come to me with evidence to the contrary, we'll take another look at the case."

Sage opened her mouth and then closed it. For a split

second she nearly told Thompson about the mysterious boat from a few nights ago. She didn't, couldn't. She was uncertain what to say, since she'd awakened from a blackout drunk, and as a result could not consider herself a reliable witness. Until she learned more, there was nothing to say. And, what about the money? Well, that could wait as well, then, couldn't it.

She stood up and clasped her handbag under her arm. "Thank you, Terry. That clarifies things a great deal." Using his first name hopefully kept things right-sized for the moment. Maybe it softened the fact that she may have sounded a bit sarcastic. If she did, tough noogies. "I appreciate your efforts to date. If anything comes up, I'll be in touch." He stood and nodded at her, his smile a bit less brilliant than it had been when she came in.

Out in the parking lot, Sage sat in the car and took several deep breaths to calm herself. It was so maddening. Someone had killed Ross. She knew it. And yet, as much as she disliked what the sheriff told her, he was right. Nothing they had found had turned up anything other than the obvious answer—that Ross had screwed up. Again. And this time it had cost him his life.

The sky had grown dark and fierce wind gusts pounded the car. A few large raindrops splattered the windshield. "I'm going to have to tell somebody about that boat," she said aloud. She stopped at the grocery store and headed East toward home.

On the way, her car stopped at the Hoot Owl. It was like

it had a mind of its own. At least that's what she told herself. She'd tell Andy, she decided. He got it. But when she walked in the door, her confidence left her. He'd already been on her about the drinking. And, as she already knew, she was an unreliable witness. It was raining more steadily now, and she limped from the parking lot to the door.

She entered and walked up to the bar, where she found Andy absorbed in another crossword puzzle. He heard her and looked up. When he saw her, a grin spread across his face. "Well, look at you," he said.

"Yeah, look at me," she said. "The storm has landed."

Andy's eyes twinkled. "You look kinda cute with your hair all messed up like that," he said. "What's going on?"

Sage rested her elbows on the bar. "I need a beer," she said. "I just talked to the county sheriff."

Andy pulled a draught of Coors and set it in front of her. He smiled knowingly. "Ah, Terry the Terrible," he said. "He really raised hell around here back in the day. Way before you can remember, I'm sure. And then he saw the light. They always say those guys make the best cops."

She shrugged. "Whatever. I'm not impressed."

Andy sighed. "What is it you want from him?"

Sage took a sip of beer, then gulped half of it. She set the glass down and wiped her mouth. "I want answers. I want to know about my brother's death."

Andy looked at her. His eyes had clouded over. "You're not satisfied that Ross died of an overdose."

It was a statement, not a question. Something had

shifted, but Sage wasn't sure what. "It's clear he died from an overdose," she said. "That's the science of the autopsy. No water in his lungs, blah-blah-blah. But for me, there's the question of how he got in the river, and therefore ended up three miles downstream. The sheriff says he fell off the dock. If he died on the dock, he'd be on the dock. He wasn't walking around after he died of that overdose."

Andy's eyes remained on her. "You've got a good point," he said. "There's nothing I can add to that."

Sage finished her beer. "Haven't you thought about it? Wondered?"

Andy shrugged. He didn't answer.

"How well did you know my brother, anyway?"

Andy averted his eyes for a moment before he re-focused on Sage. "I knew parts of your brother, but not all of him," he said. "Obviously I didn't know enough to save him." He grabbed the cloth from the back bar and began wiping down the bar around Sage. "I tried, though."

Sage shoved her glass toward him. "What do I have to do to get another beer?"

Andy continued his wiping. "I'm not going to serve you another beer. You need to get on home now before I eighty-six you."

Sage stood up. Fine. "Goodbye, then." She walked out the door and was hit by the wind and rain. The storm had turned into a righteous gale. She gimped to the car and got in. This was not the time to sit around thinking about what he said and what she said. She started the engine and drove the two miles home.

Yes, it was home now, like it or not, she thought as she pulled up close to the back door and headed for the kitchen. It didn't feel like home, but it was what she had. For now. She shook herself off and walked inside to find Janice and Betty seated at the table with Granny in her chair grumbling unintelligibly to her claw-like hands. With a quick "Hi, ladies," she headed upstairs to the bathroom and toweled her hair before running a comb through it to carefully disentangle the soggy strands.

When she was in her early teens she'd read about girls who ironed their hair to make it hang straight like those British Invasion girls on the television. She'd tried it once and hopelessly singed a big hunk of hair on the right side of her head. Granny had a fit, and promptly gave her a very short cut so everything matched. She'd spent the better part of eighth grade growing it back.

In her bedroom, she pulled off her clothes and dropped them into a pile on the floor. She donned dry jeans and pulled a sweater from the open suitcase on the floor. She still had to deal with the staff and her grandmother. She was cold to the bone, and all she really wanted was that glass of wine!

Downstairs, it was barely five, but almost dark due to the storm. Janice and Betty were busy packing up their things to go home for the day. "I got the garden cleaned up a bit before the rain," Janice announced. "And Mary Margaret had a good bowel movement."

How charming, thought Sage. "Thank you, Janice," was

all she said. She had never considered what the proper response to such a declaration might be. Somewhere in her own world, Granny smiled her agreement. Sage wondered if the smile was a coincidence or if Granny was aware of what was being said. She also wondered what to feed her for dinner.

Betty piped in, "We had six massages today. I just now got things in the warsh."

"Thanks, Betty. It sounds like a pretty good day," Sage said. *Now just go home so I can have a drink.* For some reason, she didn't want to drink in front of them. *Ashamed?* No, she was just being careful. What she did when they weren't around was none of their business.

Finally, they left! Sage took a bottle out of the grocery sack and opened it. Granny looked up when she popped the cork. Sage pointed a finger at the old woman. "Don't you dare say a word!" she said. Granny recoiled and said nothing.

After pouring herself a generous glass and taking a sip, Sage felt overwhelmed by guilt. She had no right to be mean to a sick person. Granny was old, helpless, and wouldn't last much longer. She set her glass down and pulled a chair up in front of her grandmother. She took Granny's hands in her own and looked her in the eye. "I am so sorry, Granny," she said. "I love you, and I am really, truly sorry I'm so agitated."

Granny stared at her wordlessly. Sage patted her hands and stood up. "I am going to cook you something really good for dinner," she said, although she didn't yet know what it would be. The only ingredient she was certain of was the wine. There were, she realized, vegetables and eggs. Twenty minutes later, she had produced a beautiful frittata and garlic toast. Granny attacked the food with gusto.

While they ate, Sage talked on. She told Granny about her visit to the graveyard. "We'll get a headstone for Ross soon," she promised. No response. She talked about her visit to the sheriff's office, and the handgun in the gun safe, now missing. Not a peep. She even told Granny about finding the twenty thousand dollars. "Do you know anything about that money?" she asked.

Granny looked up but seemed unphased by the mention of money. A little smile flitted across her wrinkled face. "I had a good bowel movement," she said.

After they finished eating, Sage carried the dishes to the sink and looked out the window. Beyond the garden, seventy feet in the air, the limbs of Douglas firs bounced and bent in the wind. The rain poured down sideways. And then suddenly, at the edge of the raised beds and closest to the trees, she saw a man standing in the rain. His long hair clung plastered to his face and neck, too wet to blow away from his head. His jeans and dirty white tee shirt clung to his body. She watched as he walked between the raised beds, seemingly undisturbed by the weather. He was a tall man, and lean—very lean. He was looking for something. The sandwich Janice left every day? This time it wasn't there. She had put a stop to that nonsense. She watched him pull some carrots from the dirt and hold them to his chest. As he looked around, Sage noticed mud from the carrots running down the front of his shirt. Then he spotted Sage watching him from the kitchen. He raised his hand and waved, then ran away from the garden toward the barn, and disappeared behind it.

What. The. *Hell?*

Sage bolted toward the kitchen door, but her sore ankle stopped her. She limped the last couple of steps, locked the door, and slowly turned back into the room. She was still too messed up to chase anyone. Her shouting would not be heard above the storm. He was long gone. It was time to get Granny ready for bed.

It had been a long and terribly unsettling day. First, there was the meeting in the cemetery. What had Andy been doing there, actually? Probably just what he said? And the more upsetting business with that dullard of a sheriff. It was a miracle, really, that Ross's body had been found—after he had jumped up from a deadly heroin overdose and flung himself into one of the largest rivers in the country! What about *that* couldn't Terrible Terry Thompson figure out?

And now there was a scary man in her back yard, having been fed by one of her employees, and probably housed by her brother. What did Andy say his name was? Phil? Crazy Phil! She finished the wine in her glass—she'd momentarily forgotten it—and turned to Granny. "Time to get ready for bed," she said, and helped the old woman to her feet. Slowly they made their way through the building to Granny's bathroom where Sage doggedly worked her way through all the steps necessary to get Granny comfortable for the night.

Maybe she'd make an early night of it, too.

Back in the kitchen, she looked out to the garden. She checked to make certain the back porch light was on. After seeing the stranger looking in at her, hand raised, the kitchen felt like a fish bowl. She walked to the office where Ross's poems waited for her on the desk.

She sat down and began pawing through the pages. The words that had made sense earlier now seemed incomprehensible. Where had the depth gone? And the beauty of Ross's precise arrangement of words? Was it the booze? Or was she simply too tired to deal with it. And then a phrase jumped out at her — "those careless barefoot summers, hidden treasure in the barn".

Sage stopped at the words. She remembered the careless, barefoot parts of their early lives, but no treasure hidden in the barn or anywhere else. She was done for the night. The treasure hunt would have to wait.

Chapter 16

SAGE WOKE UP REFRESHED. The storm had passed, and sunshine streamed into her bedroom. She checked her watch. Seven. It was early, but then she'd gone to bed early. She wrapped her bathrobe around her and wandered downstairs. In the kitchen, Janice helped Granny with her oatmeal, while on the other side of the table, Betty nursed a cup of coffee and scanned the Blackthorn log for signs of customers. They both looked up as she entered the room. "Good morning, ladies," she said.

She walked over to the table and said, "Good morning, Granny." She bent down and gave the old woman a quick kiss on the cheek. Granny was focused on her food, and otherwise unresponsive, so Sage moved to the coffee pot and poured herself a cup. It still smelled fresh. She turned around, cup in hand. "What's going on today, ladies?"

Betty sighed and met her eyes. "We only have a couple of soaks and massages at ten. That's about it."

Sage took a sip of coffee. "Put me down for a massage at noon," she said. "And I'd like to have a soak and wrap before that." She smiled at Betty and added, "I'll make it worth your time."

Betty grinned at her. "You're scheduled, Miss Sage. Be ready for your soak at eleven. It's been a while."

Sage couldn't remember when she'd last had a soak in Blackthorn's sulfurous, healing waters. Years and years. College, maybe? And she hadn't felt this good for weeks. Not only was she away from New York's harsh memories, but also she wasn't hung over. She'd only drunk two glasses of wine last night. A miracle. She enjoyed a quick moment of giddiness. *Hold that thought.* Yes. And in a couple of days she'd meet Tommy in Portland for dinner.

"Janice!" she said.

Janice's head popped up. "What?"

"Are you available for an overnight with Granny Saturday night? Time and a half."

Janice appeared to consider the offer. She helped Granny drink some orange juice and nodded. "Sure, I can do that. I'll miss bingo, but it's no big deal. I'll be happy to help out."

Sage entertained the grim memory of the wild man in the garden during last night's storm. Janice would probably feed the bastard again, but that couldn't be helped. Sage couldn't leave Granny overnight. Already she had spent too many nights in that big place by herself. It was a wonder she hadn't burned it down! "Great," she said. "I'll brief you this afternoon."

Janice's attention had wandered back to the old woman, who now wolfed down her oatmeal unassisted. "We're going to have a nice bath today, Mary Margaret," she said to Granny, as if talking to a child.

Granny slammed her spoon onto the table. "Maybe *you're* going to have a nice bath, young lady. But I'm certainly not!" She spoke clearly, and her voice was strong. "And you"—she raised a gnarled hand and pointed her index finger at Janice—"I want you to stop seeing that *man!*"

Everyone froze in place for a moment. Then, before Janice could react, Sage sidled into the chair next to Granny at the table. "What man is that, Granny?" she asked softly. On the other side of Granny, Janice had lifted her hand to her mouth. She dropped it quickly into her lap.

Granny looked around, confused. "What man? That tall man," She continued talking, but nothing else made sense.

Sage sighed. The moment had passed. Janice stood up quickly and carried dishes to the sink. Sage wished she could see her face. Was Granny talking about the guy in the garden? Had Janice let that scary man into the house? It was useless to ask. Granny saw things nobody else saw. Her damaged brain mixed things up. Still, there were a lot of questions Sage wanted to ask Janice. This was not the time for an interrogation. She'd deal with it later, when the time was right.

Sage ate a piece of toast slathered in jam and drank a second cup of coffee. She went upstairs and dressed, then limped out to the garden. The rain had destroyed the tomato plants. Many had split on the vine. She salvaged a large basket full of undamaged fruit, much of it still green, then pulled up the vines and hauled them out to a corner of the pasture where they could decompose. By the time she'd finished, it was time to prepare for her soak.

She entered the bath house for the first time in years. In the reception area, she noticed, a cardboard box decorated with flower cut-outs rested on the edge of the check-in counter. Someone, presumably Betty, had written 'tips' on the side of the box. Betty came out of a back room carrying a stack of clean, folded towels. "Just a minute, honey," she said, and stacked them in the old wooden cubicles that had been there forever. The smell of sulfur filled the air, stirring memories. Betty handed her a towel and a faded pink, sateen bathrobe that looked as if it had been around since World War II. It probably had been.

The place looked the same as it had years ago. As a child, Sage had sat in that backroom, after school and on many a summer day, quietly folding towels. In her lifetime, there had never been any other robes. She walked into the dressing room and closed the curtain on a changing stall. She undressed and folded her clothes in a tidy stack, removed the supportive bandage from her foot, and donned the ugly pink robe. Back in reception, Betty said, "This way, honey," and led her into the soaking room, which was filled with old clawfoot bathtubs. They stopped at the one where the water was running. All the other tubs in the large room were empty. Betty stuck her finger under the stream of hot water and adjusted the temperature. "It's a little hot, but it'll cool down," she told Sage. "You can adjust it, you know. I'll be back to get you in twenty-five minutes."

Betty pulled the privacy curtains around the tub and departed. Sage removed her robe and draped it across the back of a chair. A glass of cold water sat on the chair seat. She took a sip and then climbed into the tub of steaming water, wincing a little at both the heat and the acrid smell of the water. Yes, nothing had changed. It had just gotten older. Spots of enamel were missing in her tub, leaving egg-size dark patches of exposed cast iron edged in rust. Rust encircled the faucets, too. The curtains looked shabby. She slid deep into the water and closed her eyes. The ritual cleansing.

She wouldn't drink today. She was back on the wagon. Only two glasses last night. Easy-peasy. She inhaled deeply and slowly breathed out. She could do this. She felt ready now, whereas she really hadn't in previous days. She would get stronger, start exercising. She'd figure out who killed her brother. And why. And she'd get rid of this great, heaping dinosaur called the Blackthorn. Move back to the city and resume her job. Be done with this part of her life forever. She'd meet the right man, finally. She would just drink socially, and never be a drunk again. They'd be happy. She'd be happy.

It was a wonderful fantasy that continued until Betty spoke from outside the privacy curtain. "Time to get out now, Sage. Drain the tub and get dried off, put your robe on, and we'll go for your wrap." Betty had probably said those exact words every working day of her life for the past thirty years. Sage did as she was told. She felt dizzy when she stood, but gripped the tub and dried herself. Her ankle, all black and purple and still swollen, felt better from the soak. She finished the glass of cold water, donned her robe, and followed Betty into the adjoining room, this one lined with tidy white cots.

Betty held up a flannel sheet. Sage shed the bathrobe and slid discreetly under the sheet. Once again, she and Betty were the only people in the room—further evidence, as if she needed it, that it was time to abandon the sinking ship. She thought of Tommy's generous offer. They could talk about it more Saturday night. Betty covered Sage with another light blanket and tucked her in tightly with her arms by her sides. Then she covered her with a thick, fluffy blanket, said, "Sweet dreams," and left the room.

Sage began to sweat profusely. She couldn't move. This was the way it was supposed to be, right? It had been so long. She didn't remember it being so uncomfortable. Sweat was a good thing. The Indians had sweat lodges for a reason. *Quit being such a pussy*! She took a deep breath and tried to relax. Better. She dozed until she was awakened by Betty.

Two massage therapists worked at the Blackthorn. Sage

had heard their names in the kitchen—Misty and Lucas. Today, Sage was scheduled with Misty, a scrawny woman about her age, who showed her to a room containing a massage table with a small side table for lotions. Misty wore a long, loose, flowered dress that resembled a sack. Her blond hair was pulled back in a thick braid that hung nearly to her waist. Bing-bong music played softly in the background. Introductions performed, Misty left the room and Sage arranged herself face-down on the table with her nose in the hole of the headrest and pulled the sheet up to her shoulders. She was loose as a wet noodle and ready for a delicious massage.

Misty quietly entered the room and placed her hand on Sage's back. It felt warm and comforting through the sheet. "You're Ross's sister," was the first thing she said.

"Yes, I am," said Sage. No longer in wet noodle mode, her mind jumped to attention.

Misty folded back the sheet covering Sage so that her back was exposed, then began rubbing oil into her back and shoulders. The pressure felt wonderful. She relaxed into the moment. "We were good friends," Misty said. The way she said it indicated they were more than good friends.

What the hell, Sage thought. The anticipated relaxation of the massage vanished. But, since this was about Ross, she needed to pay attention. "That's great," she mumbled. "He was a wonderful man—and brother."

Misty pushed down hard on Sage's left shoulder. Something popped and then everything in her body felt freer. Great! Sage breathed out and relaxed into it. "I just wanted you to know that," Misty said. She sounded a bit choked up.

Following the thread, Sage asked, "What did you two like to do together?" More things popped in her shoulder.

"Oh, you know," said Misty. Was that a little giggle?

Jesus! And yes, Sage knew. She had to stop herself from shaking her head. Where was this moronic conversation going to go? She knew her brother was human, and he'd always been attractive to women. He was handsome and kind, and needy. Girls had always been hanging around, ever since he was thirteen, wanting to fix him. Wanting to make him feel better about himself. Stevenson and surrounding areas had been crawling with them. They had been like piranhas. Sigh.

Misty began working on her right shoulder. "Sometimes we'd go, you know, on hikes. Or down to the Owl on Saturday for drinks." Something popped in Sage's right shoulder. "Oooh!" said Misty, "that was a big one." She rubbed in quick little circles around the pop. "But mostly, you know, we just hung out."

And screwed, thought Sage. She wondered how that went down with Granny around. Even with her dementia, Granny could be very sharp at times, according to Ross, until recently. And the old gal had never missed much. "Well," she said, "that must have kept things interesting for both of you around here." *Just shoot me if I must listen to any more of this.*

Misty worked her way down Sage's spine, and

continued, undeterred. "Yeah." Misty sighed, and Sage noticed a small break in her rhythm. "But, you know, he got different. Toward the end, I mean. He got really paranoid and stuff."

Really, Misty talked like she was still in high school. Sage once again resisted the urge to shake her head. "Maybe it was all the dope he was smoking," she suggested. It was a shot in the dark, but he had relapsed, and marijuana had been a part—a large part—of his story. At least the part she knew about.

"Maybe," said Misty. She covered Sage's back with the sheet and began working on her arm. "But, you know, I don't think that changed. He did drink a lot. I'm not that much of a drinker. He was just, you know, different."

"Different."

Misty shook out Sage's left arm and rested it at her side, then moved to begin the right arm. "Yeah, different."

Maybe this was going somewhere, and maybe it wasn't. "How so?"

Misty snuffled a bit as she finished Sage's arm. She moved down to her leg and adjusted the sheet. "It was like, you know, he didn't want me around anymore."

Maybe that's because you're boring as bat shit, Sage thought. And yet she soldiered on with the interminable conversation. "How long had you been seeing each other?"

Misty lifted Sage's leg and gave it a good tug. Another significant pop. Hip joint. "About a year. It was just so wonderful. I thought he was the one. And then, you know, he just didn't seem that interested anymore."

Sage sighed. Nothing here. "Well, these things happen sometimes. And people just have to move on."

Misty covered up Sage's leg, and with a little squeak, left the room. Sage lifted her head out of the headrest. What in the hell had just happened? Bing bong music notwithstanding, she could hear Misty crying outside the room. Slowly she got up from the massage table and put on the awful robe. She opened the door and said, "Hey, come back in here."

Misty wiped her eyes and re-entered the room. "What's going on?" Sage asked. "How can I help?" She didn't feel the least bit helpful. She wanted to smack the little fool for ruining what should have been a perfectly good massage. She'd dealt with drama queens by the dozen at the magazine. In those situations, getting angry had never proved productive.

Misty sat on a chair in the corner of the room. She grabbed a tissue from the little stand with all the lotions on it and blew her nose loudly. She dabbed her eyes with another tissue and looked up at Sage. Her face was blotchy. She looked pathetic. "I'm so sorry," she said. "I just miss him so much."

Sage nodded, she hoped sympathetically. She reached out and touched Misty on the shoulder. "Yes, we all do," she said. "He never should have died."

"I just can't figure out how he was so stupid to, you know, drown," Misty continued. "I saw him earlier that night, and when I left he told me he was going to bed."

Sage leaned against the massage table. "About what time was that?"

Misty thought about it as she dabbed her eyes again. "Maybe nine. It wasn't late, it was still light out. I didn't think much about it. Sometimes when he'd had a lot to drink, you know, he just got sleepy."

"And you didn't stay with him?"

"Not that night. He said he wanted to make it an early night because of, you know, your grandmother."

Oh, whatever. "So, he was drunk, you say?"

"Yeah, he was fairly drunk. I've seen him worse, though."

Sage's mind struggled to know what to ask next. She wanted to ask the question that had bothered her ever since she found out about Ross's relationship with Misty—had Misty seen the boat?—but she couldn't summon the nerve. "Did you stay here often?"

"No, not really. Ross didn't like me to stay most of the time. He didn't want her yelling at us."

"Her?"

"You know. Your grandmother."

Then she thought of something she did have the nerve to ask. "So, how many times did you two use heroin together?"

Misty's mouth dropped open, apparently in shock. "Heroin? We *never* used heroin. *Ever.* I've never *met* anyone who uses heroin. We smoked a little weed. I smoked more than he did. And he drank. He drank a lot."

"But you never did heroin?"

"Oh my God. No. Ross liked his scotch. We never did any other drugs, ever."

Sage pulled a twenty-dollar bill from the pocket of her robe and placed it in Misty's hand. She closed Misty's fingers over the money and patted it while the woman looked at her in dismay. "I'm sorry you had to go through this, Misty," she said. And she meant it. "Thanks for the massage." She left the room and closed the door behind her.

Now what? Sage marched down the hall, sore ankle be damned, and into the reception area. Betty wasn't in sight, probably having lunch. The place was empty. Someday soon, Sage would get a complete massage without a bunch of yapping. But this had been rewarding. It had been good, and useful. If she could believe Misty. They'd been an item. Ross had become distracted. But they didn't do drugs—at least they didn't do hard drugs.

She walked into the dressing rooms and took a hot, sulfurous shower. Half of a massage was annoying. But Misty the lovelorn had just told her Ross didn't do heroin. Ever. Misty was a pothead, which meant she probably wasn't great on details of what happened when. But Sage knew a lot of folks in New York who smoked pot all the time. She worked with many of them. It didn't seem any worse than drinking. It always just made her sleepy. But if you were a heroin addict, you shot heroin. Right? And Misty wasn't so screwed up that she wouldn't notice that. So, if Ross was a heroin addict, he'd done a pretty good job of hiding it from the clingy girlfriend.

Sage was grateful for what she'd learned, but she also knew that if she had to listen to Misty again, she'd become a heroin addict herself. That was beside the point. The woman was hurting as much as she was. They could relate on that level at least. And Sage knew that Misty would never again in her life meet a guy like Ross.

Well, enough of that. Sage dressed and ran a comb through her hair. Suddenly, she was hungry as a wolverine.

Chapter 17

BETTY HAD JUST FINISHED HER LUNCH. Janice was off in the bedroom putting Granny down for a nap. There was nothing in the refrigerator that Sage wanted to eat.

"How'd the massage go?" Betty asked as she sipped her post-prandial coffee.

Sage shut the refrigerator door and sat at the table across from her. "Not so great. She spent my time talking about my brother. Then she burst into tears and we had to stop."

Betty nodded. "Them two was close."

"It doesn't seem that they had much in common." Sage realized she sounded snarky.

Betty's eyes twinkled. "Sometimes that don't matter, honey. Sometimes it's the opposites that attracts."

Oh my God, sex again. "Yes," said Sage. "I get it."

She rose from the table and walked to the reception area, where she picked up the phone and dialed the Hoot Owl. Andy answered on the first ring. "Do you make fish and chips?" Sage asked. She hoped she sounded pleasant.

Andy paused a minute, then said, "Ah, Sage Blackthorn. Yes, we make fish and chips. Salmon or halibut, with our own special sauce."

"Good. I'll be right over."

In the fifteen minutes it took Sage to dab on some makeup and drive to the Hoot Owl she made up her mind first, not to drink alcohol, and second, to learn from Andy everything she could about him and Ross, Ross and drinking, and Ross and drug use. If they were such good buds, surely Andy would be able to answer her questions. Or, maybe Andy was an addict of some sort too. She doubted that. He appeared to be the picture of health and centered alertness.

She pulled into the parking lot and got out of the car. Only three other cars dotted the lot. Today the sunshine felt good, but its intensity had weakened considerably. The weather had changed. Fall was in the air, crisp and beautiful, her favorite time of year. She experienced another little jolt of giddiness. It wasn't because of the massage, she knew that. Misty hadn't even worked on her sore ankle.

Inside the Owl, as Misty had called it, Andy stood behind the bar talking to a guy whose butt crack showed over the top of his jeans. He looked up from his customer and nodded as Sage approached the bar. "What'll it be, Ms. Blackthorn?"

She sat at the bar, leaving several seats between herself and the guy and his crack. "Diet Coke," she said. Andy raised his eyebrows. "And I think I'll try your salmon fish and chips."

Andy wrote her order on a piece of paper and stuck it in the window to the kitchen. He poured her a Diet Coke and set it on a coaster, then returned to his conversation with the other customer. Sage looked around the room. A couple of old boys were back in the corner eating hamburgers and drinking beer. She figured they'd be gone soon. She took a sip of her beverage and fiddled with stuff in her purse. In a few short minutes, Andy set a basket of steaming fish and chips in front of her. She tucked into the coleslaw—delicious—while the fish cooled.

Butt crack finished his lunch and got up from the bar stool. There were loud goodbyes and back slapping with the other guys in the place, and then relative calm returned. Sage dipped a piece of deep-fried salmon into Andy's special sauce and took a bite. As she savored it, Andy sauntered over to where she was sitting. He wiped a beer schooner with a towel, textbook central casting. He smiled at her with those even white teeth. "So, what brings you out on this lovely day, Miss Sage?"

Sage licked the sauce off her fingers and smiled back. "I got bored," she said. "Granny had a really good bowel movement yesterday. This morning I got half a massage and a lot of weeping and wailing from a woman named Misty. There was nothing at home I wanted to eat. Take your pick.

And these are the best damned fish and chips I've ever eaten!"

Andy chuckled and looked pleased with himself. "Ahh. An old family recipe," he said. "I've always preferred salmon to whatever else is around. Tradition, I guess."

Sage chose a large fry, dipped it in ketchup, and took a bite. "A wonderful tradition." Another bite. More finger licking.

Andy put away the glass, and then returned and watched her for a couple minutes. She obviously was enjoying herself. "So, you just came down here to eat?" he asked.

"Sure. Anything wrong with that?"

Andy laughed again, a bit insincerely Sage thought. Then he said, "I think you have something on your mind."

She considered him for a few seconds and ate another French fry. "I do, actually. How wise of you to notice. Misty said she and my brother used to drink here."

Andy nodded. "They did, as a matter of fact. Fairly often. I had to kick them out a few times when Ross had too much and got rowdy."

Sage looked up at him, wondering how to proceed. She finally said, "Yes, I remember. You told me that when we had our charming breakfast together. I'm curious about whether you ever noticed anything else. Did he use other drugs? And what was your part in all this?"

Andy put his elbows on the bar so he was eye level with her. "Sage, don't get me wrong here, but your brother was such a mess it was impossible to *tell* if he used anything else. At the end, it was just nonstop hell for him. I was his friend.

Other than that, I had no part."

Sage jerked back, food momentarily forgotten. "Well, why the hell didn't you do something then? If you were such good friends?" She slammed her hand on the bar.

Andy glanced at the other patrons. Sage looked over her shoulder. The good old boys were paying attention. *Fuck!* She came close to flipping them off but decided the better of it.

"Were you or were you not good friends?" she hissed at Andy.

He reached out to touch her hand, but she pulled back. "We were good friends, Sage. Really close for years. I loved your brother, but I couldn't help him. He knew what to do, but he couldn't or wouldn't do it. I did what I could, believe me. It's just such a personal thing. He wouldn't go to AA. He was enmeshed in the Blackthorn situation, and with your grandmother. A person must want to get well—more than anything else in the world. Ross had a lot of guilt, and I don't think he had that much faith in himself. I couldn't do it for him."

Sage drew in a deep breath. She did remember. She'd told Ross the same thing. He'd been through treatment twice, she'd told him. He was powerless, wasn't he? She couldn't do it for him. Those late-night telephone conversations had gone on and on. She breathed in and out, trying to regain calm, trying not to cry. Again, Andy reached across the bar, and this time when he rested his hand on Sage's she didn't pull away. Tears rolled down her face. Andy pushed a couple napkins in her direction. "Poor little Misty," Sage snuffled into the napkins. "She was so in love with him. And she said he changed."

She dabbed her eyes. She really wasn't going to cry. Every time she saw Andy she managed to be in some sort of mess. He probably thought she was an idiot.

He patted her hand. "Go ahead and cry," he said. "I still do sometimes." Then his eyes bored into her. "What did she mean, he'd changed?"

Sage dabbed her eyes and blew her nose in the napkin — a righteous, loud honk. There. "Misty said he lost interest. Something was bothering him. I asked about other drugs, and she said Ross never did heroin, or she would have known" she said. "But Skamania County's finest told me yesterday that Ross died of a heroin overdose."

Andy's face clouded over, his brown eyes turned black and opaque. "Yeah, I know." His eyes searched the room and paused briefly before looking at Sage again. "And they have the science to prove it."

Sage no longer felt like eating but dragged another fry through the ketchup and popped it into her mouth anyway. She made a face. "So, I guess if he never did drugs around Misty and you don't know anything, I'm still puzzled. I don't like it."

Andy just said, "No." He didn't elaborate. The connection flickered out. He was somewhere else.

Sage felt there was something he wasn't telling her. She thought briefly about the phantom cabin cruiser, about mentioning it to Andy. But she didn't trust him. Even though he seemed like a good guy, there were too many unknowns. Were he and Ross involved in something together, them being such good friends and all? What was he holding back? Disappointed, she said, "I'm going now. Can you box this for me? I'll have it for dinner."

Andy looked at her with a half-smile. "Sure thing," he said. He was still somewhere else and had closed up tighter than a clam. He carried the basket to the kitchen and returned with her box of food.

He handed it to her and she shoved some cash across the bar. "Catch you later," she said.

"Sure."

Sure? Just sure? Sage walked out of the tavern and got into her rental car. "That was the weirdest conversation I've had in a long time," she said aloud as she fastened her seatbelt and started the engine. "One minute he was there, and the next he wasn't."

She drove back to the Blackthorn. Janice's car was gone. She found Betty in the bath house shoving towels and sheets into the laundry cart. Betty looked up when she entered the room. "Oh, hi, Sage. Mary Margaret is sleeping, so I sent Janice home. I'm about done here, got all the tubs scrubbed out.

Sage looked at Betty. Her face was flushed from exertion, and strands of gray hair rested untidily on her shoulders. "You can go whenever you want," Sage said. "I'm home for the afternoon. I'm going to work in the office."

Betty nodded and continued her work. As Sage repaired

to the hotel kitchen, she wondered what Betty and Janice would do when she closed the Blackthorn for good and moved Granny into residential care. They were getting old, they had been employed here all their working lives. They were, essentially, family members—of which she had very few, she reminded herself. She sat down with her box of fish and chips and promptly finished them. She dipped her fries in the remaining special sauce. Andy may have been in a mood today, but she would get that recipe from him before she returned to New York. And she'd get her other questions answered, too.

But now, on to other things. She tidied up the kitchen and walked to the office. She peeked in on Granny before she settled in. Snoring like a hibernating grizzly. All was well with her, at least.

The windowless office felt dismal. Sage sat, turned on the banker's light, and stared across the room at the photo of her mother with Sonny. If Ross had sat in here and looked at that day after day, it was no wonder he relapsed. Remembering their funny, bright mother and how she died was enough to send anyone after the booze. How often had she relived that day? It had been a wonderful day, one of the best of their childhood, until it wasn't.

Suddenly a noise erupted in the reception area. Someone was banging on the little bell there. Someone shouted, "Anybody home?" Sage jumped to her feet and limped out to see what was going on. A tallish man of around fifty, big but doughy, with watery blue eyes and sparse but vigorous chin growth, stood at the counter. His face was veined and puffy, and strands of greasy blond hair stuck out from under a dirty green baseball cap. Sage approached the counter. "I'm afraid we're closed for the day," she said.

He leaned down, his face close to hers. She looked into his faded, red-rimmed eyes. He smelled bad. "It's you I want to see," he said.

Sage took a step back, the better to avoid his breath. "Really? Do I know you?"

The man scratched at the whiskers. "Sure you do. I'm Donald Powers from up the road. I heard you was here. We have something to discuss."

Sage remembered Donald Powers. When she was in high school, everyone had called him Donald the Pothead. She knew there was nothing in the world she needed to discuss with him. "How can I help you, Mr. Powers?"

Donald got right to the point. "You owe me some money." He nodded to himself in seeming self-satisfaction.

Really? "Do you mean me, personally? Or does the Blackthorn owe you money?"

"Your brother owed me money," said Donald. "He's dead, so now you owe me money."

Sage shook her head. "Wow, I don't know anything about that. Perhaps you could explain."

Donald managed to look concerned and angry at the same time. "Your brother bought something from me and he never paid for it. I kept trying to get the money from him, and he always had an excuse. You need to make good on his debt."

Sage wanted to believe her brother didn't hang out with people like Donald. But, if marijuana was involved, she knew better. "What? Did he buy some pot from you?"

Donald looked abashed. "How did you know?"

"Donald, you've been selling pot since I was a kid. How much did he owe you?"

Donald scratched some more, then leaned toward her as if to tell her a secret. He lowered his voice. "Fifteen thousand dollars."

Again, Sage recoiled from the smell. Her mind raced. The money in the drawer? That would cover it. And, what in the world was Ross doing with fifteen thousand worth of pot? *Well, stupid, he was dealing.* "Wow, that's a lot of pot," she said, trying not to show how upset she was. "I don't know anything about Ross's personal debts. Is there an invoice?"

Donald rolled around on the balls of his feet and started sputtering. "Invoice? Hell no, lady. There wasn't no invoice. What do you think this is? The First National Bank? We didn't do nothin' on paper!"

Sage thought for a moment. The guy was shifty. No. He was sleazy, and that was worse. "I can't do anything about this right now," she said. "You say Ross owed you a lot of money. Ross isn't here to say yes or no. Plus, it doesn't work that way. That's his debt not mine. What am I supposed to do? Pull fifteen thousand dollars out of the air?"

Donald slammed his fist on the counter and Sage jumped. "That brother of yours was no good! He owed me fifteen thousand, and I'm gonna get it."

At that moment, Betty walked through the front door carrying a load of kitchen towels. She looked at them, her eyes widened for a moment, then she collected herself. "Well, hello there, Donald," she said as he turned around to see who'd come in. "What brings you out here slummin'?"

Donald looked as guilty as a kid caught upsetting the outhouse. Neither he nor Sage knew if Betty had heard him slam the counter. "Hi yourself, Betty. I'm just talkin' with Sage here about a little business I done with her brother."

Betty shifted the load of towels from one arm to the other while she looked him up and down. She did not look pleased with what she saw. "Humph," she said. "I just bet you are." She started toward the kitchen, and called over her shoulder, "You just let me know if you need anything, Miss Sage."

"I will, Betty. Thanks." Sage looked back at Donald. "Well, I think we can end this conversation right now. I can't help you with a debt when there's no paperwork. And it's not my debt to pay. It sounds to me like it was a highly illegal transaction, and there's no tangible evidence it even happened. You may leave now."

He glared at her. "You'll be sorry about this." He said it softly. "You are going to be very sorry." His menacing words chilled her, but she didn't change her expression. She stood there watching him until he turned around and went out the door.

Sage stared at the closed door for a moment, feeling

shaken. Donald the Pothead had just threatened her. She locked the door behind him. Her gut told her Ross did owe him money. For contraband. It was none of her business, but she didn't want him coming after her for something that was none of her business.

She made her way to the kitchen. Betty sat at the table folding the clean towels. Sage collapsed into the chair across from her. "Did you ever see Donald Powers around here when my brother was alive?" she said.

Betty shook her head and kept folding. "Can't say as I did," she said. "But if them two was up to something, they probably did it when I wasn't around."

"I remember him from years ago," said Sage. "He was selling pot back when I was in high school. Now he says Ross owed him money, and if I don't pay him, I'll be sorry."

Betty picked up the towels and stowed them in a bottom drawer at the counter. She turned around. "I wouldn't believe anything that asshole says," she said. "Pardon my French. He'd lie when telling the truth is easier."

"No pardon needed, Betty. You and I are on the same page. But frankly, I am a little worried. He was angry when he left. Which reminds me, when are you going home?"

Betty grabbed her sweater and purse from the entry and said, "Right now, honey. You have a good evening, and don't you worry about that old goat."

Chapter 18

BUT SAGE DID WORRY about the old goat. She secluded herself in the office with the door open, so she could hear Granny if she woke up. She used the time wisely. By the time the old woman woke two hours later, Sage had filled several empty grocery bags with old papers that should have been thrown out years ago. She'd burn them in the barrel that evening.

As she worked, she thought about Donald and their disturbing conversation. If Ross really owed that clown fifteen thousand dollars, it meant old Donald wasn't just selling nickel bags. He had an operation going. And if Ross was buying that much pot, he was doing something with it that might or might not be linked to the boat she may or may not have seen the other night. Which could explain that great wad of cash in the envelope near her right knee. Or not. On one level, Sage found Donald's revelation and its implications deeply disturbing. On the other, if one distanced oneself just a little, it presented an interesting conundrum. What became of all that marijuana? And who was behind it?

The scene she had witnessed at the boathouse came to mind. She was certain it was real. It still felt real. Could she trust herself? She was glad she was sober today. Her relapse had lasted only a few days, but her body had gone back to craving alcohol like she'd never quit. So far, she hadn't suffered major withdrawal symptoms as she had when she'd quit cold turkey a few weeks ago. But she was still new at this. By the time five o'clock came around, she was aching for a drink. Aching was too mild a word. She was ready to gnaw off her left foot.

She heard her grandmother stirring. Time to get her up and cook a meal. Sage took a deep breath, walked into Granny's bedroom, and opened the curtains. Then she stepped near the bed. "How are you doing, Granny?" she asked, surprised at the softness in her own voice.

Granny rolled her red-rimmed eyes to meet Sage's. "Well I'm fine, Susan. Did you get that laundry done?"

"It's all done, Granny." Sage didn't bother to correct her. It only led to more confusion. "Time to get up and move around a bit." She helped Granny to a sitting position, and then to a stand. They made their way to the bathroom.

"Whatever happened to that cowboy?" Granny asked as they toddled across the floor.

"Which cowboy?" said Sage. She was barely paying attention.

"Who do you think I'm talking about?" Granny demanded. "The one who got you pregnant!"

Holy shit! Sage stopped abruptly, and Granny stumbled. She quickly grabbed the old woman, so she wouldn't fall.

My father? Ross's? "I can't remember what he looked like," Sage said.

Granny waved her free arm in the air. "Oh, you remember. That tall, red-haired boy. Useless as tits on a bull."

Sage's hopes momentarily soared. They were talking about *her* father! "I forget his name," she said, hoping for more information, but by the time they reached the bathroom, Granny was on to something else. And thus, it continued for the next two hours while Sage prepared pasta with vegetables and bits of leftover ham and walked Granny around the dining room several times. Granny needed to move more.

Sage longed for a drink. Her body continued its war with her mind. She ached like she had the flu. So much for no withdrawal! She wouldn't drink tonight, she told herself, as she completed her laps with Granny. Maybe Saturday, when she had dinner with Tommy, she'd have a glass of wine. Something good. But not tonight. She'd be all right tonight if she could have wine soon. Just not now. She would make it through the evening, and tomorrow, and on Saturday she'd reward herself. She could manage a few days, couldn't she? She could manage tonight. Granny yakked on about something that made no sense, but it brought Sage back into the room. Granny was tired. Sage walked her into the kitchen and sat her in the awful chair.

Night closed them in. It got dark earlier every night. Before Sage helped Granny to bed, she asked another question about the man who might be her father. It was met with no response. Seven-thirty found her pacing the kitchen. She thought about the partial bottle of wine left over from her trip to Stevenson yesterday. She felt desperate—like she had something crawling around inside her, beneath her skin. She was not going to drink, and that was that.

She walked around the place, locking doors. She thought of Donald the Pothead and made certain the windows were closed and locked as well. Upstairs she donned her nightgown and searched the meagerly stocked bookcase in the family living room. A dog-eared copy of Daphne DuMaurier's *Jamaica Inn* lay on one of the dusty shelves. Sage had read it years ago, when she was in high school. She remembered very little about the story, except that it was dark. Grim. And it took place in an old inn on the Cornish moors. How suitable. She picked up the book and carried it into her room.

She jerked awake in response to something outside her realm of consciousness. She had heard something. And then she heard it overhead—the creaking of old boards. The building settling? Not so fast. It was footsteps, one and then another. Right above her bedroom, someone crept slowly across the floor as if making every effort not to wake her. Floorboards creaked every time that someone took a step.

Sage froze in place. Vulnerable. She waited. *Get a grip.* The third floor had been closed up for years. No one ever went to the third floor. Certainly no one had since she'd been back. There was no reason, nothing but old, dusty rooms with bare lightbulbs hanging from the ceiling. Worn out plumbing, rusted fixtures. Single beds with chipped metal frames and tattered chenille bedspreads. Memories of vacations taken by people long deceased.

Another board creaked above her. She tried to listen over the sound of her pounding heart. Was it that man from the garden, "Crazy Phil"? Or Donald the Pothead? Couldn't be. She'd closed and locked everything tight. Then she remembered the open window on the third floor she had spotted the day she arrived. It was near the fire escape. Had Donald hauled himself up that fire escape so he could kill her in her sleep? Had he gotten in through that window to look for the money he said she owed him?

She had no idea what time it was. She reached for the clock, but it had stopped at twelve-thirty—a.m. or p.m., it didn't matter now. She had left her watch in the bathroom. She closed her eyes, breathed out. *Oh God, what should I do?* She climbed out of bed and tip-toed through the living room and into the hall. It was dark and empty. She listened. Above her the floor creaked again. He was in a different room now. She moved back into her bedroom and, in the dim light from outside, she located and quietly eased into the clothes she'd worn that day. She slid into her shoes and tied them.

The shotgun. It was downstairs in the office. *Not that you'd know what to do with it.* Quietly but swiftly, she located the key to the gun cabinet and made her way downstairs to the kitchen. She located the flashlight under the sink. By the time she'd reached the office, she was furious rather than frightened. Nobody had any business invading her home. And whatever they were doing, she knew they were up to no good! Drug dealers in the boathouse, weirdos demanding money. Sage couldn't remember ever feeling murderous in her life, but she did now. She'd had enough.

With flashlight in hand, she opened the gun safe and grabbed the twenty-two. She knew how to shoot the smaller gun, it was easy. And at close range it would get the job done. If necessary. She tried not to think about what the intruder might be carrying. Or, for that matter, who the intruder might be.

Soundlessly as she could, she eased up the front stairs and into the second-floor hall, clutching rifle and flashlight. She felt none too steady on her feet. Breathe, she told herself. *Breathe!* Old boards creaked beneath the hall runner as she crept along the long hall. She stopped to listen. Above her and farther down the building from where she stood, she heard a step, and then another. Again, a board creaked.

She readied the rifle, then continued slowly and steadily down the hall. She paused to listen again before reaching the back stairway to the third floor. She heard more movement.

The person was still up there. Of course he was. It was a person, not an animal. She took another deep breath. She set down the flashlight on the bottom stair next to her foot. And then, praying the door to the hall didn't creak, she slowly opened it and started up the stairs, one terrified step at a time.

The third floor was unfamiliar territory. It had been closed to guests since she was in her early teens and her grandmother had shut it off. Sage couldn't remember how long it had been since she had been up there. Years. She wondered if Ross had ever gone up. What reason would he have? As she stepped on the third step of the staircase, the tired wood creaked under her foot. She froze. But the person upstairs hadn't heard her. The shuffling above her continued, slow, methodical, ominous. Her mouth was dry. What was the person looking for? How had he gotten into the building without her noticing? She swallowed and took another step.

The seventh step creaked as well. Sage carefully placed her feet at the far sides of the steps, moving slowly, mindful to hold the gun in one hand and grip the railing with the other. At the top of the stairs, she allowed herself to take another deep breath and quietly exhale.

And then it was upon her. The closed door. With her left hand, she opened the door, and the damn thing creaked. She gripped the doorknob and exhaled the breath she'd been holding. She watched and listened for a moment, and then slipped into the hallway. Light shone from the doorway to the third room on the right. The door was ajar, which seemed very careless on the intruder's part. She thought she heard more movement, another tentative step. Her heart banged so loudly in her chest that she couldn't be certain.

Nearly frozen with fear, Sage wondered if she could get her body to move. She wanted to turn around, but she couldn't. She had to know who was up here, searching, threatening. She should have called 9-1-1, she told herself. But she hadn't. She wasn't thinking straight, and now here she was, loaded rifle in hand. She took a step down the hall, and then another, the twenty-two held tight against her shoulder ready to fire if necessary. When she reached the door, she shoved it open with her foot, then stepped to the side of the doorway and waited, expecting the worst.

Absolute silence. A bit of shuffling, and then a querulous call. "Susan, is that you? Do you have those sheets?"

Granny! For fuck's sake! Granny somehow had made it to the third floor of the hotel in the middle of the night! It was almost unbelievable. Sage laid the gun on the hallway floor next to the wall and clutched her stomach with both hands. *Oh my God, oh my God!* She walked into the room, body shaking with relief. She had almost killed her grandmother! She was an idiot! "Granny!" She hugged her bewildered grandmother. "How in the world did you make it up all those stairs?"

The old woman looked around, clearly confused, and then collected herself and bristled. "I've been waiting all day for those damn sheets. What took you so long?"

Once again, her grandmother was in her own world—

one that had little to do with anyone else's. Still shaking, Sage took her by the arm. "Let's go downstairs."

Granny jerked her arm away and refused to budge. "What about the sheets? We have a full house tonight."

"Betty has taken care of it," said Sage. Hopefully that would work. She didn't want to have to drag her from the room.

Granny stood quietly for a moment, and then her shoulders slumped. "I'm tired," she said after a brief pause. "Where the hell am I?"

Again, Sage took her grandmother's arm, and this time she didn't resist. "You're on the third floor, Granny. We need to get downstairs to your bedroom. Let's go."

They descended the two staircases, each step grindingly slow. It was difficult for both of them. Granny groaned so pitifully that Sage wondered how she had managed her perilous ascent. Stubbornness, she presumed. For her own part, Sage held on to the railing and walked backwards one step ahead of Granny, easing her down each step and holding onto Granny's hand so she could catch her if she stumbled. It seemed as if they would never get to the kitchen, but at last they did. Sage turned on the lights and led Granny to her chair, where she promptly collapsed.

The kitchen clock ticked just past five a.m. Sage had retired so early the night before that she now was wide awake. Granny quickly fell asleep in her chair. Sage shook her head in wonder. She made a pot of coffee. There was no point in either of them going back to their beds.

She drank coffee as the skies began to lighten. She grabbed a notepad from the office and scribbled notes. Her first note to self: call Stevenson Gardens and set up an appointment. Before she could do anything else, Granny must be relocated to a place set up to look after her around the clock and deal with her cognitive issues. Once she was safe and well cared for, Sage could move on to other things— like listing the property or selling to Tommy and his partners. Then she could go back to her life in New York City.

Granny snored in her chair, head tilted back, exhausted from her middle-of-the-night excursion. As the sky changed from black to a deep inky blue, Sage wandered down the lane, wearing only a tee shirt and jeans, to fetch *The Oregonian* from its little metal box. The damp, cold air nipped at her through her clothes. She grabbed the newspaper and returned to the hotel.

She skimmed the headlines. Finding nothing of immediate interest, her thoughts turned to her dinner date with Thomas Kitt. Tommy. She felt a little flutter in her stomach. Portland's most eligible bachelor had asked her out for dinner and even booked her a room in a newly renovated hotel. Most guys in New York weren't that classy—certainly not the ones she'd been hanging out with, at any rate.

Sage grimaced. The shame and horror of her last drunk in New York left her feeling paralyzed. What if? She knew what the hotel room in Portland suggested. Implied? What were Tommy's expectations? He wanted to spend time with her, see her socially. Obviously. What did that mean? How did that translate for him? Was she being naïve to think that he'd booked that room only out of concern for her safety? She supposed he could have, but she couldn't be certain.

She stood up and walked to the coffee pot, poured herself another cup of the strong brew, and considered. Tommy was attractive as hell, no doubt about that. He was there to help her, right? They shared a familial closeness that spanned many years. He was like a brother, wasn't he?

She wasn't so sure about that, particularly after their last telephone conversation, when he had sounded a good deal more like a suitor than a brother. She took a sip of coffee and paced around the kitchen. Hell and damn! She wanted to go out for the evening, relax, and not try to second guess someone else's motives. But there was the horrible memory of that night in New York. It was still painfully fresh. Sage was scared even as she anticipated what might be a lovely night out.

Perhaps there was real potential for Tommy to be more than her friend. Isn't that why he had invited her to dinner? She wasn't getting any younger. Neither, in fact, was he. But it didn't seem to matter as much for men. They could, and often did, choose younger women—especially wealthy and desirable bachelors when they became willing to think about progeny and settling down. She was right back where she had started.

And hadn't she always been looking for Mr. Right? Maybe her methods hadn't been the best. Getting drunk and going to bed with someone you met in a bar had not yielded any tangible results. Yet it seemed, no matter how she tried to do it differently, she always ended up drunk. That translated into poor choices. She shook her head. Yes, she felt pain daily, physical and mental. The injuries suffered during that last stupid drunk were raw. Whatever his intentions, Sage was clear about hers. No matter how she felt about Tommy, she was not ready to bed another man.

As full daylight returned, the back door rattled, and Betty let herself in. Her eyes widened in surprise when she saw Sage and Granny in the kitchen. "Good morning, honey," she said. "Is something wrong?"

Sage attempted a laugh. "Oh, no, Betty. Everything's fine now. Granny took a hike last night, all the way up to the third floor. She woke me up and scared the living hell out of me, but we're both all right."

Betty walked over and inspected Granny, who had her head thrown back, mouth wide open. "She don't look so good. It's early for her."

"She wore herself out," Sage said. "I can't imagine how she made it all the way up there. I had a hell of a time getting her down those stairs."

Betty donned her apron and helped herself to a cup of coffee. She nodded in Granny's direction. "I don't know what we're going to do about her," she said.

"We're going to find her a nice, safe place to live where she has around the clock care," Sage said. "She has a bit of money in the bank to cover it."

Betty stared at Sage. "News to me," she said. "All I ever heard was how broke she was."

"Well, it's her money that's been paying you for quite a while now," Sage replied. "This place isn't making enough to keep the lights on."

Betty sat down, stunned. "I guess that means we won't have a job much longer."

"I don't know," said Sage. "I'm meeting Thomas Kitt Saturday to discuss more details about this place. He's in the process of bringing me up to speed. For now, just keep doing what you're doing. Do we have any customers today?"

"A few," said Betty, her face grim.

Chapter 19

IT RAINED ON AND OFF for the remainder of the day, but the next morning dawned sunny and fresh. It was Thursday, and Sage began to count the hours until her dinner date with Tommy. She slogged through the day-to-day at Blackthorn as best she could. She was finished cleaning out the office. It had yielded little of interest, mostly old records from when the resort was a real business. She burned the trash paper and neatly filed the information she believed was useful or might be worth a second look. She cleaned and polished Mom's trophies and rearranged the family photos. The space was tidy and efficient. She could find what she needed.

She made a quick run to Stevenson to pick up groceries and a bottle of wine to celebrate. What she wanted to celebrate was unclear, but it seemed like a good idea at the time.

Sage was a decent cook—Granny had seen to that—but not an inspired one. She did not cook much in the city. There were dinner meetings with the editorial staff, or drinks and a bite after work just for fun. There had been the Friday nights at Paddy's, nights when she hardly ever ate anything. Taking care of her grandmother meant regular meals. Even with Janice getting Granny fed twice a day, there was always dinner. She concentrated on healthy basics—protein, starch, vegetable—and Granny seemed satisfied.

The dinner hour was the hardest for her, and that had nothing to do with planning and cooking a meal. This was when wine sang its siren song, the time she wanted that cocktail—or six. Every day, often from as early as two o'clock, she struggled with cravings. By Thursday she was nearly crazy. Bored to near screaming, she took off at lunch time to grab a burger at the Hoot Owl. She looked forward to seeing Andy, who'd been absent since they met in the cemetery. She hoped she could pick up the conversation from a couple days back when she'd gone to have fish and chips and he'd gone all weird on her. When she arrived, she was surprised to find that Andy wasn't there. "Well, where is he today?" she asked the bartender after placing her order.

The bartender, who looked like he was fresh off the farm, pushed back a lock of greasy blond hair. For a poignant moment, Sage felt like she was looking at her brother when he was young and healthy. He was that kind of handsome. "I don't know, ma'am. He just said he wasn't coming in today?" he said.

"Ma'am?" said Sage.

The kid shrugged, set her Diet Coke on a coaster, and disappeared into the kitchen. She waited for her food and had just tucked into her juicy cheeseburger when three youngish Mexican guys walked into the bar laughing and chattering in Spanish. The bartender waved and nodded to them. "Andy's at his house today," he said. They waved back at him and left. Sage munched a French fry and wondered what they wanted with Andy. Then she let her mind wander again to thoughts of her date with Tommy.

She recalled the electricity she'd felt when he touched her in his office and for the umpteenth time allowed herself to relive the moment. It had been an unexpected jolt to feel that kind of response. There had been some chemistry between them. He had felt it too. Otherwise, why would he have asked her on a date? He had matured—as had she. He was well-educated, well-employed, in charge of his life, and, let's face it, damned good looking. Sage smiled to herself and finished her burger. Of course, whatever might happen was nothing that would go anywhere. And nothing would happen. Her job was in New York, but still, it was fun to fantasize.

That evening, Granny took it upon herself to be oppositional. Sage prepared a lovely dinner of chicken breasts with artichoke hearts and a salad. She set their plates on the table and took her place. Granny cast a suspicious eye on her food. "What's this crap, Susan?" she said. Before Sage could respond, Granny grabbed her plate and threw it on the floor.

"You miserable old witch!" Sage burst out before she could stop herself. "I worked for an hour on that." She jumped from her seat, grabbed the garbage can from under the sink, and began tossing the food and broken plate into it. She cut her finger and swore viciously.

"You're a slut, Susan. A drunk and a slut," Granny yelled from her place at the table.

"And you can go to hell," Sage retorted as she ran cold water over her cut finger and wrapped it in a towel.

Looking back, an hour later, she realized they'd sounded like kids on a playground. But by then, she was drunk. She'd given Granny some graham crackers to shut her up, and then had organized her quickly into bed. She'd locked the place, turned on the outside lights, returned to the kitchen, and opened the wine.

Over the course of the evening, she drank the bottle of wine. She stared at it. She talked to it. Gradually she felt herself relax. This wasn't the end of the world. Nobody had died. Granny was sick. Hell, Sage was sick. It would be all right. She'd be better in the morning, and Janice would be here to deal with things. Wasn't it Scarlett O'Hara who said, "Tomorrow is another day."? She didn't remember going to bed.

There it was, that noise again! Sage sat up in bed. That purring inboard motor. She crawled out of bed and carefully made her way to the window. She was still drunk. And nauseated. Again. Her room was cold, but she didn't close the window. She wanted to be able to hear everything. As her eyes adjusted, she saw movement among the lights down by the boathouse. A gentle rain fell. It was difficult to see anything clearly.

People with flashlights moved in and out of the boathouse. Their voices were hushed, but she thought she heard them speaking Spanish. As she watched, she made out four people working, loading packages off the boat this time, into the boathouse. Sage thought of the men who'd been looking for Andy at the Hoot Owl. *No, please, no!* She thought about the shotgun, of going down there armed to have a word with those trespassers! She quickly realized she was in no shape to talk to anyone. She had no idea how to operate the shotgun. If these characters were transporting drugs, they were armed. She pulled on her bathrobe and sat on the bed. What was she going to do? What *could* she do?

She could call 9-1-1! She started down the hall, intending to use the front staircase to reception. *Yes, dumbass. You go right ahead and call them and slur your words.* She stopped at the top of the stairs. She opened her mouth and said, "The quick brown fox jumped over the lazy dog." It sounded okay to her. She clunked downstairs and picked up the phone. Dialed it.

"9-1-1. What is your emergency?"

Sage suddenly felt awkward. Her words tumbled out. "People in a boat are down at my boathouse. They're putting things in it. I don't know who they are, but I think they're drug dealers."

The dispatcher asked her several questions, got the Blackthorn's address, and assured her that someone would be there very soon. Sage took a shaky breath and thanked her. Now came the waiting part.

She hobbled upstairs to her bedroom and looked out the window. All she could see in the darkness was the falling mist. The boat had disappeared into absolute darkness. "Darker than the inside of a dog," she could remember her grandmother saying. *Shit!* Nobody would get caught red-handed, but at least whoever answered the call would find whatever it was those trespassers had left in her boathouse!

She pulled on jeans and a sweater and went downstairs to the kitchen. Ten minutes later, several cars with their lights off pulled into the parking lot. She walked out into the drizzle to meet them. Both the sheriff's department and the Washington State Police had responded and were ready for action.

"Down there," Sage told the first deputy out of his vehicle. "They were down there, four men and a boat. By the time I got off the phone, the boat was gone."

"Get inside, miss," said the sheriff's deputy, unfastening his holster. By now, the others had joined him. "Go inside and stay there."

Sage nodded and did as she was told. From the kitchen window she watched the men fan out across the field and walk slowly toward the boathouse, guns drawn. By the time they got there she could barely make out their dark forms.

She eased to the back door and cracked it enough that she could hear what was happening. One of them banged on the boathouse door. "Police. Come out with your hands raised." Several men stood poised to shoot.

Nothing. Not a sound. It was so quiet she could hear small droplets of rain as they hit the ground.

The officer banged on the door again and shouted. Again, nothing. He shot the padlock off the boathouse door, kicked it open, and stepped back to the side of the entrance.

Sage held her breath. Nothing. The other men crept forward quietly and carefully. They looked inside and holstered their guns. The scene lit up with flashlights. Two men went into the boathouse while the others prowled the dock and surrounding grounds searching for clues. Sage wondered if the wet dock would yield anything of interest. She had not seen the trespassers step onto the shore. She watched and waited.

Fifteen minutes later, Deputy Clark introduced himself at her back door. Sage turned on the light and invited him into the kitchen. Clark stood just inside the entry, dripping water onto the kitchen floor. "We didn't find anything, miss." His eyes wandered from hers and looked over her shoulder. Sage followed his gaze to the empty wine bottle lying on its side on the table.

Mortified, Sage looked back at Deputy Clark. Their eyes met again. The deputy gave a barely perceptible nod. He asked her a few questions—had she seen the boat before? What was the boathouse used for? General things. And then he said, "We have nothing to report, miss. Try to get some sleep." He turned and walked out. Engines were started, and tires crunched on gravel as the law enforcement vehicles moved one by one out of range.

Sage collapsed onto a kitchen chair, humiliated. *What?*

She had seen them out there, moving back and forth, carrying packages that looked the size of ten-pound bags of sugar into the boathouse! They had made several trips in the short time she'd watched them. She asked herself again and again why the cops had found nothing. It wasn't possible. All those packages couldn't just disappear.

Then the panic hit her, the self-doubt. Had she hallucinated? Her entire body cringed as she thought about it. She wasn't losing her mind. She couldn't be losing her mind.

She got up from the chair and retrieved a flashlight from the kitchen junk drawer. At least one thing in her life was where it was supposed to be. She slipped into one of the jackets that hung in the entry and headed outside and down the hill, careful not to fall this time.

Part of the door frame to the boathouse had been shot away, along with the padlock, but at least the door was open. She looked in and shone the flashlight around the room. She visually explored every corner and cranny. Nothing. *Nothing!* It was as if the place had been scrubbed clean. She walked inside and noticed dark, rusty-looking patches on the floor— old fish blood, no doubt—but the place was cleaner than she could ever remember seeing it. That was weird, Sage realized, as the Blackthorns had never been the tidiest of folk. She looked up to the rafters and shone the light everywhere. Nothing there but rafters. How was this possible? Where had those packages gone? Baffled, she walked out and pulled the door closed, hunched her shoulders, and trudged back to the kitchen through the drizzle. She locked the door and slowly made her way upstairs and to bed. Sleep did not come easily.

Chapter 20

FRIDAY MORNING SAGE ROSE EARLY. She showered and dressed for the day. Downstairs she threw away the empty wine bottle, put on the coffee, and ate a piece of toast to calm her acid stomach. When Janice and Betty arrived, she greeted them with all the enthusiasm she could muster, which wasn't much. Her head pounded, and she felt like shit. She felt the shame of her encounter with Deputy Clark and his men. He knew her little secret. Her credibility was zero with the local authorities, and she deserved it. But she knew. Someone—some*ones*—had been doing things in the boathouse. She just couldn't prove it.

Her choice for what to wear to dinner at the Heathman was an easy one—a black cocktail dress she'd brought with her from New York, and a filmy little wrap. Why she had brought such items with her to the Pacific Northwest the gods only knew, but she felt satisfied and a bit smug that she now would have the opportunity to wear them. She planned to leave the Blackthorn early the next day, but not too early. She couldn't check into the hotel until three, but she wanted to do a little shopping before dinner, which was set for seven. She had not packed any dinner date shoes; she'd buy something appropriate before she met Tommy.

Her date promised to be a wonderful distraction from the weirdness at the Blackthorn. She'd have to deal with these problems eventually, but not today. With a special evening awaiting her, she thought more about Tommy. He had changed beyond recognition. His teeth, for example. When they were in school together, he was a nice-looking kid until he opened his mouth. His teeth had been horridly crooked. Tommy's teeth had been terrible, but his family couldn't afford to fix them. At some point he's spent a lot for his flashing smile.

She could understand why he'd wanted to change his looks to the extent that he had. Being the poor kid was no fun. He had not made friends easily, and she wondered how the bullying he'd suffered during his early school years affected him now. He'd made good marks in high school, he was smart, and studies came easily. But mostly he became known on the baseball field. That stuff mattered to kids in Stevenson. If a kid excelled at sports, he was popular even if he was a complete dickhead, which Tommy most certainly was not. She shrugged. The way of the world, she supposed.

After packing, she set aside her suitcase and went downstairs. Her ankle, though still a little swollen, felt better and she was getting around well. The day hummed along— Betty supervised the bath house, Janice puttered around the kitchen, Granny napped. Sage wasn't needed for the moment. She threw on a jacket and walked out into the crisp fall air.

Without a destination in mind, she started walking. The air had been rained clean, and she could smell the fresh pungency of conifers. She walked past the barn and Sonny's old paddock behind it, past the graveyard, across a field, and finally into the woods. There was an old trail through the wooded area that had been there forever, probably the route used by deer to move between open spaces. She and Ross had spent their summers in the woods exploring, building forts, pretending they were explorers like Lewis and Clark. They chose to believe Lewis and Clark had traveled this exact trail through their woods nearly two hundred years before.

Sage took her time. She didn't want to aggravate the ankle, but it felt good to be outdoors. It felt exquisite to be able to walk almost pain free, and to be away from the Blackthorn and its troubles. The smell of the earth, wet leaves, the rotting sweetness of forest duff, the sounds of birds and of small animals scurrying in the brush, filled her with peace. She felt she had taken a break from the rat race her life had become, even here in nowhere Washington. Everything was a mess, but right here and right now, all was well.

She didn't know how far she'd walked, but suddenly she became aware that it was time to turn back. Her ankle complained about the exercise. It was time to put her foot up for a while and ice it. In the old days she would have known the shortcut home, but years had erased that memory, and in the forest, it was easy to get confused. Rather than even think of an alternate route, she simply turned around to retrace her path. It was then that she saw him.

He stood about a hundred feet away from her on the trail, a tall, gangly man, over six feet, with matted brown hair and haunted brown eyes. His face was young looking, hidden behind a long beard. His pants were too short, and he wore sandals on his feet. They looked homemade. Sage realized he'd been following her.

She cringed with fear as their eyes locked. Why was he following her and what did he want? They stared at each other for several seconds. She couldn't run and risk hurting herself again. It wouldn't work anyway. With his long legs, he'd overtake her in seconds. She detected no malice in his silent staring, so she began walking toward him. Tentatively. "Hello," she said. She hoped she sounded matter-of-fact, as if meeting a wild-looking man in the woods was an everyday occurrence for her. Her courage faded as she neared him. He stood his ground, blocking the path. When she was about twenty feet from him, she said, "I'd like to go past you if you don't mind. I'm going home now."

The man nodded and stepped to the side of the trail.

"You're Sage," he said.

Sage stopped, nonplussed, and looked at him intently. Up close, she saw the tentative look in his eyes. He was ill at ease, too. Close to her age, she guessed, tattered, but clean enough. At least he didn't smell bad. "Yes, I am," she said. "Who are you?"

"I'm Phil Curran," he said. "I live here. Ross told me about you."

Was this really happening? Just another day in paradise. "Pleased to meet you, Phil Curran," she said. She wasn't at all pleased. This was Crazy Phil, the guy Andy had mentioned. The guy Ross had given permission to sleep in their barn. She was scared, but as she took him in more fully, she had no sense that he wanted to hurt her. She decided to play along and try not to screw it up. If she had to run, she realized, she'd have a real problem.

"You're my sister," Curran said. It came out of nowhere.

"What? I beg your pardon?"

"You're my sister," he repeated. "Ross was my brother. That makes you my sister."

Oh, yeah, whatever. Sage shrugged. "I don't even know you," she said. "It's not possible. We're not related."

"Ross told me we were brothers and we'd always be brothers. He helped me. That makes you my sister." Curran's eyes darted anxiously.

Sage didn't want to quarrel. In New York, she had heard of people with PTSD attacking strangers for no reason. This man did not appear to be someone who was in tune with the world. She could give him the one thing he seemed to want from her. She couldn't see any harm in that. "I hear what you're saying," she said. "Brother."

Curran reached out his right hand. They shook. He smiled at her, and then he turned and walked into the woods. Sage watched him go. One minute he was there, the next he was gone without making a sound. The apparition from the garden had become a real person.

Sage stuffed her hands into her pockets and trudged toward the hotel. Now, wasn't this just the weirdest thing? A vagrant trespassing on the property had just called her his sister. In fact, he probably camped in the barn since the weather had changed. In a few weeks she'd be gone. She'd be happy, of course, if she didn't run into him again. They'd said what they needed to say to each other. She was no longer afraid of him. He wasn't a threat.

Or was he? She knew nothing about the man. He had mental health issues. He was a veteran with PTSD. He said he was friends with Ross—another one of her brother's mysterious connections—but was he? Companions? Brothers in arms? Where did he fit into the puzzle that had been Ross's life? Was he a benign soul who lived on the fringes, or was he involved in whatever nastiness was going on out here? It was impossible to tell. Phil. Donald. Andy. Misty. Janice. Sage realized there could be more, and that she didn't know much about any of them. She pondered the tangled web of characters for the remainder of the day.

Chapter 21

FINALLY, IT WAS SATURDAY. Sage got up early. She ate her breakfast and attended to morning chores. The minutes crawled, and finally it was noon. She carried her bag downstairs and set it behind the reception desk. It was long past time to deal with the rental car. She needed to get rid of it. She hoped Tommy would have the time to bring her home in the morning.

In the kitchen, she dug in the drawer where Granny used to leave her car keys. She wondered if the old beater still ran. If it didn't, she faced another set of problems. She walked out to the barn, pushed the sliding doors open, and found Granny's Buick unlocked. It was covered with dust. She settled into the driver's seat, inserted the key; the motor turned over and began purring nicely. Excellent!

She noticed a filthy worn paper bag on the passenger side of the seat. As she lifted it to throw into the back seat, she was surprised at its weight. The bag ripped open, releasing a cloud of dust. Chunky packets of paper landed on the floor and seat. Sage picked one up and took a closer look. It was a thick bundle of one hundred-dollar bills. Bound packets of bills littered the car's passenger seat and floor. Thousands of dollars. She heard herself squeak. What should she do? What *could* she do? Call Terry Thompson?

She thought about it. Calling him seemed to her the most useless option, even more so after last night. He was an idiot, but by now everyone in his department thought she was the idiot. She tried to wrap her mind around the surprising discovery and the problem it created. If that didn't solidify her suspicion that Ross had been involved with drugs, nothing would. "You dumb shit," she said aloud. "What were you thinking?" She turned off the ignition.

The place had needed money. Hell, Ross had needed money and there had been little. Then he was presented with the opportunity to get lots, and he'd gotten in over his head. He'd been vulnerable. And weak. The question was, who was he involved with? Ross couldn't have done this on his own. An operation of scale to leave sacks of money would require, mobility, contacts, and capital to start. Ross had never had any capital. The director of such a project would have people to transport the goods, and a place to store the goods, not to mention distributors, a network. She thought about the boathouse. Yeah, the boathouse. It could be one place to store inventory in a larger network, even though she had found nothing to indicate drugs were stored there. Another mystery, since she had seen people unloading parcels into the boathouse. Was Ross collecting rent from those characters in the boat, or was he involved even more deeply in a deadly operation?

And what about Sheriff Thompson and his deputies? He'd told her they'd searched the place. Well, they hadn't done a very good job. The car had sat there unlocked for months. Here she was, tripping over money that was sitting right under their noses. She snorted. Some searchers they were. Had they searched, or did Sheriff Thompson just make up that part?

Ross had brains, but the Ross she knew was a dreamer. He'd always had trouble focusing—which had been a big problem for him during his growing up years. A business on this scale took organizational skill, and Ross had never been organized. He'd been a fucked-up alcoholic at the end, and—she now had to admit it—probably an addict. Heroin? Cocaine? Neither sat well with Sage. But where else would money like this come from? And had it been paid to him or did it belong to someone else? Donald wanted his cut. His deal was marijuana. But—she looked at the money again—this haul represented more marijuana than Donald ever was capable of handling. And, as it was in Granny's car, had it been put there, possibly by her late brother? Or had it been planted?

Sage got out of the car. She searched the barn for an old burlap bag, something strong enough that it wouldn't break when she dumped all packets of cash into it. It didn't take her long to locate a bag—a couple of small holes in it, but nothing serious. She loaded the cash into it, climbed up to the loft, and stashed the bag in a corner behind an ancient bale of straw. It would be safe there for now. Heck, it had sat in the car almost in plain sight for at least two months. She wondered again how the money had not been discovered by the sheriff or his deputies. Well, she knew Terry Thompson, and his stupidity explained a lot.

She climbed back into the Buick, started it, and drove out of the barn and down the road toward the highway. Once on Highway 14, she stomped on the accelerator. Everything sounded good. The car drove fine. She drove all the way to Stevenson and back to assure herself the vehicle was reliable. Now all she needed was a ride from that nice Avis kiosk at Portland International Airport back to the Blackthorn. She was certain Tommy would help her with that.

Back in the hotel, Sage found Janice in the kitchen looking wary. No doubt she and Betty had been talking about their shared futures as unemployed persons. "I fed Mary Margaret, and she's having her nap," Janice said.

"Great," said Sage. "What do you need from me before I leave for Portland?"

Janice pointed to her overnight bag waiting in the entry. "Nothin'. Don't worry about us. We'll be fine."

Reassured, Sage finished tidying upstairs and thought

about Andy. Since she'd decided not to talk to the sheriff, maybe she should confide in Andy. She liked him well enough, even if he did have the aggravating habit of being blunt with her. He seemed to have good sense. And he'd been friends with Ross. Or said he had. And what did good friends mean, anyway? Did it mean they were pals? Drinking or fishing buddies? Or had they been partners in this dirty little business Ross had been involved with? With his bar and restaurant, Andy had access to everyone in the county. The Hoot Owl was a natural meeting place. Sage decided to put that one on hold for now.

And finally, there was Tommy. Family friend, confidante, lawyer, investment maven. And, she sighed, Portland's most eligible bachelor. She would tell him tonight, depending upon how their evening progressed. If they talked about business, and Ross, it would only make sense. He would need to know what was going on. He would know what to do.

But what if they didn't talk business? Her stomach fluttered, throwing her brain off course. Maybe this was entirely social. Maybe it would be fun and flirty. In which case, she could postpone the money revelation for a few more days. That cash would still be sitting in the loft behind that bale of straw the next time they talked.

She decided to tell no one, and to wait. She didn't know who she could trust. There seemed to be no urgency at all. If anyone had missed all that money and seriously looked for it, it would have been long gone before she arrived on the scene. Now it was in the loft and she could forget about it for a few days.

Sage threw her things into the back of the rental car and headed for Portland. It was a pleasant drive. The day was cool as the region cycled into October, calm and sunny, with intermittent clouds. The storms would return for winter soon enough. Driving through the Columbia Gorge, she marveled at the changing oaks, alders, and maples, colors that glowed against the dense, dark green of Douglas fir. Soon there would be rain, and a lot of it. And the wind and gloom. By then, she'd be back in Manhattan doing the work she loved.

She made good time to Portland. At the Heathman, Sage let the valet park the car. She left her overnight bag at reception, threw on a light jacket, and hit the street. Her ankle felt much better, and there was much to see. Broadway was abuzz with shoppers. She wandered through the new Nordstrom store and came out at Pioneer Courthouse Square. Dubbed Portland's Living Room, it offered a sweeping red brick amphitheater of welcoming space that filled a full city block. It had replaced one of the ugliest parking lots that ever blighted the Rose City.

During her early years, Sage's trips into Portland had been few. And then she left—for college, and after that her new life in the magazine industry. While Portland was still a small city, it seemed to have gained an energy she didn't remember. She felt excitement and anticipation for its future, even though she wouldn't be here to see it.

By the time Sage returned to the Heathman and checked in to her room, she felt the excitement worthy of a big date. She toured the beautifully appointed, spacious room on the fifth floor. She tipped the bellman and closed the door behind him, bolting the door. Then she turned back, hung out the "do not disturb" sign, closed, and re-bolted the door. She sighed and set a shopping bag on the floor. Her explorations through the heart of downtown Portland, had netted her a sexy pair of shoes to show off her cocktail dress.

A bottle of champagne chilled in an ice bucket on the coffee table, two flutes beside it. On the side table sat an ostentatious display of flowers. She walked over and opened the attached card. Tommy. Of course. This only made her more nervous, and she looked at the champagne longingly. After Thursday night, she was through with drinking. This time she meant it. Too much was happening out in her neighborhood; she couldn't let her guard down.

Drinking won't solve anything, she told herself. She peeled down to her underwear and crawled into the king-size bed. Propped against very plump pillows, she pulled the covers up to her chin and laid there, eyes wide open. She was a bundle of nerves. She took a deep breath. What the hell was going on?

And then it struck her: she had never, *ever*, gone on a date sober. Even in high school, there always had been booze. And, where there was booze there was sex. That was how most of her dates had ended up from age sixteen onward. She'd been careful in high school. Going steady, as it was called back then, offered protection. If the guy talked, he knew he'd get cut off.

Since she'd moved to New York, there had been those rare occasions when a one-night stand turned into a short fling. But after a couple of months at most, it was over. Sage never understood why. She'd chosen men badly in an alcohol-induced haze and found she had nothing to talk about when they were sober. As quickly as an affair had started, it was over. Then it was back to the work of relentlessly prowling the bars until she found the next one. It occurred to her, as she sat in her room, that this was a pattern she'd like to change. She also realized that tonight could end up like all the rest of those dates.

But it wouldn't. Tommy was different. Tommy had what she wanted. Or he was at least as close to what she *thought* she wanted as she had ever seen. She didn't know what she'd do about her job if they did get together. Here she was, projecting, creating imaginary futures, as she so often did, her mind running like a squirrel cage. She did know, after spending the afternoon in downtown Portland, that she could end up in worse places. Tonight, though, she would be sober. She would be classy. She could do that for one night— a few hours. She *could* control herself and her impulses. One drink, and she'd be off to the races. She knew that she had to be better than that. She sighed again and scrunched down under the covers, tossing one of the pillows to the side.

When Sage woke up and looked at the clock, it was after six. She leapt from the bed, tidied it, and took a fast shower.

The champagne still beckoned, but she now was pressed for time. She needed to fix her hair, apply makeup, and get dressed before Tommy came to her room to pick her up. The nerves were back, but she managed to ease herself into sheer black pantyhose without putting her thumb through them. She shimmied into her black cocktail dress—black with a very low neckline—and donned her only expensive piece of jewelry, a diamond pendant. In the bathroom she gathered her hair, pulled it back from her face, and secured it in place with rhinestone-embellished combs. She paused for effect before getting out the war paint.

At seven on the dot there was a knock on the door of Sage's room. She peeked through the spyhole before unbolting it. Thomas Kitt entered the room and kissed her lightly on the cheek. He stepped back and looked at her with deliberate admiration. "You are beautiful!" he said, and Sage felt a familiar tummy flutter.

"Thank you, Tommy. You look pretty wonderful yourself." Thomas wore an elegant dark suit. Italian? His shoes were polished to a high gloss. Not a hair out of place. His cologne left the faint aroma of lime in the air—just a hint, but enough that Sage felt herself long for a gin and tonic. Her mouth watered.

Thomas looked her up and down again and smiled. "Mmmm," he said. Then he looked at the champagne, forlorn in its sweating bucket. He raised his eyebrows at her. "What? You didn't have any of the champagne?"

Sage glanced at it. "Regrettably, no. I needed a little nap

after all my shopping. But thank you so much. And the flowers are lovely. Truly." She was not at all certain she sounded like herself.

"Would you like a glass before dinner?" he asked.

Sage shook her head. "Not now," she said. "I'm starving."

Thomas smiled again, and his eyes registered surprise. "Suit yourself, then," he said. "Let's go put the Heathman's new chef to the test."

As they entered the dining room of the new and improved Heathman, Sage noticed that several heads, mostly female, turned. The buzz in the air was anticipatory, exciting. Portland's well-heeled were out to try the food and then critique the new chef in the bar after dinner. Tommy smiled and nodded to several people as the host escorted them to their table and presented heavy menus.

When a server approached the table and asked for drink orders, Tommy nodded to Sage. "Tonic with lime," she said. She noted the look on Tommy's face. More sensitive than he should have been about not drinking, Sage wondered if it was her imagination or if her order surprised Portland's most eligible bachelor. He was accustomed to her drinking her share and then some, and she was certain he'd noticed.

Thomas ordered himself a Maker's Mark on the rocks and surveyed the room full of Portland's beautiful people. It amazed Sage how much she noticed when she wasn't drunk. Colors. Delicious smells. The muted sounds of fifty conversations. The faint clinks of cutlery and wine glasses. The stiffness of her date's posture. He picked up the wine list and studied it for a moment. Then he said, "I think we should make this a Burgundy evening."

Sage smiled at him across the table. "Whatever you like." He relaxed and flipped to the next page of the wine list. *Amuse bouches* arrived with their drinks. Thomas ordered a bottle of 1978 Puligny-Montrachet and the waiter nodded his approval.

He then raised his drink to Sage and said, "To our evening." He moved like a robot.

She clicked her glass with his, took a sip of the tonic, and then tucked into the small morsel of crostini topped with chanterelle mushroom compote on the plate in front of her. She sighed with satisfaction. No hotel, no Granny, no guilt. It was heaven to be away. "It's going to be a grand evening," she said. Thomas smiled broadly for the first time that night.

Meanwhile, something niggled at her just outside her carefully controlled awareness. Part of her edginess, if that's what she could call it, was watching Thomas navigate his grand new lifestyle. It had happened over years—years when she was not present. When they had met up on school vacations, he was still just one of the kids she grew up with, and she had always been thrilled to see that he was doing well. But this was something else again. It was if her childhood friend had sprung fully formed from Zeus's thigh as a wealthy, powerful, and confident man. On the outside, at least. She wondered how long it had taken him to get comfortable in the role he had carved out for himself, as a person others looked up to. Something told her he wasn't yet entirely at ease. Or perhaps he wasn't at ease with her.

While she pondered these things, their waiter brought the bottle of wine to the table and poured a taste. Thomas swirled it in the glass, smelled, tasted, and nodded his satisfaction. The waiter poured for them. Sage put the wine glass to her lips and then set it down. Thomas didn't notice. His eyes cruised the dining room taking inventory. Who was here and who wasn't? Anyone important? Who watched them? They were not on a date, she realized. They were on stage. He looked at her and smiled. "Have you noticed how people are looking at you?" he said after the waiter departed. "They're wondering who the stunning redhead is."

Sage tossed her head and laughed. She took a teeny sip of wine. It may have been the best wine she'd ever tasted. And she was *not* going to get drunk. "More likely, they're wondering who is the strange woman with Portland's most eligible bachelor? Is she important? Is she good enough for him?" It was Tommy's turn to laugh.

"Do you remember when nobody looked at us?" she asked. "Nobody noticed any of us until you and Ross started winning all those baseball games."

Tommy shook his head, grinning. "I remember pegging my pants really tight, because it was in style, you know. I knew nothing about sewing, and there was nobody around to show me. I was in English class my junior year, and I heard this popping sound. It was the stitches in my pants giving up the ghost. Both legs!"

Sage burst out laughing. "I never heard that one!" she

lied. "Why did you guys never tell me?" It was an old story, but it sounded new coming directly from him. She laughed until she snorted, the ice finally broken. It felt good.

"I was mortified," he said. "I made Ross promise not to tell you. I made him swear! Being cool was such a big deal then." He shrugged. "And now it's not." He swirled his wine and took an appreciative sip. Now he was the liar.

They chatted easily about other memories from the Stevenson High days. Sage took pretend sips of her wine and hoped Tommy wouldn't notice. And he didn't. His eyes again worked the room. As they finished their first courses, a distinguished-looking older couple came in and were seated near the front of the restaurant. "Excuse me for a minute," he told her and left the table. Sage looked around and located a large potted plant behind her chair. She hoped no one noticed as she dumped the Puligny-Montrachet into the pot.

When Thomas returned to the table, he seemed pleased to see her glass empty and refilled it. He ordered an equally showy red wine to go with their main course, then poured some of the white into a spare glass and excused himself once again. Sage could see him across the room talking to a man about fifty, offering him the glass of wine. Somehow, the contents of her wine glass again ended up in the potted plant. She smiled to herself. If she had to be sober, she might as well make a game of it. She questioned why she felt it necessary to deceive him because she didn't choose to drink. But the answer felt difficult somehow, and far away, and complicated. So, she focused on the task at hand—getting through the evening sober. She could figure the rest out later.

Tommy was back just in time to taste and approve the red Burgundy—a Beaune Clos de Mouches (yes, Sage had studied up on wine a little bit!)—and her duck breast and Tommy's steak arrived at their table.

The duck was fabulous. Once again, her date's eyes roamed the room. Time to send you back to charm school, Sage thought. However, she said, "Thomas, I really would like to talk a little business tonight, if you don't mind."

He started at the formal sound of her voice. She took a pretend taste of the red wine, savoring the aroma. And then, he reached across the table and laid his hand on hers. "My dear Sage, I really hoped to just keep this social tonight. We can talk business any time."

She looked at him and smiled. "All right, then, let's *be* social." She gently withdrew her hand.

Thomas frowned at the implied correction of his behavior and picked up his fork and knife. "You're right," he said. "I've told you that I want to get to know you better, and I meant it." He gave her a helpless look. "I guess I'm just not sure where to start."

Sage felt her heart soften a little. Maybe they were on the same page, after all. Why was she feeling so standoffish? Shyness? Fear? What could go wrong with Tommy? She took another bite of duck as he attacked the steak. She felt a little lighter somehow. "Look, it's been a long time since we spent any time together," she said. "We've become very different people than we were back in high school. So, let's get caught up. I'll show you mine if you'll show me yours."

Thomas laughed—not the genuine, booming, healthy laugh like the kind she remembered, but at least a laugh without pretense. After that, their conversation became easier, light, friendly. She managed to get through the meal with only a couple of tiny sips of wine, and another sleight-of-hand dump into the potted plant before they ordered dessert. Her subterfuge so amused her that Sage almost forgot she wasn't really drinking.

Almost, but not quite. Her body craved more of the delicious wines she had tasted. Even though she was sated with food, she felt the empty, familiar longing for alcohol. As Tommy provided detailed stories of his transformation to Portland's-most-eligible, she found herself staring at the half-full bottle of red Burgundy that sat, now untouched, on the table. She also noticed that, along with his new-found success, her old chum had become a cold fish with a formidable ego. This was not the awakening she had anticipated or hoped for.

By nine-thirty Sage was exhausted by the performances—both his and her own. She sipped a cappuccino. Across the table, Tommy enjoyed a cognac while hers sat, forlorn, in front of her. She had managed a fake sip to be polite, and now struggled with her urge to slug down the rest in two gulps. This sort of non-drinking was very difficult for her. It was right in front of her screaming her name. If she was going to stay sober, she needed to be away from it altogether, at least for a time.

And then her prayers were answered. Thomas made a trip to the men's room. She felt a moment of guilt for upsetting the ecological balance of the Heathman's stunning new dining room. But as she emptied most of her cognac into the plant she assuaged her guilt by thinking, *better it than me.*

Upstairs, at her door, Sage turned to say goodnight. Thomas drew her toward him and nibbled her neck with his lips, sending a thrill down her spine. Without thinking, she felt herself lean into him and it felt comforting. So close to him, she caught a delicious whiff of lime and sandalwood. "Let me come in for a few minutes," he murmured. "It's early."

Sage drew back and keyed her door open. Sober, she realized she had walked into unfamiliar territory. She wanted to be by herself now, but somehow could not tell him that. "Come in, then," she said. Her heart pounded as if it would burst from her ribcage. Inside, she closed the door and walked to the loveseat. Behind her, Tommy locked and bolted the door. Sage's heart moved to her throat. In seconds, she'd gone from excited to wary. She watched him cross the room and sit beside her. He leaned toward her, took her face in his hands, and kissed her—gently at first, and then firmly, probing with his tongue.

When she could stand it no longer, Sage drew away from him. His eyes registered confusion, but he moved closer toward her and surrounded her with his long arms. Then panic seized her. She felt as if she might be drowning. As he moved in to kiss her again, she pushed him away. "No!"

Tommy withdrew as if he'd been slapped, and again Sage saw the confusion. And anger. "I can't," she said. Tears welled up in her eyes. It had gone all wrong, somehow. She felt she had done something unforgivable. Like something was her fault.

Thomas sat back, pulled out a handkerchief, and dabbed his brow. He had changed his expression now. "What did I do, exactly, to upset you?" His voice was detached, robotic.

Looking into his eyes, Sage could see the dark anger that gave the lie to his firmly calm expression. Something else lurked there, too. Something unreadable. The look touched her at gut level. She no longer felt in the wrong. She no longer felt safe.

She laid a hand on his arm. Had he seen her fear? "It's not you, Tommy," she said with a gentleness she didn't feel. "You didn't do anything you shouldn't have done."

"Well?" Another flash of anger. And that other thing.

"Something happened to me in New York. Something horrible. Five weeks ago. I can't talk about it now. It's too raw. But someday." Her voice trailed off.

Thomas looked away from her. Then back. "I have feelings for you, Sage. I want you to know that. And I want you to care for me, too." His dark eyes had softened, making him appear vulnerable, no longer the predator. He folded his handkerchief and returned it to his pocket. "Do you think you could care for me?"

Had he even heard what she said? Sage wondered as she drew in a breath. "Of course. I care for you already, Tommy.

You know I do. I've always felt you're special. You just have no idea what I've been through."

Thomas reached out, put his arm around her shoulders, and pulled her nearer on the loveseat. She felt herself stiffen, and she breathed in deeply in an attempt to relax.

"I know how hard it was to lose Ross," he said. "I've felt it too. As for whatever else is going on with you, I can't do anything but offer you my help and support. If I can do anything, or when you want to talk about it, just let me know. I'll be here for you."

So, he had heard some of what she'd said. Her tension eased a bit.

He gave her a little squeeze and slowly stood up. "I'll go now. And I'll meet you downstairs in the dining room at nine tomorrow morning. We'll have breakfast here before we go to the airport to return your rental."

Sage sighed. She stood to walk him to the door. "I'm so grateful you have the time to drive me home tomorrow," she said. "I didn't know what I'd do."

Thomas smiled. It was a thin-lipped smile. "Anything," he said. "I'm happy to give up a golf game at Waverley to help get your business settled."

The little jab stung her. Or was it the name dropping again? Sage pretended she hadn't noticed and treated him to a warm smile. "Excellent, then. I'll see you in the morning."

Chapter 22

ONCE THE DOOR WAS SAFELY LOCKED and bolted, Sage removed her cocktail dress and pantyhose carefully. Then she rushed into the bathroom and vomited up her lovely dinner. The panic she'd felt with Tommy in the locked hotel room during the previous several minutes had unnerved her completely. She'd felt trapped and helpless as all the terror and pain of that Friday night five weeks ago engulfed her. She'd found strength during those few tense moments on the loveseat, but now that strength vanished. She was weak and scared. She leaned against the cool tile bathroom wall while she allowed herself to let go and cry.

She sobbed until she shook, and then sobbed some more. She sat on the broad side of the tub. What was *wrong* with her? She'd never felt so helpless and demoralized in her life. And she'd had some rotten days during the last few months.

After a time—she had no idea how long—Sage got to her feet, drank some water, and rummaged in her overnight bag for her nightgown. She removed her makeup and washed her face. She brushed her teeth and felt a little better. She ate the chocolate truffle placed on her pillow at turndown, brushed her teeth again, drank more water, and then slid between the cool, inviting sheets. Lying in bed against plump pillows, with her reading light on, she thought about the evening.

Great food. Too bad she hadn't kept it down. Delicious wines. Too bad she didn't drink them. But she was pleased that she'd made it through the date without getting drunk. Sober, she could assess Thomas Kitt, her friend, her lawyer.

Why hadn't she felt a thrill being with him? Was she a snob about his humble beginnings? Her own were pretty humble, so she knew it wasn't that. Was she put off by his rudeness in leaving her at the table while he wandered around the restaurant talking to Important People? Yes, that certainly irked her. But in the big picture it was no big deal. If she felt truly interested, she would have talked with him about it after dinner when they were alone.

Sage had felt excitement and anticipation earlier when he'd said flirty things to her. But tonight? Much had fallen flat. She had felt all evening that she was observing him from a distance, watching a play in which Thomas Kitt was director, producer, and star. Somehow the script wasn't real. There had been missed cues and awkwardness. He had been so wrapped up in his performance that he had not been present for her. She had wanted to get closer, to discover the sort of man her old friend had become.

Sure, they'd talked, about their lives during and since high school, but it seemed superficial. He had been watching the room. Always watching the room. And, she felt he was taunting her with alcohol, as if he expected her to get drunk. Well, she'd done it when they had lunch, so maybe that was justified. He'd had made certain there was more than enough alcohol at every juncture--the champagne, the cocktails, the wines, the after-dinner cognac. Yet he hadn't over-indulged. He wasn't much of a drinker at all. Had he expected her to drink all that wine? Was it a test? Or was he just showing off to all the other important people in the room? Was it part of the performance? Or was she paranoid?

Sage could not be certain. She knew she was over-thinking a simple dinner, but the whole evening made her uncomfortable. She had not wanted to feel flat. She had wanted to feel swept up into Thomas Kitt's amazing and exciting life. She had wanted to be dazzled by his intelligence, his ideas, his successful world. She had wanted him to be the man she'd been seeking all her life. Instead, she had found him arrogant and boring and by-the-book tedious about his look good. She was disappointed. He was not available in any real sense, despite all his talk of being there for her. That had been a very sad surprise.

She realized she was defensive about not drinking. *Everybody drank.* It was how people socialized. And yet at some level she knew that for whatever reason drinking wasn't the same for her as it was for most other people. She couldn't think of one other person who had been gang-raped in her own apartment in the middle of a blackout drunk. Normal people didn't get themselves into messes like that. There. She'd put the thought into words.

That was it! It wasn't him. It was her. She was uncomfortable about not drinking but afraid what would happen if she did. She feared people would notice and exclude her for not drinking, think she was square, or a religious fanatic. She had judged people that way. If she did drink, however, she turned into someone else, someone she didn't know. Or like.

She had been crazy to let her imagination run away with her before their date, crazy to entertain ideas of romance. It might look good in her imagination. It might be tempting from a distance. But when the rubber hit the road, as it had tonight, she had panicked.

Sage wasn't ready for a relationship, and she certainly wasn't ready for sex. Yet she'd felt the invitation lurking between them, unspoken throughout the evening. She wasn't even ready—yet—for dating. It was too much pressure. She didn't know what she wanted right now, or even who she was. She was out of balance, and afraid. So many challenges faced her—moving Granny, dealing with the Blackthorn, all that cash, people creeping around the old boathouse in the night, people showing up at the hotel demanding money for drugs.

She would talk to Tommy about it later when she'd made some sense out of what was going on around her. How much would she tell him? After tonight, she wasn't sure. He hadn't fit with her. Despite his pleasant words and physical gestures, he'd felt distant, cold. She felt a discomfort with him that she didn't understand. Truth be told, her old friend had become someone else, and it was not someone she liked.

She had to live with the memory of the violence done to her. Three thousand miles wasn't far enough away from the scene of that horror. But that notwithstanding, cold sober she saw that she never, ever would be attracted to Thomas Kitt. In some ways it was regrettable. But it was the truth.

Then she thought again. She treasured Tommy's friendship, but after tonight she knew his need for adulation surpassed any attraction she might have for him. He needed to be on stage. He needed to be important and looked up to. He had wrapped himself in artifice, and she hated that about him. All in all, though, he was a good lawyer. He could still be her lawyer, couldn't he?

She thought about her apartment, wondering whether she could continue to live there. Could she go back and feel safe? That was one of the many problems she faced when she returned to New York. She thought about returning to her job and what that meant, suspecting as she did that one of her assailants was a co-worker. She didn't know if her imagination had blown that up or if her subconscious knew something her conscious mind couldn't remember. That was why she had to stay sober. She was doing it to save her own life. Nobody else was going to do it for her. She was very certain of that. The idea that Tommy could swoop in like Prince Charming and save her from her past had been a fantasy and nothing more.

Sage rolled over and turned out the reading light. She snuggled down under the covers. She heard the traffic out on Broadway muted by double-glazed windows and thick draperies. Out there, it was still early for some people. As she closed her eyes and drifted toward sleep, she thought she heard voices murmuring around her. She was too tired to listen. They seemed benign, soothing.

And then she was screaming. Her body jerked upright, and she grabbed for something, she knew not what. Had she screamed? In her dream she had been trying to scream. The men had been hurting her again. She had fought with all her strength. And screamed. Wordless, paralyzing silence as she had urged her lungs to push out the air to make the sounds that could save her. No sound had come out of her. Nobody would know she needed help. And, she had seen him. She had recognized him. She had known him for just a second and then he was gone.

Sage turned on the light and sat at the edge of her bed gasping for breath. *Oh, that was a good one.* Her chest heaved, and she looked about wildly. After what seemed like a long time, she remembered where she was, and why. She felt a trickle of sweat between her breasts as she tried to calm her breathing. Her hands kneaded the bedding. She closed her eyes and saw the face again. It came closer, but no matter how hard she tried to see who he was, the face wouldn't come into focus—except for those dark, dead eyes. She knew him. Who was it?

She got up, used the bathroom, and drank a glass of water. She pulled open the curtains and looked down on the city. The traffic on Broadway was minimal now. Four in the morning. She let the curtains drop and paced the room. She felt tired, but on high alert. Was she ever going to get a decent night's sleep? *Do dreams mean anything? Or are they just dreams?* Since Ross's death, and since the rape, she'd experienced an unending series of nightmares. She checked the bolted door, and found it was still sufficiently bolted. She was safe here. This wasn't New York City, and she was alone. Safe. Awful as it was, this was just another dream. She crawled back into bed and turned out the light. She lay there, eyes closed but awake. She finally drifted off to sleep and groaned when the wakeup call came through at seven-thirty.

Chapter 23

WHEN SAGE ENTERED THE HEATHMAN dining room promptly at nine, she spotted Tommy across the room by the window reading a newspaper. She turned on a perky smile that had nothing to do with the way she felt and crossed the room. He wore a blue and white striped shirt under a yellow V-neck cashmere sweater. He looked impeccable, nary a hair out of place. He stood to greet her—tall and slim, handsome—so handsome diners turned in their seats to look at him. He kissed her lightly on the lips and seated her across from him in the booth.

Outside, in the early fall sunshine, people bustled up and down the street looking busy and important. Everyone had somewhere they were needed. Sage picked up her menu and said, "What are you having?"

Thomas looked across the table at her. "I'm told the salmon hash is killer."

She set down the menu. "That does it, then. Salmon hash."

Their server brought coffee and took their orders. They chatted about the weather, and about the ways Portland was changing. Sage watched him and saw that Tommy was as he'd been the night before. Pleasant, bland, wooden. She knew she'd lost the friend she'd once known, that he was not coming back. Unfortunate, yes. But she could live with it.

"How long has it been since you've been to the Blackthorn?" she asked.

Tommy took a sip of coffee. "Nearly three months. Since Ross's funeral. I lost interest in going out there after he died. But, as I told you last week, I'm very interested in the property. Otherwise, I've had no reason to go there until today. I'm a busy guy."

"You must know those hundred acres as well as I do," she said.

"I played there as a kid, and I walked it with Ross many times—until he got too sick."

Sage held back a shudder. Thinking of her brother as sick had proven difficult. But he had been sick. A man with a disease—the disease of trying to kill himself with alcohol. Obsessed. Just like her. "I have trouble thinking of him as 'too sick'," she said.

Tommy shook his head. "You have no idea."

It was nearly noon when they pulled up to the Blackthorn in Tommy's sleek Mercedes. He jumped out of the car, opened her door, and collected her bag from the trunk. As they walked toward the kitchen door, Tommy stopped her, turned her around, and pulled her into an embrace. As he kissed her, Sage heard tires on gravel. She pulled back as a pickup rolled into the parking lot and stopped next to the Mercedes.

Thomas released her, and they both turned to see Andy walking toward them. He smiled, but not convincingly. His furrowed brow and flashing hazel eyes registered his disapproval.

"Oh, hi Andy." Sage realized her own voice sounded tentative.

"I came by earlier, but nobody was home," said Andy. He nodded to Thomas, who nodded back.

"Do you two know each other?" said Sage.

"Yeah," Andy drawled.

"Through Ross," Thomas agreed. Neither offered a handshake.

Sage turned to Thomas. "Well, again, thanks so much," she said. She tried to sound breezy.

"No problem," he said. "Is there anything else I can help you with?" Sage shook her head. "Okay, then." Another thin-lipped smile. He looked at his expensive watch. "I'll still have time for a round of golf when I get back. I'll call you."

Thomas headed toward the Mercedes and got in. He waved at Sage, turned the car around, and drove past the building and out of sight.

"What's he doing here?" said Andy. He sounded angry.

"Why the hell do you care?" Sage retorted. *And why is it any of your business?* "What are *you* doing here, all puffed up and pissy?" She picked up her bag and headed toward the kitchen door.

Andy followed her to the door. "I was a little concerned this morning to find nobody around and the place locked up," he said. "Where's your grandmother?"

Sage let them into the kitchen and set her bag on the floor. She turned to face him. "Janice spent the night with her," she said. "I had to return my rental car. I had dinner with Tommy last night. He graciously agreed to bring me back. Is that a problem?"

Andy glared at her. "Of course not. Why should it be?"

"Well, I don't know. You seem so angry."

"I'm concerned because I came out here earlier and nobody's around," he repeated.

"Janice is here somewhere," Sage said. "She's probably doing laundry or something. I'm sure Granny's fine." She walked through the kitchen and dining room toward Granny's bedroom with Andy close on her heels.

Sage walked into the bedroom, which was dark and smelly. Alarmed, she pulled open the curtains to let in the light and dashed to Granny's bed. Andy stood in the doorway watching as the old woman began flailing her arms and crying out.

Sage leaned over her. "Granny, what on earth is going

on?" She lifted her shoulders up and put her arms around her. "I'm here now. It's going to be all right."

"Susan, where were you? You left me here alone, and I've pooped my pants. Were you out drinking again?" Somehow it always came back to that.

"No, Granny. It's Sage, and I'm here. I haven't been drinking. Where's Janice? She's supposed to be here. Have you had breakfast?"

"Hell, no, I haven't had breakfast! And I stink! Do something!" Well, at least she'd regained a sense of her surroundings, thought Sage. Granny looked around, wide-eyed, and saw Andy in the doorway. "Who's *that*?" she demanded.

Sage smiled. "That's our friend Andy. He and Ross were close." How true that was remained to be seen. "Let's get you out of bed and cleaned up."

Andy stepped into the room. "Ma'am," he said, and nodded at Granny, who gave him an angry yet fearful look. Then he said, "Why don't I go start some breakfast while you deal with things in here. I'm also going to check upstairs."

"Thank you," Sage said over her shoulder. She got her grandmother up and led her into the bathroom.

Twenty minutes later, they all were seated at the kitchen table. Granny, now clean from a very quick shower, shoveled scrambled eggs into her mouth while Sage and Andy sipped coffee. "Where did Janice go?" Sage asked her grandmother.

Granny looked at her blankly. "Who's Janice?" she said. "I don't know anyone named Janice."

"She was spending the night with you." Sage felt herself growing tense. Something was really off the tracks.

"I told her to go home. I don't need anyone spending the night with me."

"Granny, her car is in the driveway. Please don't give me any more crap." Sage looked at Andy and said, "She wouldn't have left. At least I don't think she would."

Andy stood up. "It was all clear upstairs. I'll go out and look around some more," he said. He took a gulp of coffee and headed out the back door.

Sage turned back to Granny. "When did you last see Janice?" She was not optimistic about getting an answer that made sense, but she was running out of ideas.

Granny looked at her squarely. "I'm here by myself while you're out running around with men," she said. And then her face shut down. Nobody home. *Great.*

"All right," said Sage. "Let's go for our walk."

She got Granny to her feet and they took a couple of slow laps around the dining room. Then Granny stopped in her tracks. "I'm tired," she said. Sage eased her back into the kitchen and sat her in the infamous chair.

Andy came inside, looking puzzled. "Well, I walked all around out there and didn't find anything," he said. "It's just the damnedest thing. She wouldn't walk home, would she?"

Sage shook her head. "Do you know Janice?" she said. "She hates walking. Plus, she lives more than two miles from here. I really don't think so. Did you check the bath house?"

Andy nodded. "It's locked."

"What about the laundry?"

"What laundry?"

Sage looked at Granny in her chair. Well-fed and comfortable, she was beginning to nod off. "I think she'll be okay," said Sage more to herself than to Andy. "Let's go check the laundry. She might have fallen or something."

They checked the bath house, and then trudged down the drive to the laundry, neither of them speaking. Sage carried the ring of hotel keys, but when they got to the large wooden doors below the bath house, they found one of them was ajar. Not surprising, thought Sage, since nobody ever locks anything around here. Who'd want their old towels, anyway? She thought of Crazy Phil. He might need a towel. They really should lock the place. She didn't want him sleeping in the laundry.

She shoved the wide door open and walked inside. Andy followed her into the cavernous room. "Where the hell is the light switch?" Andy muttered. Sage patted the wall inside the room until she found it, and an explosion of fluorescent light illuminated the room. They looked around, but no Janice. Sage called her name. The washer door was open. She walked over and closed it, then noticed the red light blinking on the front of the dryer. It was full of dried clothes.

So, Janice had been down here drying towels—unless Betty had forgotten to get the laundry out Friday afternoon. She pulled open the door to check the dried items. She screamed.

Andy leapt to her side as Sage covered her face with her

hands and moaned. "Oh, no! Oh *noooooooo!*

There were no towels in the dryer. The crumpled heap was Janice. Her bloodied face was bruised black and blue. Bloody, matted hair stuck to her face. She stared at them, wide-eyed, her mouth a grimacing mess of pain and broken teeth.

Sage held her hands over her face and screamed again. Andy dashed to open the dryer and checked for a pulse. After a moment, he turned away from the mangled body. "She's stone-cold and rigor has set in," he said. "She's been dead for several hours."

He took Sage's arm and walked her up the drive to the kitchen. She collapsed at the table, too numb to think. "I don't understand it. I just don't understand," she moaned. She felt nothing. Her mind rejected what she had seen. It wasn't real, and yet she knew it was real and would have to be dealt with. A little song ran through her mind. It told her, "Life is but a dream."

She heard Andy leave the room. She could hear his voice talking to someone, telling them to get here quick. He returned to the kitchen. "I just talked to Terry Thompson," he said. "Help is on the way."

Within half an hour, an armada had arrived at the Blackthorn—Sheriff Thompson, along with an ambulance, a fire truck, and full back up. "Where is she," he demanded. Again, Andy held Sage's arm as they led Thompson and his entourage to the laundry.

For a time, everyone clustered outside the laundry

room—except for Sheriff Thompson and one of his deputies. Andy and Sage stood in the background and watched as officers secured the scene both inside and out. The coroner arrived. Forensic investigators quickly followed. They donned white suits and headed into the laundry room to begin searching the grim scene for evidence. Sage's knees felt wobbly, particularly when Janice's body was removed from the dryer. As if sensing her distress, Andy touched her arm, and they walked back up the hill.

In the kitchen, Andy made a fresh pot of coffee. Granny, awake now, demanded a snack. A few minutes later, Sheriff Thompson lumbered into the room. He tipped his hat at Granny and said, "Afternoon, Mrs. Blackthorn." Mouth full, Granny grunted in response. Then she munched cheese and crackers and watched the proceedings with her usual vacant expression.

Andy handed the sheriff a cup of coffee, and Thompson settled his large posterior onto a chair across the table from Sage. Andy offered a little pat on Sage's shoulder and sat down next to her.

Thompson cut right to the chase. "Young lady, we have a situation. I want you to tell me what's going on here," he said. He took a large gulp of coffee. "And Andy, if you don't mind, I want to talk to Sage alone. You'll get your turn soon enough."

Andy nodded, got up, and left the room. "See you later," he said over his shoulder—whether to Sage or the sheriff was not clear.

Sage waited until Andy was out of the room. "I drove into Portland last night to have dinner with a friend. I planned to stay the night, so I hired Janice to spend the night here. She's the one who takes care of Granny most of the time."

Thompson scribbled in his little notebook. "Who were you meeting?" he asked, not looking up.

"Thomas Kitt. He's our family attorney and an old friend."

Thompson looked up and grinned. "Tommy Kitt! We played baseball together. He and I and your brother. They were sophomores when I was a senior."

Sage nodded.

"So, you were spending the night with Tommy Kitt!"

Sage resented the implication. "I didn't say that. I had dinner with him. I stayed in a hotel. He left after dinner for his own home. He drove me here this morning because I needed to return my rental car at the airport. And then he returned to Portland. When I got here, I couldn't find Janice anywhere. Granny was a mess. Andy showed up, unexpected, and after looking all over the place for Janice, we found her in that horrible dryer."

Thompson raised his eyebrows at Sage. "And that's it?"

"I'm afraid it is."

"What about Andy? What's his place in your story?"

Sage snorted. She wondered if Thompson imagined them in bed together as well. "Andy comes around frequently. He was friends with Ross, and he comes by to check on us. Sometimes I go to his tavern for a burger. I don't know why he showed up today, but I'm glad he did."

Thompson made a couple more notes. Sage wished he'd go away, but she was afraid to have him leave. She needed to put Granny in bed for her nap, and she wanted to lie down herself for a few minutes. She felt confused, but more than confused, she felt fearful.

Thompson looked up from his note taking and intercepted her impatient look. "So, you're sure there's nothing between you and Kitt?"

Sage drew herself up. "No there's not. And if there were, I'd say it was none of your damn business."

Now it was Thompson's turn to be offended. "Listen here, young lady. I'll decide what's my business in this investigation.

"Sheriff *Thompson*," said Sage. She got to her feet, assuming the superior position. "I am *not* 'young lady'. We went to the same high school years ago, in case you have forgotten. We are peers. Don't you get all uppity with me. I saw the shit you pulled in high school. Kindly choose questions that are related to Janice's death. Now, if you don't mind, my grandmother needs my attention." Granny snored in her chair.

Sheriff Thompson looked at Granny and stood. He gave Sage an oily smile. "I don't like your attitude," he said with as much dignity as he could muster. "I'm finished for now, but I'm sure I'll have more questions as our investigation proceeds. I'll get back to you soon. Meanwhile, don't you take off for New York or get any ideas about traveling anywhere."

Sage rolled her eyes. "Since my grandmother's an invalid, you needn't worry. I'm stuck here for the time being."

She walked with the sheriff to the front door of the hotel. He made a move toward his cruiser and then turned around. "You might not be aware of this, you bein' away all these years, but we've got a huge drug problem around here."

Well, duh! Sage thought of the money in the barn. In the desk drawer. She felt her body go numb. She looked straight at Terry Thompson, eyes wide, and said nothing.

"We think it's coming up the coast and through this area somehow on its way to Yakima. And from there it goes to Seattle, and Spokane, and Boise, and Canada. And God only knows where else. Just so you know. Out here all by yourself, you might want to keep your eyes open." He nodded to her, got into his cruiser, and pulled away from the building.

In the kitchen, Granny snored without a care. Sage found herself struggling just to breathe as she walked to the sink and drew a glass of fresh well water. She drank, set the glass down, and sat at the table. She folded her hands in front of her on the table and looked straight ahead at nothing. *Shit shit shit! Shitty shit!* A bag of bundles of hundred-dollar bills in the barn. Why hadn't it been found when the deputies searched the place? Twenty thousand in cash in the desk drawer. Would they be able to find their own back ends without a map and compass? And there was Ross. Always Ross. He was dead, and she did not believe the stupid cops' theory.

She felt herself dizzy for lack of oxygen. Dizzy at the

thought of *her brother* and his role in this huge mess coming down around her. She sucked in a big breath. She knew there was a drug problem. That's why she'd called for help the other night. And nobody found anything then either. Where were the damn drugs? She had seen those men carry things into the boathouse. And what had Ross been doing? She didn't want to think of her brother as one of the low-life scum who made their fortunes ruining people's lives. It was beyond her imagination. Ross had never cared about money. He hadn't had a vicious bone in his body.

Yet, here was the evidence. Piles of money. His mysterious death. And now another mysterious death, this one an obvious murder. At least with this one, nobody would try to tell her that Janice had crawled into that dryer, closed the door, and turned it on! Should she tell the sheriff about her discoveries, her thoughts, her fears? If she trusted him, she might. But no. He could be involved in this as well. Who could she trust?

She walked to the front door of the hotel, stood on the broad veranda, and looked down the drive. Below the bathhouse, out of her line of vision, the full force of Skamania County law enforcement worked the scene. They would be there for hours. Thompson was down there — he'd driven the entire fifty yards! — and was out parading around barking orders at his subordinates. Truth be told, Sage thought Terry Thompson was just a wee bit short of an idiot. He'd been an okay shortstop, but he'd also been a world class doofus. Still was. He was the principal law enforcement officer in Skamania County. He talked down to her. She knew and appreciated that there were many competent people in law enforcement. Maybe some of the state troopers who'd shown up could help. Someone she could talk to who had a functioning brain. Other people solved cases every day, just not Terry.

She went inside and shut the door. What had Janice been doing that someone had to kill her? With her furtive behavior, Sage knew she had been up to something. Stuffing sandwiches under basil plants was not motive for murder. So, either she'd been up to something no good or knew about the drug trafficking—and who was behind it. Between working for the hotel, and more recently taking care of Granny, Janice had spent every working day of her life here for nearly thirty years. She knew everyone in the area. One of those people had murdered her. There had been no evidence of a robbery, no hint of a disturbance in the hotel. Someone had targeted Janice and had wanted her to die horribly. Janice had lived a secret life beneath the one Sage knew. A life of stashed sandwiches and who knew what else? She had become a problem, a threat to someone. And now she was dead.

But who had killed her, and why? Was it linked to Ross? The money? The drugs? Her mind stopped. Andy. Had Andy just happened to show up this morning? Or had he planned to come back to remove the body and bury it in the woods where it would never be found, to just remove Janice's car from the premises?

Who would miss Janice anyway? Her husband was deceased. She never mentioned children or grandchildren. How long would it be before anyone even knew she was gone? Oh, Sage would know. It would be a great inconvenience. But would she have done anything about it? She wasn't certain. If Janice had wanted to leave her job unannounced, what could Sage do about it?

She thought of Betty. Betty surely would raise the alarm if Janice disappeared. They were—had been—close. What was it her grandmother used to say about Betty? That she was "regular as the rain". Betty was strong, much stronger than Janice.

Sage looked at Granny, snoring and drooling in her chair. She walked through the dining room to the telephone and dialed Betty's number. Betty picked up on the fifth ring. "Hi, Betty. It's Sage. I wonder if you could come over here for a few minutes. I need your help."

"Sure, honey. I'll be there in fifteen minutes." Yes, regular as rain. No questions or complaints. Now, how to deal with her. Telling her about Janice would be tough. Sage was not looking forward to it.

Granny stirred from her slumbers, and Sage was grateful she was present. The old woman had experienced a traumatizing morning. "Hey, Granny," she said, and knelt in front of her. "Let's go to the bathroom, shall we?"

Granny looked at her, and Sage could see her trying to orient herself. "I guess so," she said. Together they toddled off to the toilet, then they returned to the kitchen for

Granny's snack just as Betty came in the back door.

Betty looked around. She was wary, nervous. "Where's Janice?" she said. "What's goin' on down in the laundry with the sheriff and all?"

"Take a seat, Betty," Sage said. She cut a banana, set the pieces on the plate, and placed it in front of Granny.

Betty sat, eyes wide, her attention on Sage complete.

Sage sat at the table. "I'm sorry to have to tell you that Janice is dead." Betty's hands flew to her mouth. She gasped.

"We found her in the dryer," Sage continued. "Somebody put her there. I don't know if she was alive or dead when she went in. I got home late this morning and she wasn't around. I looked all over and found her a while later. She'd been dead for several hours. I'm just so sorry. I know you two were close."

Betty shook her head, her apple doll face crumpled. She began to cry. Sage handed her the nearest dishtowel and sat back down across from her. "I don't know what to say," Betty said. "Me and her was like sisters."

Sage reached out and touched her hand. "I know," she said. "You guys were the real deal together. Does she have any family? Who should we contact?"

"Nobody close," said Betty, wiping her eyes. "I was the closest to her, even though we ain't related." She shook her head again. "I just don't get it."

"Why would anyone want to kill her?" Sage asked. "This was deliberate. It wasn't a robbery. Nothing was out of place here when I got back about noon. I just couldn't find her, and

Granny hadn't been tended to. Do you know anyone, *anyone*, who had it in for her?"

Betty thought about it for a minute and shook her head. "She had her feathers up about somethin', but she never told me what. She was just actin' real antsy the last couple of weeks. But she did have her moods."

"What about those sandwiches she left in the garden?" Sage said.

"I don't know much about them," said Betty. "Probably that homeless guy who was hangin' around. Crazy Phil. I think Janice felt sorry for him. We never talked about him, though."

"Would he have any reason to kill her?"

Betty shrugged and blew her nose in the towel. "He's some distant relative of Janice's who was in the military and got that shell shock. He lives in the woods. I seen him talkin' to Ross a couple times. He didn't look like he'd hurt anybody, and Ross seemed to like him, so I didn't pay much attention."

"We'll have to tell the sheriff," Sage said. "And they're going to want to talk to you since you were close to Janice."

Betty nodded. "Well, they know where to find me." She stood up. "I need to be by myself now. I'm goin' home. Will you be okay?"

Sage smiled. "I'll be okay. I'm going to close the place down. Nobody will come here after a murder, and I don't want anyone here."

Betty nodded and stood up. She wobbled on her feet. "I understand," she said.

"I'd be very grateful if you would stay on for a while," Sage said. "I've got a lot to do here before I can return to New York. And I'll need help with Granny until I can get her relocated."

"I'll be happy to help you, Miss Sage," said Betty. Regret tinged her voice. "We've all had a long time here together, ever since you was a little squirt." She stood up and began gathering her bag and jacket.

Sage stood and hugged her awkwardly. She felt Betty's warm tears against her own face. They hadn't hugged since Sage had left for college. Betty dabbed her eyes and headed out the back door. She walked slowly, like a very old woman.

Chapter 24

SAGE STRUGGLED THROUGH the rest of the day, alternately caring for Granny and watching from the hotel's front porch as crime scene investigators worked down the hill. She couldn't see what they were doing and didn't have the energy to go down the drive to watch. The image of Janice's body in the dryer was painfully vivid in her mind. She felt depleted, numb. She did not need to be reminded of what she had seen. She felt no curiosity. *I'm in shock. That's it.*

The day plodded on. She couldn't relax, she feared closing her eyes. She sat and drank coffee, then she watched from the porch some more. And thought. Who could have done this? The first person who came to mind was Donald the Pothead. He'd visited recently, acting more like a hothead than a pothead. Was Janice mixed up with him and his marijuana business? People had been killed for less. Then there was Phil. Yes, he'd been courteous to her, but she'd read about Vietnam vets and the toll the war had taken on them, the guilt many carried after the war. The horrors they had witnessed. Phil was known to suffer from PTSD. Had he gone nuts and killed Janice?

Then Sage thought about the big picture, what she had witnessed down at the boathouse. Was Janice's murder tied to those activities somehow? She couldn't imagine an older person like Janice getting mixed up with drug traffickers. If she had been, she was out of her league. These were high stakes players. Sage thought some more. Who was the guy in the shadows, the one who ran the show? The one who knew the area, who lived here and could keep his finger on the pulse of what was going on in the county, all the while seeming to mind his own business? Who was friendly with Ross? And perhaps could influence him and use him? Who had access to Janice? She closed her eyes and listened to the cacophony in her brain. Andy.

No! The thought chilled her. Andy had helped her when she hurt herself. She liked him. His directness was refreshing even if his observations often made her uncomfortable. He seemed like a straight up good guy, someone a person could rely on. And she believed him when he said Ross had been a friend. And yet. And yet, Andy with his tavern was in the middle of everything, filled all the requirements for someone capable of running such an operation. Smart, capable, part of the landscape.

Andy's place was the watering hole for the area, and it drew people. People came and went—the locals, people passing through. Outsiders. Nobody would ever think twice about someone frequenting the Hoot Owl. It was a place where business could be done. People could sit at their tables, sip their drinks, and hatch all kinds of despicable plots, and nobody would notice. Ross used to drink there. Ross, who had been very sick during those months of his final relapse. Ross, who could justify things when he was drinking that he'd never buy into sober. Sage knew how that worked. She'd practically written the book.

By six-thirty, the sky had darkened, and floodlights blazed near the laundry's entrance. Rain began to fall, first as a bit of a mist, and then in earnest. Sage fed Granny and put her to bed. Then she turned on lights in the kitchen, dining room, and reception area. After eating a bit of toast and jam, she turned on the light to the office, retrieved the gun safe key from its new hiding place, and opened the safe. She removed the shotgun from its home. She sat down and placed it across her knees. It sat there on her lap, and she felt its weight. Now, if she just could figure out what to do with the damned thing.

This was war. Janice's death made that very clear. Her brother had been killed because he was involved in whatever was going on down at that boathouse. He had become a liability. Janice had known something as well. Twitchy and nervous, she always had acted as if she expected the other shoe to drop. And then it had. Janice had become dispensable. Two lives thrown away like yesterday's trash. Who would be next? Sage stood and lifted the gun to her shoulder. She looked down the barrel and put her finger on the trigger. Now what?

The phone rang. She screamed and dropped the shotgun. *Jesus!* She marched into reception and picked up the receiver. "What!"

There was a silence, and then "Sage?" It sounded like Andy. "Sage, are you all right?" It was Andy.

She let out a breath. She felt like she might wet her pants. "Yes. Hi, Andy. What's up?" She could hear Sunday night tavern noises. A woman's laugh tinkled in the background, light over the men's voices. *How the hell is business, Andy?*

Sage heard his intake of air. "I'm checking on you," he said. He sounded tentative. "How are you doing? What's going on over there?"

Sage sighed. "I'm not a happy girl," she said. "I had to tell Betty about Janice. A bunch of men are down by the laundry with floodlights going through the scene with a fine-tooth comb. That poor woman I've known most of my life was murdered, dead in a dryer! My life is fucked, frankly."

"It sounds like you could use some company," Andy said. "Maybe I should come over?"

"No thanks." It came out sounding harsh. "I'm sorry," she said. "I'm on edge. Thank you for the kind offer, but I'm going to take a hot bath and head to bed. I just got Granny settled, and it's been a long day."

Another silence. More tavern noises. "All right, suit yourself," Andy said. "I'm a little concerned about you after what's happened. I don't like it that you're there alone."

I bet. "I'm fine," Sage said. Fine. Such a useless word. "Don't worry. Every able-bodied lawman in Skamania County is currently on the property. Plus, nobody has any reason to come after me."

"You don't know that," Andy said. "The sheriff and I talked this afternoon. He's all worked up about drug traffickers in the neighborhood."

"Well, they wouldn't have any use for me," she said. "I don't know anything. And I'm not going to worry about drug scum right this minute. I'm going to find a place where my grandmother can be safe. Then I'm going to sell this whole mess—land, buildings, everything—and get out of here. I'll go back to New York City where I belong. Have a good night."

Sage hung up the phone without saying goodbye and wrapped her arms around herself. "Oh, my God, my God," she said. "What am I going to do?"

She walked out onto the hotel porch. Through sheets of rain that seemed to grow heavier by the moment, she could see the crime team packing up to go home. She saw the yellow tape surrounding the lower part of the bathhouse as they dismantled their floodlights, vehicle headlights were turned on, and rigs began their slow exodus toward Highway 14. In a short while she would be here alone. With Granny. She almost called the Hoot Owl and told Andy she'd changed her mind. She knew he'd come.

But what if he was the one? What if he had killed Janice? *What if he had killed Ross?* She'd reckon with him later. Right now, she couldn't think straight. She needed to rest.

The phone rang again. "Dammit!" She picked it up. "Hello?"

"Hey Sage, it's Thomas. I just wanted to check in and thank you again for coming in to town last night. It was great catching up. When can we get together again?"

"Oh, Tommy. I don't know. The most awful thing happened." Sage's body relaxed, and at last she allowed her eyes to fill with tears. She told him the details of finding Janice dead and everything she knew that had happened afterward. He would know what to do.

Thomas listened. He interjected a question here and there for clarification. When she was finished with her story, he said, "What an awful shock you've had. Would you feel safer in Portland? You could stay at my place. There's plenty of room."

Sage groaned. It was so tempting. "I wish I could, but there's Granny. She has to be taken care of."

"Call Betty and ask her to stay with your grandmother."

Sage's mind jumped hopefully. Then she stopped herself. "No, I'm not going to do that—not tonight. Betty's really upset about Janice and she's not up to taking care of anybody. I sent her home for the night. I'm going to stay put, but thanks for the kind offer. Tomorrow I'm going in to Stevenson to check out a place for Granny. I really just want to get out of here."

"I understand," Thomas said. His voice sounded tinged with regret. "The offer to stay is always open. Call me any time of the day or night. I can drive out any time. I can come out now if you want me to. Just say the word."

"No thanks, Tommy. I've got Granny settled for the night. We'll be all right for another few days, and then I'm out of here. It would help, though, if you'd call me tomorrow."

They said their goodbyes, and Sage returned to the office and the shotgun. She was tired. She needed to sleep. She padded around the hotel, rechecking locks on all the doors and windows. She left the back and front porch lights on, and even the old floodlight that illuminated the weed-grown front parking lot. She left the light on above the kitchen sink, and the light in the hallway to Granny's room. Small comfort. Outside, trees were silhouetted against the sky, their limbs tossed in the wind. Even with the doors closed and locked, she could hear rain pelting the ground like buckshot. It was a terrible night. A terrible, lonely, scary night.

Finally, Sage went upstairs to one of the long-abandoned guest rooms and pulled a thin mattress from one of the twin beds. She dragged it down the stairs and into the office. Upstairs again, she procured her pillow, toothbrush, and clean sheets and blankets from a linen cupboard. She made up a bed on the office floor and brushed her teeth. Then she laid the shotgun alongside the mattress and crawled under the covers. It was comfortable enough, she told herself.

When she closed her eyes, she saw through the dryer's glass door the bloody stumps of Janice's teeth, her silent awful scream. She opened her eyes and squirmed on the mattress. She listened for sounds. Would Granny feel her restlessness, or act upon some restlessness of her own, and try to climb those stairs again? Why had Janice been killed? Would she and Granny be next? It was very late before she was able to sleep.

In her dream, someone was banging. It was so loud. Why didn't it stop? Then Sage realized she was awake, on the floor of the office. Someone banged relentlessly on the back door. "Sage, open up. It's me!"

It took her a minute to realize where she was. And why. Sage groaned and staggered to her feet, disoriented. "Shut up," she muttered under her breath. The noise was from the back. She picked up the shotgun and made her way through the dining room and kitchen. She could see Andy's head outside the kitchen door window. She threw open the door. "What do you want?"

Andy's eyes popped wide open when he saw the shotgun. He cradled a grocery bag in one arm. "Whoa!" he said. "What the hell are you doing?"

Sage blinked in the daylight. She leaned the gun against the wall. "What do you mean?"

Andy started laughing as he came toward the door. Sage stepped back to let him in. "It looks like you've gone all Annie Oakley on me," he said.

"I don't think that's funny. What are you doing here,

anyway?"

Andy set the bag on the table, removed his jacket, and draped it over the back of a chair. "I brought you breakfast," he said. "Could you make a guy a cup of coffee?"

Sage found a filter, put it into the coffee basket, and poured in grounds, all the time aware of his eyes on her back. She felt grouchy and off balance. Her clothes were rumpled and slept in, and she had to pee. She turned the coffee maker on. "I'm going to check on Granny," she said, and left the room.

She scurried into the bathroom, brushed her teeth, and combed her hair. It was sticking out everywhere. There was little she could do without spending time on it. She pulled it back and secured it with a rubber band. Granny stirred in her bed. Sage got her up, took her to the bathroom, wrapped her in her old heavy bathrobe, and was back in the kitchen in fifteen minutes, Granny in tow.

Andy stood at the stove turning bacon. It smelled divine. The coffee was ready, and Sage saw pancakes on the griddle. Better than she would have done the day after a murder. She sat Granny at the table and poured herself a cup of coffee. She stood beside Andy at the stove. "Looks like you found everything," she said.

"I'm used to this kitchen," he replied. "Remember, I hung out with your brother."

Yes, Sage remembered, and wondered if that meant they'd been business partners. It was not a comforting thought. She retrieved three plates from the cupboard and put them on the counter beside the stove. Andy flipped pancakes and broke eggs into a cast iron frying pan.

She stared out the window at the dormant garden. He broke into her reverie. "Do you want to learn how to use it?"

"Huh? What do you mean?"

Andy nodded toward the entry, where the shotgun stood on its butt, then refocused on his cooking. "After we eat, I can take you outside and show you how to shoot that thing. If you're going to lug it around like some stagecoach robber, you at least should know how to use it. Otherwise you're more a danger to yourself than others."

Sage looked at the gun. She hated the thing, but stuck like she was here alone with Granny, and a murderer on the loose, it probably was a good idea to know how to shoot it. "I guess," she said. "I don't want to shoot my foot off."

Andy laughed and slid eggs onto the plates. "That's the spirit," he said.

They sat down to eat. Sage cut Granny's pancakes into small squares and doused them with maple syrup before passing the bottle to Andy. "After you," he said. The food was delicious, and the friendly combination of coffee and carbs elevated her mood.

By the time they'd finished eating, there was a sunbreak. "I'll get Granny down for a little nap, and then let's go shoot that sucker," Sage said. Andy nodded his approval.

They walked out behind the barn, through tall, wet grasses and weeds, to what once was Sonny's paddock. Above them, Sage heard the cries of geese heading south. A long V with purpose, just like every year of her childhood. The autumn air sparkled, scrubbed clean by a night of rain. Andy hauled an old sheet of plywood from the barn and rested it against the fence. He seemed unaffected by going in and out of the barn. Did he know about all the money that was in there? Had anyone known, besides Ross?

"This is not going to be any fancy target practice," Andy told Sage. "I'm going to teach you how to safely load and shoot this thing. A shotgun scatters the shot, so you have a fairly broad target from a distance. Up close it's more concentrated. And it's lethal. Never forget that this is not a toy. Hopefully, if you're shooting at anything, it will be in the air, to keep something—or someone—away. Just to put the fear of God in them, so to speak. These things will do a shitload of damage."

Sage nodded and fidgeted. Here he was, showing her how to use a gun against the enemy. She appreciated the irony, but the fact that he was teaching her something useful was not lost on her either. Maybe he wasn't a drug trafficker. But who knew? The county was full of likely suspects. She supposed she could keep an open mind, at least until the lesson was over.

Andy paced off twenty-five feet and helped Sage position herself with the gun at her shoulder. "This is a four-ten, which is about right for someone your size," he told her. "A twelve-gauge would knock you on your butt." He showed her how to load the shells, how to pull the stock tight against her body. He had her aim at the plywood and fire the gun.

The butt made a bruising thump against her shoulder a nanosecond after she pulled the trigger. Despite Andy's warning, she was surprised at the kick. The piece of plywood shuddered. They walked up to it and Andy pointed out the spread of buckshot that surrounded a significantly larger center hole.

Target practice continued until the ammunition they'd brought outside ran low. Again and again, Andy had Sage load and fire the shotgun. When they finished, her shoulder ached, and she felt exhausted. She knew she would never be friends with firearms. Andy returned the shredded plywood to the barn and carried the shotgun back to the hotel for her. In the kitchen, Sage poured them each a cup of coffee. Her arms were tired. Her shoulders ached. She dropped into a chair and looked at him.

His face was flushed from the chilly morning. His eyes were bright. He grinned at her, a warm, easy smile. She smiled back. "That was quite a session," she said. "Thank you."

Andy joined her at the table. His face lost its smile. He took a sip of coffee and looked her in the eye. "I'm glad we did that," he said. "I'll be able to sleep a little better now."

"What are you talking about?" she said, although she already knew. His eyes had grown dark and his face registered concern.

"After what happened to Janice? Sage, wake up. You're not safe here. I'd feel much better if you left the Blackthorn today."

"That's easy for you to say," she bristled. "I'm taking care of a frail old woman with dementia. Right now, I have not arranged anywhere to put her, and she's not going to New York with me." She paused for breath. "And why does everyone want me out of here, anyway?"

Andy held up his hand in surrender. "Okay. All right. I get that. Arrangements must be made. She's your grandmother, and a very important person in her own right. Yesterday someone was murdered here. On your property. Did it ever occur to you that you could be next? Maybe someone wants you out of here."

Sage shrugged. She was scared. But why would anyone want to get rid of her? "Thomas Kitt called last night and invited me to come in to his place in Portland."

Andy thought about it. He looked more angry than thoughtful. Finally, he said, "It's not a bad idea. Except for your grandmother, of course."

"That's what I told him," Sage snapped. "It's not like I can just take off."

She jumped to her feet, unable to continue the conversation sitting down. "I'm terrified, and yet I can't believe someone's after me," she said. She paced the floor. "I'm sleeping in the office with the shotgun. What else can I do? I can't leave Granny. I can't imagine trying to take care of her anywhere else. She's lived here all her life, she doesn't like change, and in her condition, she doesn't understand it. This will take more than a few days. Even when I find a care facility, she'll be difficult to get settled there. She yells and cusses when she's afraid."

Andy spread his hands in a gesture of supplication. "Come to my place," he said. "Both of you. Please. You'll be safe there. And welcome."

Her reaction surprised her. "No! I won't do that. Granny'd be too shook up, even if she knows you some of the time. We'll be fine here a bit longer. We'll have to be."

"You're scared to death, and for good reason. You don't know if you're going to be fine, or even okay." Andy's lips had become thin lines. His eyes flashed dark with anger. "And I don't blame you. You don't know who's out there or what they're after."

"You're just making me feel worse," she said. "I can't imagine why anyone would want to harm us. My grandmother doesn't know what day it is, and I have nothing to do with whatever Janice's death is about. I don't know anybody. I'm not involved in any local drug fights. I need to find a place for Granny, settle the Blackthorn business, and maybe figure out what really happened to my brother. Then I'll leave in peace."

"Come to my place," Andy said again. "Please."

But Sage couldn't go to Andy's house. As much as she wanted to, she didn't feel safe with him. She shook her head. "Nope. Staying here."

Andy stood and carried his coffee mug to the sink. He rinsed it out. Slowly. He turned around and looked at Sage, his face clouded. "Do you think I'm the bogeyman?" he said.

Sage's mouth fell open. She searched for words. "Why no.

Of course not," she said. But she had paused a second too long.

Andy looked at her for a moment, then made up his mind. "Thanks," he said. He walked out the door and closed it firmly behind him without saying goodbye.

For the second time that morning, Sage fell into her chair. "Shit! What did I just do? And you're talking to yourself. You're as bad as Granny." She sat there for a while. No answers. Just bloody teeth. Andy was right. They weren't safe. Somebody was out there. Someone had killed Ross, and now Janice. Certainly, that someone or some*ones* wouldn't risk another killing. It would just bring more attention to the place, more cops combing the area.

She thought of the pile of money in the barn. Just take it and go away, she thought. She didn't know why it was abandoned there—unless it was to draw attention to her dead brother and paint him as the person behind the county's drug problems. Yes, find all that money. And Ross was dead. Ergo, county drug problem solved. The real person or persons behind the trafficking would be free to continue as usual. With her and Granny gone, nobody would be there to watch them move their wares.

"Ugh!" Sage said aloud. That blasted cash. Did the someone behind all this even know it was there? Yes, she decided, someone did, even if she couldn't prove it. The boat in the middle of the night. Donald the Pothead and his demands. What was Donald's role in this, or was he just some yokel who grew pot? The way her brother had died by jumping off the dock after he'd overdosed! That was the best one yet. The madman Phil wandering around the property knowing what, doing what? And Janice's murder. There, she'd put the word out there. Murder. She needed to get out of this place sooner rather than later.

Sun was drying the grass; it was a beautiful fall day. She finished the cup of coffee and went upstairs to take a bath. When Granny woke, they'd get to work.

Chapter 25

SAGE'S DAY BEGAN A SECOND TIME when Granny got up from her nap. Sage had called Stevenson Gardens and the person in charge there told her to bring Granny over for lunch and a tour. That meant getting the old woman presentable. When she walked through the dining room to wake Granny, she noticed fresh activity down by the laundry. A couple of sheriff's department cars. Men with big beer guts walking around. One of them was the sheriff. He spat on the ground and looked up toward the hotel.

Sage moved out of sight and into Granny's bedroom. She wanted nothing to do with whatever was going on down in the laundry, and nothing whatever to do with Thompson. She located a respectable dress in the closet, one from

Granny's church-going days. She helped Granny into it, helped her sit at the table in her bedroom. Sage brushed her hair and pinned it up. Then she rummaged in the bathroom and found some loose powder and lipstick.

"What are you doing to me?" Granny demanded.

"I'm fixing you up to go out," Sage told her. "We're going out to lunch."

"I don't want to go out to lunch. The food here's just fine," Granny complained. "We have the best food in the county. Have you tasted Janice's pies?"

"Janice's pies are the best, but we no longer have the best food in the county, so you can put your mind to rest on that one."

"I'm staying right here."

"You most certainly are not! There's something I want you to see."

Granny's moment of sharpness, the brief glimpse of the feisty woman she once was, once again quickly faded to something else, and she became petulant. "I'm hungry," she said.

Sage began walking her out the front door and toward the barn where the car was parked. "That's why we're going to lunch," she told Granny as they walked slowly across the parking lot.

They drove past the two men. Sage waved, pretended a smile, but didn't stop. The wind whipped up whitecaps on the Columbia, and she drove against a stiff breeze into Stevenson. Stevenson Gardens sat slightly uphill from the short street that was downtown. The building had an amazing view of the river. Sage pulled up to the front, stepped inside, and secured a wheelchair for Granny. When she opened the car door to help Granny out of the car, the old woman took one look at the wheelchair and screeched, "I'm not a cripple for chrissakes!"

Indeed.

Sage had never heard her grandmother come anywhere close to taking the Lord's name in vain. As she paused momentarily to collect herself, a heavyset woman came outside to greet them. "Hi, you must be Sage Blackthorn," she said. "I'm Marion Pence, and I'll be the one to show you around today." Everything about her was cheerful and hearty. She pumped Sage's hand and then leaned down through the open passenger door and said, "Why, Mary Margaret Blackthorn, welcome to Stevenson Gardens. I've been hearing about you for years, and I'm so glad to finally have the chance to meet you."

Granny looked puzzled for a moment, and then grinned from ear to hear and stretched out her veiny right hand to Marion. "Why, thank you," she said.

Marion helped her from the car to the wheelchair without eliciting another curse. "Come inside, Mary Margaret. We've fixed you a lovely lunch."

Not wanting to break the spell, Sage said nothing. She followed her smiling grandmother and Marion through the lobby and into the dining room, where several elderly diners, many in wheelchairs themselves, sat hunched at four-top tables. Marion rolled Granny up to one of the empty tables and sat down next to her. Sage took a seat as well.

At the end of a bland but nutritious meal, Marion took charge of Granny and the three toured the "gardens". Granny dozed off, but the tour was mainly for Sage's benefit anyway. She watched, asked questions, listened, and took mental notes. Residents seemed well cared for in their various declining states of health. Nobody was left alone, drooling, in the halls, and nothing smelled bad. When the tour ended in the lobby, Sage said, "When can we move her in?"

"There are no beds available at this time," Marion informed her, and Sage's shoulders slumped. "However, we expect to have an opening in a couple of weeks." In other words, some poor soul was on his or her last leg.

Sage thought about it, about two more weeks in the Blackthorn. What choice did she have? "I think Granny would do well here," she said. "I'm sure of it. I need to get back to my job in New York, so was hoping to find something sooner than that. I'll need to keep looking."

"You're welcome to leave a deposit and we'll reserve the next available bed for your grandmother," Marion said. "If you find a place somewhere else, fine, you get your deposit back. If not, you've got Mary Margaret's space reserved for our soonest opening here. In these facilities, you never know when there will be an unexpected vacancy."

You never know, thought Sage. The folks who left the Gardens would go out feet first. She pulled out her wallet and gave Marion eight hundred dollars in cash. Better to spend her found money on Granny than give it to some drug dealer. Or some asshole sheriff she didn't trust. She pocketed the receipt, and then she and Marion loaded a groggy Granny into the Buick.

On the way home, Sage pulled into the parking lot of the Stevenson grocery store. She quickly debated the wisdom of leaving Granny in the car alone, and practicality won out. She dashed inside, leaving the old woman in the locked car, quickly picked out some items for dinner, and ran back outside. Fortunately, Granny hadn't stirred.

Back home, Sage left Granny in the car to finish her nap. She'd pulled the Buick up far enough that she could see it from the kitchen window, and she kept watch as she rustled things together to prepare a simple evening meal. The die was cast. Granny would move into Stevenson Gardens—not today, and probably not tomorrow, but soon. Sage felt she had done a good day's work. She hoped things would move forward quickly now so she could get home to New York.

She looked up from her prepping to see Granny stirring in the front seat of the car. She dried her hands and walked outside, opened the door, and helped her grandmother to her feet. "Where in the hell am I?" Granny demanded. "I just peed my pants."

Ah, those moments of clarity. Sage eased her toward the kitchen door. "It's all right, Granny. You've got on your Depends. We'll have you fixed up in no time, and then you can have a nice snack." No time took twenty minutes. Sage's arm and shoulder ached from the morning's shooting lesson.

She was tired, but there was no time to be tired now. Evening was fast approaching. "No rest for the wicked," as Granny used to say. She settled Granny in the chair and cut up some fresh fruit for her to nibble. Thank goodness Granny still liked to eat.

Sage performed her chores like an automaton. The endless night lay ahead. Last night the place had been swarming with investigators. It had been a horrible business, but people were around. She had been scared, but tonight was different. Once Granny went to bed, she was on her own. It was not a comfortable place to be alone.

The sheriff had come and gone. She was grateful she hadn't needed to deal with him. Now she wished him back, as a sense of deep foreboding washed over her. She wanted a good hot meal, prepared by someone else, and a warm fire, and a television. Yes, a television would make noise. There would be the comfort of human voices, background music, even commercials. She was tired of Granny's senile prattling. She wanted to be warm and held and comforted.

It was not to be. Dinner finished, Sage went through the motions of Granny's care and tucked her into bed. And then she turned on all the lights in the hotel and did a great big walkaround. She went up to the third floor, the place of Granny's adventuring a few nights previous, and looked in every room. Had the old woman been looking for something in a moment of clarity, or just wandering? As she walked down the hall, Sage remembered the twenty-two she'd carried up with her that night. She'd left it on the floor just outside the door to the room where she found Granny. It wasn't where she'd put it. Or where she *thought* she'd put it. Nor was it in the room where she'd found Granny. It wasn't in any of the other guest rooms either. She searched them all. It wasn't in the bathrooms.

Sage turned out the lights on the third floor and walked down to the second. She searched each of the guest rooms and bathrooms. Nothing amiss anywhere. But no rifle. She knew where she'd left the thing. Her sense of foreboding only worsened. Someone had been in the hotel. Someone was messing with her. Was it the person who murdered Janice? Or Ross? For all she knew, he could be here now.

She walked through her living quarters, carefully looking at the items scattered here and there. Everything looked normal, the way she remembered leaving it. She left a lamp on in the living room and went down to the kitchen. Thank God she was sober. Thank God.

The porchlights were on, back and front. The doors had been locked. Nobody else was in the building. Just her and Granny. Nobody there who shouldn't be there. She looked out the front of the hotel. It was raining again. No light, no activity from the laundry area. She pulled in a deep breath and let it out slowly. Relax, she told herself. Relax.

Leaving lights on in key places, Sage repaired to the office. She could finish going through the papers in the desk. She would do something useful until she was tired enough to go to bed. She sat in the well-lit room and thrummed her fingers on the desk. It was no good. She couldn't focus. She began digging around on the desktop, through the neat stacks of papers she'd sorted earlier. She felt unmotivated to continue. She sat back in the old desk chair. She remembered the book, *Jamaica Inn,* sitting partially read upstairs. She shuddered. It was dark and creepy and rainy on the Cornish moors just like it was here. People had died at that inn too.

The phone rang. The muscles in her chest tightened. Her breathing became shallow. She listened. On the fourth ring she stood up and walked into the reception area. She dreaded to pick up the phone but pick it up she must. "Hello."

"Hi Sage, how are you doing?" It was Thomas Kitt, and he sounded entirely too pleased with himself.

What was wrong with the man? This murder had made the front page of the *Oregonian.* Did Mr. on-his-toes-about-everything think she was having fun out here? "How the hell do you think I'm doing, Tommy? After finding a body in my dryer? It's not like anything's gotten better. There's still a murderer out here somewhere."

Thomas's voice became sober. "Of course, Sage. I was thoughtless. Have you talked to anyone since yesterday? Does the sheriff have any idea what happened?"

Sage sighed. "Aside from a cold-blooded murder? No. It seems like I've talked to everyone in the county. There were people all over the place late into last evening, and more of them out here today. In the hotel, in the laundry, all over the property. Everyone was questioned and re-questioned. They poked around a bit today. They're gone now."

"Did they find anything?"

"I don't know, since I didn't talk to them. I drove into Stevenson with Granny. We looked at a place where she can stay. I paid a deposit."

Thomas paused for a moment, "That's great progress, Sage. I'm proud of you. Really, are you doing okay out there?"

No. "I'm doing as well as I can, Tommy. I need to wind things up here, get Granny settled, and go back where I belong." Same old mantra.

"I hear you, sweetheart. In the meantime, I'd like to take you to lunch or dinner this week. Let me know what day is good for you and we'll make it happen. It's important that I see you soon."

Sage shook her head violently. She did not want to be in a restaurant with Thomas Kitt or alcohol. "What's this about, Tommy? I'm very stressed out just now."

Thomas Kidd continued undeterred. "It's personal. Not something I can divulge on the telephone, so please bear with me. When can I see you?"

It was Sage's turn to sigh. She couldn't think of such things now. "I'll check my calendar and get back to you, Tommy. Thanks for calling." She hung up.

"I'm in the middle of a crisis, losing firearms, going crazy, dead people, and he thinks he needs to see me," she sputtered as she marched back to the office. "Maybe I'll just drop everything and drive into Portland, so he can parade me around the Heathman again. Selfish ass." She was talking out loud to herself. That had to be bad.

She walked into the office and saw her mother. Sat down

and flipped through Ross's poems. And there it was again:

With Blackthorn staff
I draw the bound.
All malice and bane,
I thus confound.

The words leaped off the page, and this time she got it. He had drawn the line and been killed for his trouble. He hadn't had the opportunity to "confound the malice". He'd probably gotten drunk instead and opened his big mouth. That's what happened with alcoholics. They said and did dumb things. And she was just like him. There. She was an alcoholic just like Ross.

She thought about what Andy had said—about Ross being a good person with a bad disease. He had been a person whose life was out of control, and someone had decided he needed to go away. She felt a stirring grow inside her. Who? Who had wanted Ross to go away? Andy? She couldn't quite put her head around him being a bad guy, but who could tell? Her picker had never been the best. Person or persons unknown? Who had staged that stupid murder? Certainly not the person in charge of moving all those drugs—and money. That person would have gotten someone else to do his dirty work.

Sage imagined there had been hell to pay for the fool who'd botched the murder of her brother so badly. The only person stupider was the sheriff of Skamania County—

popular with the locals, well known, a good old boy. Hell, he could be involved, but he wasn't smart enough to be a major player. Still, it might explain why the investigation into Ross's death was such a farce.

She picked up the Rubik's cube on the desk and messed with it until she almost got two sides done. *Click, click, click.* She thought of Terry Thompson, so certain of his command of all things Skamania County. *Click. Click.* She flipped the cube over and under and around. Thompson didn't want her poking around. He didn't want to be challenged. She needed to talk to him, see if she could get him to trip up. Maybe tomorrow. She'd sleep on it and figure out what to say. She looked at her watch. It was past eleven. She'd sat there for hours and gotten no further, either with the cube or the mystery.

Sage made her rounds of the hotel. Upstairs again, she looked in every room on both floors and double-checked that all the windows were locked tight. She checked on Granny. All was well. She left on the lights she'd need if anything stirred. She retrieved the shotgun from the cabinet, loaded it again, and laid it on the floor next to her mattress, comfortable to know that at least now she knew how to use it. And then, satisfied that she'd done everything she could, she turned in for the night.

Chapter 26

SOMETHING AWAKENED HER. Sage turned over on her mattress and rolled onto the floor. Wide awake and alert, she stood up, peeled off her nightgown, and pulled on the jeans and sweater she'd worn the day before. She picked up the shotgun and silently walked into the kitchen.

She looked out the kitchen window. Outside was dark and ominous, and she couldn't see anything but mist around the boat house. But she knew she'd heard something. She climbed the stairs to her bedroom and looked outside. From a better vantage, she saw lights bouncing in the mist and heard the unobstructed purr of the cabin cruiser moored at the dock. They were at it again! She moved downstairs to the front of the building, which was invisible to anyone at the dock. She turned out the porch light and stepped outside.

Her mouth felt dry, and she realized she was shaking, as she tip-toed around the building toward the back door and almost banged into the parked pickup. She squeaked in surprise, just as she noticed a dark figure standing by the back door. It turned and walked swiftly toward her.

"Andy." Sage swallowed hard. "What are you doing here?" She whispered harshly lest her voice give her away.

Andy grabbed her by the arm. "Get inside," he hissed.

She jerked away from him. "I will not," she whispered. "Tell me what you're doing here."

Andy reached for her again, and this time he grabbed the shotgun as well. He held her arm firmly and marched her around to the front of the building and into the hotel.

Sage pulled away from him, furious. "Leave me alone."

"What did you see?" He spoke in normal tones now, but his shadowed face registered concern and something else. Was it a fear that matched her own? She'd caught him red-handed.

Sage looked at him. In the darkness she couldn't see him very well. Her own fear overwhelmed her so that she had trouble getting the words out. "I saw what you saw," she spluttered. "I know what you guys are doing down there."

In the near darkness, Andy drew his hand across his face. "Whoa. You've got it wrong, Sage. It's not me."

"Then what are you doing here?"

He walked up close to her, so she could almost read his expression. In the faint light from the hallway, he looked pale and grim. "I was sleeping in the pickup. The boat's engine woke me up."

"Sleeping. In your pickup. What the fuck, Andy?"

His expression turned sheepish. "I'm worried about you. So, I've been coming over after the bar closes. I sleep here until it starts to get light. You wouldn't let me stay here, and I didn't want to make you mad." His voice trailed off.

Sage had no response to that. "Let's go upstairs," she said. "We can see better up there."

Still carrying the shotgun, he followed her up the front staircase, and down the hall to her room. They arrived at her bedroom window just in time to see the boat pull away into the mist. Its light shone on the water as it headed toward deep water. "Shit," said Andy.

"Who was it?"

Andy shook his head. "I'm not sure."

"But you think you know."

"I think I know, but my knowledge is circumstantial. I have to be certain." He paused. "You thought it was me."

And maybe I still do, Sage thought. "Let's not go there," she said. She headed out of the room and down the back stairs. Andy followed.

They stood in the dark in the kitchen, which was dimly lit from the back porch light. "What time is it?" Sage asked.

"Four-fifteen."

"I'm freaking wide awake."

"Me too."

"Is it too early for coffee?"

"It's never too early for coffee."

She flipped on the light over the sink and spooned grounds into the coffee maker, poured in cold water, and turned on the machine. Then she sat at the kitchen table, head in hands. "I think I'm losing my mind," she said. "This happened twice before, but I thought I'd imagined it."

Andy joined her at the table. The coffee maker burbled in the background. "What's different this time?" he asked.

"I'm not drunk. I've been dry for four days."

He reached across the table and covered her hand with his. It was warm and strong. "That is great news. Keep up the good work."

His hand lingered over hers for another moment, and for that moment Sage felt a little stronger. And safer. "It's not much, but four days is four days," she said. "I've been so scared."

Andy looked at her and nodded. "You need to be scared," he said. "Ross was scared, too, before he was killed, but he wouldn't talk about it. I don't want anything to happen to you."

Andy had said he "was killed", as opposed to "he died". They were on the same page about that. She poured them each a cup and returned to the table. "How close were you, really, to Ross?" Sage asked.

Andy tested the coffee and blew on it. "As close as he let me be," he said. "We reconnected when he came back here to live. He'd come in for a burger. Sometimes we'd hang out over here, cook, entertain your grandmother. She was a lot more with it back then. We fished a few times. We mostly did what guys do, grunted and scratched, didn't talk a whole lot. But it was good. He let me read some of his poetry. It's very good, actually. He went to AA meetings for a while, and I supported him in that." He paused, took a sip of coffee. His mind seemed to stray somewhere else.

"And then?" Sage prompted.

"And then. I don't know what happened. One day everything seemed all right, the next he was in the bar drinking."

"You served him? How could you?" Sage was furious.

Andy shrugged. "Am I going to tell a man in his thirties he can't drink if he wants to? I asked him about it, and it became apparent he'd already been drinking. So, I told him if he'd give me his car keys, I'd serve him."

"I can't believe you did that!"

"Listen Sage, if a man is going to be sober, it's his job not mine. I'm not the temperance committee. I made sure he got home safe that night, and many other nights. Then he took up with that massage therapist, and she drove."

Sage shook her head and looked toward the kitchen window. It was still dark.

"You quit drinking on your own here," Andy said. "Would it have helped any if I'd tried to get you to stop drinking?"

Sage glared at him. "I would have told you to fuck off."

Andy emitted a humorless chuckle. "Of course, you would. My point exactly."

"I'm not as bad as he was."

"You can think that, Sage, but don't pretend to tell me you haven't gotten into serious trouble because of your drinking. I've wondered if that's not why you're here, taking all this time off from your big, important job. You didn't come here because you love your grandmother."

Sage winced. Andy's comment hit her like a sock in the gut. She knew he was right. "Nice talk," she said. "What do you think you know about me?"

Andy again reached across the table, but she pulled her hand away. "I run a bar, Sage. I've seen every kind of drunk there is. You're not special or different. They all get into serious trouble because of their drinking, and usually that's the only thing that will wake them up enough to make them stop. That is, if they don't die first."

"Like my brother."

"Like your brother. Yes."

Sage walked to the coffee pot and warmed her brew. Andy joined her. She felt him close to her and didn't know whether she like that or not. Could she trust him or not? She turned and faced him. "Do you know what Ross was involved with that got him killed?"

Andy leaned against the counter. "It was the drugs. I believe he was approached by a certain someone who wanted to use the boathouse for a transfer station, to move stuff inland from the coast. Ross got paid for it, probably very well, and he needed the money. Somewhere during that time, he relapsed. He felt guilt for his part in this. Drinking made it easier for him to look the other way. Have you found anything that might prove this theory of mine?"

Sage walked back to the table and sat down. "Well, I learned the other day that we—the hotel and Granny—have money in the bank. Quite a lot of it. And, I found some cash. Then a few days ago, that guy we used to call Donald the Pothead showed up here and said Ross owed him fifteen thousand dollars. That's a lot of pot."

Andy whistled low. "No kidding. I've always thought of Donald as a small-time dealer. I had no idea he had access to that much. Shows what I know. What did you do?"

"I told him I couldn't say whether Ross did or didn't owe him money, and that since I hadn't found an invoice from him I had no reason for Donald to think he had money coming. Then I sent him on his way. He wasn't happy."

Andy began pacing around the kitchen. "I don't imagine he was. Anything else?"

Sage hesitated a moment. "Well, I have been thinking about our sheriff. When I went to his office a few days back, he acted like it was perfectly normal for Ross to fall into the Columbia River after he died of a heroin overdose. He didn't show any interest in investigating his death any further. When he told me the investigation is closed that was a red flag."

Andy finally settled at the table again. "Old Terry never was the sharpest knife in the drawer," he said. "Hell of a linebacker, though. He's a good old boy and does a reasonably good job out here. Folks know him and like him."

"Yeah, whatever," said Sage. "I think he's a dipshit, and I've gotten pretty sick of good old boys, truth be told."

Again, Andy chuckled without mirth. "He's not smart enough to run a drug operation," he said. "However, that's not to say he wouldn't take a few bucks to look the other way. I think your instincts may be good on that."

Sage snorted. "A lot of good that does anyone. There seems to be a lot of looking the other way out here." They sat for a moment, then she said, "There's another man."

Andy popped to attention. "Who?"

"Phil. You told me about him, remember? I met him in the woods the other day. He seemed harmless at the time, but who knows?"

Andy broke in. "Yes, Crazy Phil. He's a mess, but probably not a drug dealer. Since Ross always let him sleep in the barn, you likely have a tenant you don't know about. Ross talked to him a few times, started calling him Crazy Phil."

Sage thought momentarily about the burlap bag filled with cash. Phil could do all right on that, if he were to find it. She looked to the kitchen window again. The sky had lightened to a deep, luminous indigo. The sun would be up soon. "Well, that doesn't mean a thing," she said, looking back at Andy. "Unless you think Phil murdered my brother."

Andy shrugged. "I'm dismissing Phil as the murderer, although I wouldn't say he's harmless. He was a sniper, and he's a seriously damaged soul. However, if he were to kill someone, it would not be with a lethal injection of heroin."

Sage shuddered at the thought of a sniper living in the barn. "That leaves us exactly nowhere," she said. "I'm going to send you home now, so you don't run into Betty. We wouldn't want to cause gossip."

She said it sternly, but he smiled at her. "Yes 'm," he said. "I will check in with you later. I want you to think very seriously about how you and your grandmother can get out of here within the next couple days."

We'll see about that, Sage thought, and closed the door behind him.

She carried the shotgun back to the office and locked it up, then hid the key under one of Susan's trophies. It was lighter outside now, and soon Granny would be stirring. She went upstairs and brushed her teeth and took a quick shower. She dried her hair and put on clean clothes.

When she returned to the kitchen, Betty was letting herself in. "Good morning, missy," she said. She walked over to the coffee pot and inspected its contents. "You been up early, looks like," she said as she poured herself a cup of coffee.

"Yeah, I couldn't sleep," said Sage. "I've been up thinking."

"'Bout what?"

"About Janice, and that man she was feeding. What can you tell me about that, Betty?"

Betty closed her eyes and let out a sigh. "Oh, him. He's her first cousin once removed. They wasn't close, but when he came back from Vietnam things got pretty hard for him.

It's a long story, and you probably don't want to hear it all."

Sage leaned against the counter, watching Betty's face. "I probably don't want to hear everything," she said, "but I would like to know how he ended up here."

Betty settled in at the table and took a sip of her coffee. "Well, as I understand it, he had a family. But after he'd been home a while, it's like he wasn't himself. He'd get all paranoid and crazy. So, his wife took off with the kids and divorced him. They was livin' in Puyallup then, and her folks was in Vancouver. When he lost the house an' all, he came down here, and he was homeless. He knew Janice was here, so he came out to see if he could work here.

"Your granny hired him for a spell, but he wasn't reliable. He took off and was gone for a long time, four or five years. Then he come back here last year and started freeloading. Your brother let him sleep in the barn, which was probably a mistake."

"Knowing Ross, he felt sorry for the poor man."

"Yeah, well, he did, bless his heart. But Phil's pretty crazy. You don't know what he might do."

Sage wondered if he was crazy enough or capable of working with the drug people. "Can't he go to the veteran's hospital and get some help?"

Betty shook her head. "Janice took him there once, but he wouldn't go back. Said those A-holes ruined his life."

Sage crossed Phil off her list. Almost. "They probably did," she said.

Betty stood up. "I gotta get to work. It's time Mary

Margaret got up."

Sage said a silent thank you. "Sure," she said to Betty. "I'll get breakfast started." She started a fresh pot of coffee and pulled eggs and bacon out of the refrigerator. By the time Betty returned with Granny, the French toast was ready.

Chapter 27

GRANNY, BETTY, AND SAGE ATE BREAKFAST. Betty gave Granny her shower and she had nodded off in her chair, Sage grabbed a roll of black garbage bags and headed up to Ross's room to the one job she'd dreaded doing most since she came home.

Within two hours she had filled ten bags, mostly with old clothes. Really old clothes. Some of them going back to high school. She put aside some of the better tee shirts, jeans, socks, and a couple of jackets to leave in the barn for Phil. Winter was coming. She hauled the bags downstairs two by two and pulled the Buick up to the back door so that she could fill it with Ross's stuff and take it to the donation bin in Stevenson later that day. She drank a cup of old, burnt coffee before she went up to Ross's room to clean out the last few drawers. That's when she found it.

In the bottom drawer under some vintage socks, Sage noticed a spiral bound college rule notebook, the kind everyone had used in school and probably still did. She picked it out, threw it on the bed, and continued emptying the drawer. Only after she had carried the last bag down to the car and taken the notebook into the office did she realize its significance. It was a journal. Flipping through the pages, she discovered it was a recent one.

The entries began in August 1982, three years ago. Sage thought back to what she could remember of the time. Had she and Ross been in contact then? When had he moved into the Blackthorn? Yes, it was early summer1982, just after he got out of rehab. He'd had no job prospects and nowhere to go. Granny needed him.

The entries were pretty general—jottings about things he needed to do. One day in late September he'd gone salmon fishing with Andy and caught a big one. They'd smoked it at Andy's place. There was stuff about garden cleanup, and even reference to how broke they were even though he was working his butt off. He wondered what he was going to do during the winter when they had fewer customers. Stuff like that.

The phone rang, and Sage cursed under her breath. She shoved the journal in the desk drawer with the money and walked into the reception area to answer it. Tommy.

"Hi Sage," he said without preamble. "I'm leaving here in

a minute to drive up to Stevenson. I want you to have lunch with me. It's important that I talk with you."

Something about his tone told her not to argue. Sage looked at her watch. Eleven-thirty. She felt as if she'd been awake for a week. She had to go to Stevenson again anyway. What the heck. "Sure, Tommy, what time will you be there?"

He named a restaurant in town and told her to meet him there at one. Then he rang off.

Sage hung up the phone and wandered back to the office. Something was eating his lunch, so she might as well see him and get it over with. Plus, lunch out was never a bad thing. Even in Stevenson. She would ask him to list the property, so they could move forward with the sale of Blackthorn. That would give her an idea of fair market value. Then he could pursue purchasing it if it suited him.

Sage went upstairs, changed her clothes, and put on some makeup. When she came downstairs to the kitchen, Betty was feeding Granny. "I'm going to Stevenson for lunch," she told her. Betty nodded. Sage hauled a few remaining donation items into the car and headed for town.

It was a decent day, cool and breezy, blue sky. Fall colors along the highway did their showy best to make it even brighter. They'd be gone soon. Winter would set in, with icy winds blowing downriver from the east. Sage thought about the journal. So far, Ross was still sober. There had been no big revelations. She wondered why he'd even begun keeping the thing in the first place. She'd read the rest of it after lunch.

She dropped off her load at Goodwill and then found a

parking space on Stevenson's main drag, across the street from the restaurant Tommy had chosen. As she crossed the street, she noted the black Mercedes parked right in front of the restaurant. He'd arrived before one. How had he gotten here so quickly? It occurred to her that he might already have been in Stevenson when he called. Maybe he had clients up here?

She walked inside. Tommy was seated at a booth in the back corner of the dining room. He stood when he saw her. She walked over to him and he took her in his arms. She turned her cheek for his kiss. He pecked it, before he held her a little away from him. "Really?" he said. His smile was uneasy. He moved closer and kissed her on the lips.

Sage drew back from him and sat down. He was creating a spectacle she wanted no part of. "How lovely to see you, Tommy." What on earth could he want?

Instead of sitting across from her, Thomas slid next to her. He seemed jittery. "I'm glad you could make it on short notice," he said. "I have business in Stevenson today. And, as you know, I've wanted to talk to you."

Sage picked up the menu and glanced at it. "Sure. What's going on?"

A server approached the table with glasses of water. When Sage looked at her, she realized it was Misty, the massage therapist. Misty smiled at them. "Hi Sage. Hello Mr. Kitt. How are you today? Thanks for hiring me."

Thomas gave her a warm smile. "Well, Misty, I hope you like your new job."

Misty's smile drooped. "I do, Mr. Kitt. But it was so sad about Janice." Sage made a mental note to talk to Misty about Janice.

Then Thomas said, "Give us a few minutes, won't you, Misty." She walked away. He folded his hands on the table and looked at Sage.

Sage set her menu down. "Misty works for you?"

Thomas smiled easily at her. "Yes, I bought this restaurant a couple years ago. It's part of my fascination with the area. And, we needed a decent restaurant up here. Have you noticed all the new activity around Stevenson? People are taking up sail boarding. From here to Hood River, it's really catching on. Anyway, she answered my ad. She told me she wasn't getting enough work at the Blackthorn to get by."

Sage shrugged. "How long has she worked here?"

"A couple weeks. But that's not what we're here to talk about." Thomas took her hand in his and looked at her. "I've been thinking of you constantly, ever since you got here," he began. "I don't want you to go back to New York."

Sage wished he'd cut the bullshit. She felt prickles along her arms as the hairs raised. What on earth was he talking about?

"You remember how we talked that first week you were here. At lunch, I informally offered to purchase the Blackthorn from you?" he continued.

Sage nodded. "Sure, Tommy. I think it's a great idea. We're officially closed since Janice's murder. I've found a place that I think will be a good fit for Granny. I plan to list it, but if we can come to an agreement, there's no reason why I shouldn't sell it to you. Then as soon as I get Granny relocated, I can back to New York. I'm ready to list the place as soon as possible."

Thomas's mouth twisted, and he furrowed his brow. She remembered that expression of his from high school, when he was concentrating hard on mastering a concept in advanced algebra or defeating a foe on the baseball field. Then he smiled—a bit unconvincingly for Portland's most eligible bachelor. "You remember I mentioned my little fantasy of turning the Blackthorn into a world class resort," he said. "I've thought about this a lot, and I propose that we do it—together. We'd live in the city, of course. You don't want to live out here, and neither do I. But we could do this together. I've got the backing and you have the property."

Sage was stunned. And more than a bit uncomfortable. "If you want us to be business partners, there's no reason we can't do it long distance," she reasoned. "There are plenty of direct flights between here and New York. If we decided to do this, we'd need to talk about it a great deal more, I could arrange to come out once a month, for meetings and so forth. But I know you appreciate honesty. Running a resort, world class or otherwise, isn't something I'm interested in doing. I'd rather just sell the place."

Thomas started patting his jacket. Finally, he located we he'd been digging for. He smiled broadly. "There. I have a better idea," he said. "I hope you'll agree with me." He set something on the table and pushed it toward her.

It was a jeweler's ring box, deep green velvet. Sage felt a surge of emotions as she realized what was happening. This was the moment she had been waiting for—Prince Charming and the ring! For years. Only this wasn't the prince. For ten minutes of her life she had entertained the notion that he might be. And then she had spent Saturday night with him and come to her senses. She felt her stomach sink as she looked at it. Fighting a wave of nausea, she pasted a bright smile on her face and looked at him.

Thomas smiled at her, but his dark eyes were veiled. His smile felt as fake as her own. "Open it," he said.

Sage pulled the box to her and opened it. Her mouth formed an "o" as she looked at it—a round diamond the size of her index fingernail surrounded by smaller diamonds. It looked like something Princess Diana would wear. She gasped.

Thomas's smile grew more certain. "Put it on," he said. "Or, here. Let me put it on for you." He seized the box, removed the ring, and slid it onto her finger. "Yes, I want us to be partners, but we'll be life partners. I want to marry you, Sage. I've known it since you came out from New York. You are everything I've been looking for in my life, everything I need to make me complete."

Sage slipped the ring off, placed it in the box, and closed it. She should be flattered and go all gooey, like those women in the bad soap operas. At least that was the response he expected. Instead, she felt revulsion. For some women, this would be a dream come true. Instead, she realized, he was patronizing her. It was all about him and how he wanted others to perceive him. He didn't love her. She just happened to be in the right place when he thought he needed her.

Had he always been this way? This desperate? She wasn't sure. It didn't matter now. He was not what she wanted. This wasn't a romance. Did he realize that? He couldn't give her anything that mattered. He felt he needed her for some reason, and at some fundamental level, he believed his own bullshit. He believed he had won her.

"I can't do this Tommy," she said. "I don't even really know who you are."

Thomas looked as if he'd been slapped. "But of course you do! We've known each other since we were kids."

Sage shook her head. "No, Tommy. You went away to college. You went to law school. I chose a different direction, away from here, and I've been gone from this area since I left for college. That was intentional. We only saw each other a bit on vacations. We have completely different lives now. We're different people than we were growing up. That's not to say that with time we couldn't discover that we belong together. But for now, I don't really know you," Sage wanted to jump up and run. Instead, she behaved as a good girl should. A polite, sensible girl.

Thomas reached for the ring box, held it for a moment, then opened it and smiled to himself. He looked at Sage. "You *are* going to marry me, darling. I have everything you want, and I can give you anything you can possibly imagine."

Sage felt an involuntary thrill. She always *had* liked a

take-charge male. She saw herself sliding between high thread count sheets with the handsomest man she knew. Then, somewhere in her mind a door slammed. That trapped feeling returned. She was prey. She found his arrogance insufferable.

She managed a smile back at him. "I know you can Tommy. You have everything I have ever wanted in a man. But I can't say yes to you. I don't know you well enough to feel the way you say you feel about me."

Thomas moved the box back in front of her. "I'm very disappointed, Sage," he said. His eyes bored into hers with intent, but she saw no love there. No softness. They were dark and cold. "Give me the opportunity to earn your love. Keep the ring for now. I'm not ready to give up on you."

Sage heard the steel in his voice and felt a chill in his words. She smiled and hoped her smile signaled regret. "I don't think that's the right thing to do, Tommy."

Thomas Kitt's squirmed in his seat. He shot her a pleading look. "Please Sage, just give me a chance."

She nodded and accepted the box. She wanted the conversation to end. She wanted to go home. She slid the ring box into her handbag. "I can do that," she said.

He patted her on the knee. "Good girl."

Misty returned to take their order. In fifteen minutes, Sage found herself picking at a large shrimp salad. And it helped a little. It helped fill the hole she longed to fill with scotch. Lots of scotch. She chattered about New York. She told Thomas the things she liked about her job. Thomas sat beside her, mostly silent.

Finally, it was over. He walked her to her car, kissed her on the cheek. She got in, and he closed the door. She sighed with relief as she watched him cross the street and get into his Mercedes. Her hand shook as she put the key in the ignition. He pulled away from the curb, waved as he passed her, and continued down the street. *Sweet Jesus!* She started the Buick. And then she turned it off again. She took a deep breath and released it, got out of the car, locked it, and crossed the street. She walked back into the restaurant.

It was just past two, and Misty was taking a break in the back booth next to where Sage and Tommy had eaten. Sage slid into the seat across from her. Misty looked up from her sandwich, surprised. "Oh, hi," she said.

Sage smiled. "Hi, yourself. I'm really excited that you got this new job so quickly. It must be a huge relief."

Misty set down her sandwich half and dabbed her lips with her napkin. "It's just the most amazing thing," she said. "Mr. Kitt called me up last Friday and offered me the job just like that. It was, like, supernatural, or something."

Sage wondered if Misty knew the meaning of supernatural. But, never mind. "Just like that, huh?"

"Yeah. He said you'd be closing the place. And, you know, I just wasn't getting enough hours. And then Janice died. Not that I knew her that well. She was just, you know, around."

Sage nodded as if she understood completely. "I guess you worked around Betty more than Janice, right?"

Misty took a sip of her Coke. "Yeah, mostly," she said.

"But the massage job wasn't full time, you know. So sometimes Mr. Kitt had me run errands. Just so I could make a little more money."

Sage nodded again. "That's interesting," she said. "What kind of errands."

Misty's eyes grew large. She put her hand to her mouth. "Uh-oh. I wasn't supposed to mention it to anybody," she said.

Sage shrugged. "Oh, well. It's just us. I don't think it's a problem now," she said. "I mean the place is closed and everything, so why would it matter? That's all over with now. And you needed the money."

Misty had picked up her sandwich and taken a bite. She chewed and set it down. "You're right, I guess. I mean who cares now. It was just taking letters to people, like, no big deal."

Sage was puzzled, and more than a little curious. "Taking letters to people? That's weird."

"Yeah, I thought so too. But he paid me for my time and gave me gas money. It wasn't, you know, hard or anything." She took another bite of her sandwich and looked out into the nearly empty restaurant. "I have to get back to work in a minute," she said.

"Sure," said Sage. "I understand. But tell me, how did you get the letters to deliver them? Did he give them to you?"

Misty squirmed in her seat. "Yeah, like, he'd come out and give them to me in a big envelope, you know. And I'd take them out and deliver them."

Sage nodded at her and smiled. They were old friends now. "And why do you think he did that, Misty? I mean, why wouldn't he just call these folks, or send their letters in the mail? That would be a whole lot less trouble."

Misty looked around her, like she'd left something on her seat. She gathered her dishes together. "I guess he didn't want to send them in the mail." She looked at Sage helplessly. "I really need to get back to work now," she said.

Sage looked at her calmly and said, "I know you do, Misty. Just humor me for a second. What do you think was in them?"

Misty sighed. "Money."

"Why do you say that?"

"Well, they were fat and kinda squishy."

Sage nodded her best friend nod and smiled. "I can see why you might think that," she said. "But it could have been something else too, I guess."

Misty smiled and nodded. "Yeah, I guess, but it wasn't," she said. She slid out of the booth, relieved to be done. She stood. "My break's over."

"Sure, Misty. But how did you know it was money?"

Misty rolled her eyes. She really wanted to get going. "I like said something to one of the guys, you know, like weren't paydays great, and he said yes."

"Thanks Misty. I'll talk more with Mr. Kitt about what we might have for you in the future."

Misty stopped in her tracks. "Like what?"

Sage shrugged. "Well, you never know. He and I are

going to be doing some business together. I'll keep you in the loop."

Misty gave her a little wave. "Wow, that's great. Thanks." She grabbed her dishes and scurried into the kitchen. Sage saw herself out into the cool October sunshine and crossed the street to her car deep in thought. She didn't notice the black Mercedes parked half a block up the street.

Chapter 28

ON THE DRIVE HOME FROM STEVENSON, Sage's mind raced. Tommy! Large sums of money in the barn, in the desk drawer, in the Blackthorn bank account. Even Granny was set for life—what remained of it and well beyond. That boathouse had become an important fixture in Thomas Kitt's life. He'd made his headquarters right under their noses!

Now stop it! You're making things up!

Here he was, this up-and-comer, spending money like it was water on designer suits, the new Mercedes, and all the rest. He'd been practicing law a relatively short time. It seemed he'd become successful and made a fortune quickly, for someone so new on the scene. She had no doubt he pulled down a good salary—more than enough to have all the toys anyone could want. But to flaunt his success so publicly? That was important to him too, no doubt because of the poverty he'd endured growing up. Despite his money now, he was still learning how to behave.

Sage gave herself a good mental shake. *Yes, and you, apparently, just earned your PhD. in psychology. Get a grip, girl. You don't know anything yet. This is all circumstantial.*

Yes, he'd had a rough time. Hadn't they all, in one way or another? But Thomas Kitt had become a criminal. A drug trafficker. A murderer. And like most people who led double lives, he'd tripped up. In front of her. *Stop it. You're imagining things!* All she'd had to do was connect a few dots. She'd stumbled over the answer she'd been seeking. *You have no evidence.*

It seemed he'd been careless in other ways too, like leaving that bag of cash in the Buick for anyone to find. Although nobody had until she did. Sometimes it made sense to hide things in plain sight. Easier to put the blame on someone else. She took a deep breath. Maybe it was Ross's doing. Maybe he had been out of it, or he had wanted someone to find it. Maybe he didn't care. She didn't know. How could she possibly piece together all that had happened when the details were conjecture?

But hiring Misty the day before Janice died? and telling her Sage would close the place down? That was *not* conjecture. Neither were the mysterious packets Misty delivered on a regular basis. Sage felt the anger welling up in her. She wanted to scream.

And what about Saturday night? Who could have killed Janice? *Well, dumbbell, he did.* He simply drove out to the Blackthorn and did the deed after she was tucked in for the night at the Heathman. It would have been an easy trip with very light traffic. He'd even have time to catch a few hours of sleep before he met her for breakfast. Sage knew she couldn't prove any of it, but she made up her mind that the timing was no coincidence. It was the only time she'd been away for more than a few hours since she'd arrived here.

She pounded the steering wheel. And then, just around the bend, there it was. The Hoot Owl. She veered into the parking lot without a thought and skidded to a stop. She shook with rage. She got out of the car, locked it, and dashed into the bar.

The place was dark and empty. Thank God! Sage's legs felt shaky as she crossed the room and climbed onto a barstool. She put her head in her hands and let out a low moan. "What am I going to do?" she cried. "What can I *do?*" She'd be next, she knew it. Marrying her had been part of his big picture plan. She was having none of it, and he was angry. He'd come after her. She knew he would. She'd seen the expression in his eyes. It was subtle, but she knew him so well. *Stop it! Get a grip!*

She thought of the rape. She could not imagine anything worse. She'd been drunk at the time, in a blackout during part of it. It only became real the next day. This was real now. Tears dribbled down her face, but she made no noise. She couldn't drink. She dared not drink. There was nothing she could do to deaden the pain. The betrayal. The awfulness. Her body began to shake with sobbing.

Andy emerged from the kitchen carrying a burger in a basket and a newspaper. He stopped when he saw her, then smiled. "Hi, Sage. Hey, you must really miss me."

She looked up at him, and his smile froze in place. He set down the burger and newspaper, came around the bar, and sat next to her. He turned toward her and took her arm. "Sage, what's happened? Did something happen to your grandmother?"

Sage threw back her head and wailed. She sounded like a wild animal. "Tommy killed Ross!" she moaned. "He did it. It's been him all along!" Her scream pierced the room.

Andy jumped to his feet. "Come with me!" He guided her to the far end of the bar and down a hall past the restrooms, where he opened the door on an untidy office. He pointed to a chair across from a desk piled high with papers. "Sit here," he said. "I'll be right back."

Sage sat. Her strength was gone. She felt as if the wind had been knocked from her. She gasped several times and began crying again.

Andy came back and set a Coke in front of her. "Drink this," he said. "It's the best I can do on short notice. Then I want you to tell me what happened." He pulled up a chair, so he could face her, and sat.

Sage looked at him, eyes frantic. "He called me, said he had to talk to me, and asked me to meet him for lunch." She spoke haltingly, gasping for air. She dug in her pocket for a tissue, but of course she didn't have one. She wiped her nose on her jacket sleeve. "He's been bugging me since Janice died, wanting to see me. Today when he called, he wanted to meet in Stevenson for lunch, so I decided to hear him out, get it over with. Andy, he said he wants to marry me. He had this huge diamond and a spiel about how we'd be life partners and business partners. I was so shocked, I didn't know what to do."

"Well, I hope you said no," Andy said.

"Of course, I said no!" Sage was momentarily indignant. "He is such a phony. But he's dangerous. He's a killer."

A darkness settled in Andy's eyes and stayed there. "How do you know that?"

"Misty, Ross's old girlfriend, is working at the restaurant where we ate. He *owns* that restaurant, and he told Misty the day before Janice died that she should come to work for him because the Blackthorn was going to close up for good."

Andy's expression was inscrutable, his eyes showed no emotion. "How were you able to talk to Misty?"

Sage let out a long, shuddering sigh. "I went back in after lunch, after he'd left. Something didn't feel right. She told me she'd run errands for him over the last year or so, to pick up a little extra money. She delivered packets to people. Packets of money. It's him, Andy. I know it is. When I met him in Portland right after I got here, he told me about Ross's and Granny's investment accounts. That sounded so weird. We've never in our lives had any money for investment accounts."

Andy's face was a mask. He'd pulled inward. "You must be scared out of your mind," he said.

"I am," she said. A tear rolled down her face and she brushed it away. "I've got to get Granny out of there. He will come after me once he knows I talked to Misty. He's a very smart man. He's not happy with me for turning him down. And now I know what he did. I know."

Andy nodded. "Okay, you could be on to something," he said. "You can't be sure, of course. This is circumstantial up to a point. But I believe you."

Sage let out a shuddering sigh and wiped her eyes on her sleeve. "Thank you. I know he did it," she said.

Andy nodded again and patted her on the knee. "Here's what we'll do," he said. "We'll drive into Portland, spend the night, and visit the FBI office first thing in the morning. I'll call and tell them we're coming. We'll tell them what we know. Just the facts, like that boat we both saw, the money, things you have noticed. Then maybe they will want to look into it. Can't hurt."

He sounded so calm. Sage shook her head violently. "I can't leave Granny."

"We're not going to leave her," Andy said. "She comes with us. Go back to the hotel and send Betty home. Then pack what you both need for the night and call me. You don't need much, so don't make a big deal out of this. You don't need to dress for dinner or anything like that. Just get ready fast. I'll come over and we'll all go together. Right now, I need to find someone to cover for me and close tonight. By tomorrow at this time, this will all be out of your hands, and you'll be safe."

"What about the sheriff?"

"We're not going anywhere near him. Even if he's not involved, this is way too big for him."

"I don't have anything that links Tommy to this except my suspicions."

"Oh, come on, Sage. You know what you know. You've seen the boat more than once, and we saw it together. You'll just tell your story and voice your suspicions. When you talk to the feds, they'll probably want to question him. At least find out if he owns a boat. If it's not him, fine. But you still don't have to marry him."

Andy looked at his watch. "It's past three now," he said. His voice had taken on an urgency. "We don't have any time to lose. How soon can you be ready?"

Sage took a deep breath. You can do this, she told herself. "Okay, I need to gather some of Ross's things that may contain clues," she said. "I'll get Granny fed and ready. We should be set to go by five at the latest."

Andy stood and patted her shoulder. "Great. Now get going. I'll get my stuff together and get somebody lined up for tonight. Call me as soon as you're ready."

Sage stood and reached out to touch him. Her hands shook. Andy took them and held them for a moment. Warm and comforting. She wasn't alone. "This will be over soon," he repeated. "You won't have to worry anymore."

She left the bar and drove back to the Blackthorn, her

mind speeding faster than the car, running through scenarios. Janice. She had been close to Thomas Kitt too, it turned out, and now she was dead. Just like Ross. He had used her, and he had used Ross. They both knew too much. Either they were involved, or they figured it out. No way to know. But there was a pattern. Misty—poor obtuse Misty—would be next if she didn't watch out.

She pulled up to the back door of the hotel thinking about what she needed to pack. Inside, Betty sat at the table reading a magazine. She looked up. "Hi, missy. I just gave Mary Margaret her snack. She's in bed now. Everything's fine. Did you have a nice lunch?"

Sage smiled with an enthusiasm she didn't feel. "It was great, Betty. Couldn't have been better. I hadn't realized Thomas Kitt owned that new restaurant in Stevenson."

Betty furrowed her eyebrows. "Does he? What's he doin' out here? He used to come around when your brother was alive, but I've seen less of him since then, although he does come out now and then. Mostly he ignores me."

Well, well. "What does he do when he comes out here, then?"

Betty made a face. "Oh, you know. Sometimes he brought our checks. Not so much since you've been around. He goes down to the boathouse, pokes around here like he owns the place, which ticks me off no end. Too good for us now. But he was close to Ross. Janice had a crush on him, I think. She followed him around like a puppy." Betty snorted. "He seemed to like that. They was pals. But I've only seen him the once since you got here."

Sage wondered when that was, and why she had not been told of his visit. "Interesting," she said. She went to the sink and filled a glass of water. She drank it down and looked back at Betty. "You can go now. I'm home for the evening. And thanks, Betty, for all your help with Granny."

Betty headed for the entry to gather her jacket and handbag. "My pleasure, Miss Sage. I'll see you in the morning."

"Have a good one, Betty," Sage called after her as she went out the back door. She hadn't told Betty she wouldn't be there in the morning. Once the door closed behind her, Sage focused her attention on the project at hand: get packed, get the important stuff to bring to the FBI. She thought of Ross's journal. She hadn't even looked at it properly. She'd bring it with her. *Get out of here,* her inner voice told her. Body tensed, she was ready for action.

She dashed up the back stairs, grabbed her smallest suitcase from the closet, and filled it with a change of clothes and overnight necessities. Downstairs, she hauled it out to the car and packed it into the trunk. Then she went into the barn and up the ladder to the loft. Yes, the bag of money was still there. That went into the trunk as well. She needed it as evidence.

She closed the trunk and locked the car. So far so good. She'd pack a few things for Granny and figure out something to bring along to eat. Sage looked into the refrigerator. While she had no appetite, the old woman would need something.

She made two sandwiches and quickly put them into a bag along with some sliced cheese and crackers. And then she headed through the dining room to prepare Granny for the trip to Portland, to call Andy, to pick up Ross's journal from the office.

She was nearing the office door when she heard it. *Click. Click.* She stopped, her mouth went dry. *Click. Click. Click.* She swallowed hard, stood for a minute. It could only be Thomas. How did he get in? Since Janice's murder, she always locked the front door to the hotel. Had he sneaked in the back while she was upstairs?

Sage was only a few steps from the telephone. It would take a second to punch in 9-1-1. They could trace the call, she hoped, even if he tried to stop her. She had no other choice. She tip-toed back to the reception desk. Hands trembling, she quietly lifted the receiver and put it to her ear. Nothing. The line was dead. Of course, he would think of that. He was a master criminal. She stifled a gasp, and just as quietly she replaced the receiver. Now what? The clicking had stopped.

Chapter 29

"COME ON IN, SAGE," Thomas said from the office. "Let's have a chat."

She swallowed. Her brain spun with thought fragments until fear took over and thought froze. She walked to the office door and looked inside.

Thomas Kitt sat in the desk chair, resting his feet on the desk as if he belonged there. As if it was his desk! He had changed out of the suit and shiny wingtips. He had on a rust-colored sweater over a cream button-down shirt, jeans that someone had ironed, and running shoes. Her carefully organized piles of papers had been moved to one side of the desk. Ross's journal sat on the desk blotter. It was open.

Thomas played with the Rubik's Cube as he leaned back

in the desk chair. *Click, click.* He seemed completely at ease, attention focused on the toy. *Click.* He looked up at her, an amused half-smile on his lips. "Come on in," he repeated. "Have a seat." His eyes did not smile. Dark, bottomless holes, they followed her as she entered the room.

I'm going to die, Sage thought. She swallowed again. *Will he kill me here?* She walked toward the desk and sat in the chair across from him. She couldn't process her thoughts in any meaningful way. She hoped that she didn't look as scared as she felt. She could not feel her body. Her intuitive awareness, the sane part of her that hovered above her physical self, gave keen attention to her surroundings and what he was doing. That part of her observed without emotion. He was a killer and he would kill her very soon. Still, she tried to smile. "Hi Tommy. What are you doing here? Did you come in the back way?" Mundane questions, but she was curious.

Click, click. Thomas had turned his concentration back to the cube. "Oh, I came in the front. I have a key." Again, that half-smile. He hadn't looked at her. He seemed pleased with himself. Hardly surprising since his team was winning. *Click.* "I've had it for quite a while, actually. Since your brother and I became business partners. And guess what I found when I got here?" He nodded toward the journal. "I've been looking all over for that. It's quite interesting. Have you read it?"

Sage's heart was sinking like a boulder. She raised her eyebrows and continued to sound chatty. "Not yet. I was planning to get to it tonight. I didn't know you and Ross were business partners."

Tommy nodded. Still smiling, he looked up. "I think you did, at some level. Yes, we had a pretty good run for a while. Ross was in a financial pinch, you know. We found a way he could help me out and bring in some cash to keep the lights on here. It was a win-win situation. And then, as sometimes happens, we had to end the partnership."

"I see," Sage said. Her mouth was so dry, her throat so constricted, that she found herself unable to say more.

Thomas watched her carefully. "Is that it?" he said. "I see?"

Sage looked at him and nodded. "I would like to hear the whole story sometime."

"Oh, you will, very soon," Thomas said. His expression changed to that of the needy boy she'd known as a kid. "Why won't you marry me, Sage? It would make things so much easier." His voice managed to sound at once whiny and pleading and menacing.

At least she knew her lines for the answer. "I told you why, Tommy. We need time. It wouldn't be fair to either of us if we didn't take the time to get to know each other better before taking such a huge step." *Never mind that you're a killer.* "We've changed a lot in the past few years." *No shit.* There. That was the best she could do. It wasn't enough, but that didn't matter now.

Thomas looked at the Rubik's Cube. "This is a fascinating little device," he said. "It helps me to think. To focus."

Sage said nothing. Waited.

He looked back at her. "Do you ever play with it?"

"Sometimes I do, yes."

"Why did you go back to the restaurant? Did something Misty said get your attention?"

So that was it! Sage searched her mind for an answer. She was back in her body now, sharp and attentive. Her survival depended on it. "Actually, I need a massage," she said. "I went back in to see if Misty would come out in a couple days to give me a massage."

"Ahh," he said. "I saw you put a suitcase in the car." *Click. Click.* "Where are you going, Sage?"

She found this most alarming. She was certain it showed on her face. She couldn't fool him. He knew everything, it seemed. *But when in doubt, lie.* "I'm taking Granny into Portland. She has a medical appointment in the morning at eight, so we're going to spend the night and come back here late morning. It's been a long time since she saw a doctor. She needs a check-up before she moves into Stevenson Gardens."

"Oh?" Thomas seemed interested. "And when will that be, exactly?"

Sage shrugged. "Exactly? I'm not sure. Sometime within the next two weeks, they tell me. Then I can go back to New York, and my job, and my life."

Thomas set the Rubik's Cube on the desk. He looked at her. "You know that's not going to happen, don't you Sage. You're lying. I saw you stop into the Hoot Owl, as well. What do you say to that?"

Sage pursed her lips and shot him a look. "I'd say you're a busy guy."

"Don't get smart with me," Thomas said. "When you go away, people will think you've gone back to New York. Perhaps. It would have been so much easier if you'd just said yes this afternoon. I can think of several women who would have been thrilled with my proposal and especially thrilled with that ring. Where is it, by the way?"

Sage took in a deep breath and let it out slowly. "It's in my purse."

"Get it. Put it on. I want to see it on you."

Sage stood up and felt her knees nearly buckle. She walked over to her handbag, where it lay on the floor inside the office door. She pulled out the ring box and returned to the chair.

"Put it on," Thomas repeated. She did as he told her and laid the bottle green velvet box on the desk. The ring felt like an anvil on her finger. Thomas stood, and she thought once again how he looked like a model for the advertisers in her magazine. Sculpted, trim, handsome, immaculately and expensively dressed. Then she noticed the bulge under his sweater. A gun. Of course. He wasn't here to pay a social call.

He walked over and picked up her hand, admired the ring. He gave a soft whistle. "Excellent choice, Tommy boy," he said to himself. "It looks perfect on your hand, Sage. Maybe you'll reconsider. When I learned you were coming from New York, I realized you could provide the perfect solution to my dilemma. We'd become close, and I could do my job and continue with my business here. We'd build the resort, of course. It only made sense for us to be together, after my long association with you and Ross."

She looked up into the blank darkness of his eyes. And then she looked away. What a crock! Her words came out before she could stop them. "This seems to be all about you, Tommy," she said. "I don't want to marry you. You just want to get married so you get the property when something happens to me. When I have a little hiking 'accident' or fall overboard on our honeymoon cruise." She began tugging at the ring on her finger. "I'd help you look good for a while, and then you'd bump me off."

"Leave that alone!" Thomas's voice no longer was gentle. "Just leave it on. Indulge me."

"I will not indulge you!" Sage pulled the ring off threw it across the room. "What are you thinking, Tommy? Are you still pretending I'll marry you?"

"Shut up!" Thomas hit her in the face with the back of his hand.

Tears sprang to her eyes and she could taste blood where her teeth had cut the inside of her cheek. She put her hand to her face. "At last, the real Thomas Kitt," she said.

Thomas rubbed his right hand. "You're just like your brother," he said. "You don't know when to keep your mouth shut." He walked back behind the desk and sat down.

He was upset. Very upset. Eyebrows drawn together, he picked up the Rubik's Cube and began the infernal clicking.

Sage's face burned where he'd hit her. "Have fun," she

said. "I need to look after my grandmother." She stood and started for the office door.

Thomas quit clicking and looked up. "Get back here and sit down," he said. "And shut the hell up. I need to think."

Sage hesitated before she returned to the chair. She'd pushed him, and she didn't want him to hit her again. Or worse. She needed time. "Why don't you indulge me a little?" she said. "At least I deserve to know what's been going on here. And why you killed my brother."

He seemed to think about it for a moment, then said, "Sure, why not."

Thomas rearranged himself in the desk chair and set aside the Rubik's Cube. "I needed to grow my business," he began. "I'd been selling cocaine in Portland for years, since law school, actually. A little here, a little there, just enough to get me some of the luxuries I couldn't otherwise afford without drawing attention. It was all very quiet—me working with my source and managing the business, and a guy in Portland to handle distribution outside my immediate circle. And it was fun and profitable. I enjoyed outsmarting all those stupid people. But you know how it is. People eventually talk to other people, so I stepped back, became invisible. I was done with the kid stuff, and that meant getting my business out of Portland and turning the small things over to smaller people.

"About the time Ross got out of rehab that second time and moved back here, he looked me up. He was bored, broke, couldn't find a job. And he was worried about keeping things going out here for your grandmother. Obviously, business had dropped off. She was still mobile then, but not capable of doing much. He wanted to help her. His motives were pure, I'll give him that.

"We got together a couple times, and I could see he was hurting. My friends in Mexico were pressuring me to move more goods. But to get the business where we all could benefit, I needed a safe place where I could stash product after it came up the coast. It needed to be isolated but close to Portland and located where stuff could easily be transported in all directions.

"When I came out to see Ross one day, I suddenly thought of the boathouse. It was perfect. I offered to rent it from him—just between the two of us—no paperwork. A gentleman's agreement. I told him all he had to do was keep his head down and go about his own business. He agreed. I gave him enough cash to keep him happy and set up accounts for your grandmother and him on the side. I managed them discreetly, I was generous, and I put in money for this and that, nothing that would attract attention. The bills got paid—when he remembered—and their little nest eggs grew.

"I paid your brother very well, and it worked for quite a while. Janice had sharp eyes, but I needed a sharp pair of eyes, so I brought her in. I didn't tell her much, but I found little jobs for her to do from time to time. It gave her some extra cash. Then one night I had to take care of a guy. He'd been screwing up big time. He was part of my crew, so it was easiest to deal with him in the boathouse. Ross heard him screaming. That was in July. Ross didn't like it."

Sage sat there, sickened. She knew he was arrogant, but his cold-bloodedness shocked her. "So, you just killed that man and then you killed my brother. Is that it? What about the people you harm with all those drugs?" she asked. "None of this seems to bother you."

"Nothing makes my day like an ignorant, self-righteous little bitch." Thomas practically spat the words and moved toward her again from behind the desk. "No, it doesn't bother me. Why should it? What kind of stupid, dim person deliberately takes drugs? Everybody knows drugs kill people. If they want to die, I say let them. They're too stupid to live."

He sat on the corner of the desk, looking down at her. "As for Ross, he wasn't thinking clearly. He was drunk all the time and he wouldn't shut up. I couldn't trust him. So yes, to answer your question, I killed him. I had to."

Sage melted into her seat. There, he'd said it. It was on him and him alone. She could feel his anger, his unease. His eyes darted now. She'd gotten under his skin. Cold-blooded notwithstanding, he did not seem comfortable trying to justify having murdered Ross. Somehow, she knew it was just a matter of moments before he did something violent. To her or to Granny. Or both.

"Look at your brother!" he continued. His voice rose again. "Intelligent but weak. He went to rehab twice and still didn't figure out he was killing himself. I didn't have any problem getting rid of him. I just gave him what he wanted."

Enraged, Sage jumped to her feet. "Shame on you, Thomas Kitt, for trying to justify your behavior. Shame on you! People with addictions need help."

"Who helped me?" His voice dripped sarcasm. "Ross got plenty of help. Who helped my family when we lived out of our car?" He banged his hand on the desk and glared at her.

Sage froze in place and glared at him. "I never knew you lived out of a car. But we were always here for you, Tommy." She softened her voice. "Whenever you wanted to come out, and you were out here all the time. We were your friends. We loved you. This was your home, too. You were always welcome here."

"I don't think so," he yelled. "Not so much. You looked down on me. Both of you did!"

"Where did you get that notion? That simply is not true. Don't give me your victim shit." Sage said, trying to keep the fear and anger from her voice. "You were like our brother. You spent the weekends here when we were little kids. We ran around together in high school. What changed?"

Thomas paced around the room. He came to a stop right next to her. "Your messed up little shit of a brother was going to rat us out."

Anger rose like vomit in Sage's throat. She gulped hard. She had to keep talking, to calm him a little. If she flung herself at him, he'd only have more of an excuse to kill her. "I don't believe that," she said. "If he was going to tell anyone about anything, he would have told me first. He never told me anything about you renting the boathouse, not one single thing about you two being in any kind of business together. No, he never would have done that." But she didn't know, did she?

Thomas jammed his finger at her face and she jerked her head back. "I'll tell you what he did," he said. "When I had to get rid of that guy out here, Ross heard us, he was drunk and whimpering like a puppy. The next day, when he was sobered up, he told me I'd have to find a new place to do business. Just like that. He said he wouldn't rent to me anymore, and I should clear out."

Shocked, Sage said, "That makes perfect sense to me. You can't just go killing people on our property."

"I need this place. It's perfect. The right distance from the city, remote. I can run the boat right in here. No cops."

"So, you killed Ross as a matter of convenience?"

"He became a liability."

Thomas straightened up and was quiet for a moment. He hit his left hand against his right fist, clearly enjoying the smacking, fleshy sound. Sage found it unnerving. "Yes, I killed him, and then I took him out in the boat and dumped him overboard. He was going to ruin my business. Satisfied? Got all your damn answers? Let's go outside."

Sage shook her head. "One more question. Where are the drugs you hauled into the boathouse? I've looked. The police looked. There's nothing anywhere."

Thomas chuckled. "So, you got the cops out here? I'm surprised. I may as well tell you, since it no longer matters. There is a container we submerge. It's like a great big cooler.

Waterproof, of course. We pull it out with the hooks that come down from the ceiling—the ones that were used to bring your boat out of the water for winter, when you had a boat, that is. My crew is good. We can get product in or out of there in a matter of minutes."

Sage nodded. It made sense. Nobody was ever on the dock looking or poking sticks in the water to see if something was stashed down in water out of sight. Simple. Workable. Yes. "Thank you for the information. Now, I need to take care of Granny," she said. "It's time for her to get up and eat."

She moved toward the door, but he was ahead of her, blocking her, before she got to it. The grin on his face was menacing, cruel. "Quit worrying about your grandmother. She doesn't need you now."

"What do you mean?" Sage asked, suddenly chilled. She made a motion for the door.

Thomas grabbed her by the arm. "You know what I mean, Sage."

"Granny!" she screamed. She tried to pull away, and he gripped her harder. "You're hurting me, asshole." She struggled, to no avail. "Have you killed her? Do you kill everyone who calls you on your shit? Why did you have to kill Janice? Was she going to rat on you too?"

Thomas said nothing. He pulled her through the office door and drag-marched her through the dining room into the kitchen. When he stopped, Sage caught her breath and said, "What about the sheriff? Is he on the payroll?"

Thomas shook his head and gave her a smug look. "No, he's just stupid," he said.

Sage pulled, and he let go of her arm. "I want to see my grandmother!"

Thomas leaned against the counter, his eyes trained on her. "You can't help her Sage. She was ready to go. She hardly fought at all."

She watched his eyes, looking for the lie. But he was telling the truth. Tears streamed down her face. She might as well cry now. It might be her last chance. She was as good as dead herself. "How did a dear friend become a monster?" she sobbed. "You were such a great kid, so smart, so fun."

Thomas shrugged. "Those things don't matter."

"Well, they did to me and Ross," she said. "I thought we all were life-long friends."

Thomas shrugged. "Things change, don't they."

"What about Donald?"

"What about him?"

"Is he involved in this? He showed up the other day to tell me Ross owed him a bunch of money."

Thomas looked momentarily confused. "Oh, him," he said after a moment. He smiled to himself. "Good old Donald. I forgot about him. I guess I better get one of the guys to pay him before he starts making noise. He's a minor supplier. Ross dealt with Donald. Like so many out here, Donald doesn't know who I am."

He looked around the room. "Time to go," he said. "You might want a jacket."

"Where are we going?" she asked.

"Does it matter?" Thomas grabbed a jacket from a peg in the entry. "Here, put this on. We're going for a walk."

Sage didn't move. Thomas grabbed her arm and yanked her so roughly that she gasped. "Put it on!" he yelled. "I don't have time for this."

Sage's hands shook as she put on the jacket. It was large for her, and heavy. It must have belonged to Ross. Thomas gripped her arm again and moved her toward the back door.

Outside was getting dark and cold. Mist rose from the river, giving the landscape a magical, eerie quality, as if they had walked onto the set of a horror movie. Indeed, she thought, we have. My very own home-grown horror movie.

Gripping Sage's arm, Thomas moved them across the parking lot toward the barn. "Did you find the money I left in the barn for you?" he asked. He chuckled to himself. "Insurance money in case the law came sniffing around. Ross or you would know nothing about it, of course, but the finger would point at you."

Sage didn't answer. Such a childish trick, but it would have worked. While prosecutors built a case against her family, Tommy would have time to relocate. She thought of Granny dead as she stumbled deliberately beside him, trying to slow him down. She felt sickened, sad, and dismayed. He didn't need to kill Granny. Granny couldn't have done anything to hurt him.

She thought about Andy. By now, maybe Andy would be concerned that he hadn't heard from her. Would he try to call her and be alarmed when he couldn't get through? Andy would figure it out, wouldn't he? He wouldn't let her down. He was her only hope. She pretended to trip and lurched forward onto her knees.

Thomas pulled her up hard and rewarded her stumble with a fierce slap in the face. "Knock it off, Sage," he said. "You're not fooling me." He picked up speed, dragging her along beside him. Past the barn and paddock, across the field, past the little cemetery. She looked over her shoulder. There were no lights in the parking lot, no one there looking for her. Into the woods. Where he'd kill her without thinking twice about it. Time was short.

They followed the well-worn animal trail she'd taken on her walks and passed the place where she usually turned around. Thomas paused several times, looked around, and listened. He was on edge. And so was she. She gasped for air. She wondered what it would feel like to die. Would she see Ross in some beautiful place? Or would there be nothing? How far was this monster going to drag her before he killed her?

Sage's ankle hurt, and she lagged at Thomas's side. Every second mattered in what life she had left. Being alive mattered more than she had ever realized. A grim ending awaited her when they reached his destination. She thought of her own death with disbelief. This couldn't happen to her. It was a nightmare. Some horrible nightmare, like the many she had suffered since her assault. She'd wake up as she always had. And yet she knew this wasn't a nightmare and she wouldn't wake up. Their old good friend had killed Ross. She was next.

He swore at her as he dragged her along. She didn't speak. There was no longer any need for conversation. Nothing she said would make a difference.

She wasn't sure how far they'd gone when they entered a small clearing. A dark-colored Land Rover sat there, next to a wider trail that led out of the far side of the clearing. She remembered the rig. Tommy had owned it for years. Sage's mind clicked into action. She felt an alertness she hadn't felt since they'd left the hotel. Would he kill her here, or would he take her somewhere else? Was there a way to escape, or was it already far too late? *Think, dammit!*

She reckoned he'd driven in on the larger trail. It would lead to a paved road somewhere nearby. In the darkness she was completely disoriented. If only she could break away, disappear into the trees and underbrush, and follow the trail out. A long shot. If she did get away from him, even if she got lost in the forest, she'd be able to figure it out in the morning—that is, if he didn't catch her first. It was very cold. And wet. Spending a night in the cold. Better than being dead.

She thought of all the childhood forts she, Ross, and Tommy had built together. She knew how to take cover, how to hide. She could survive a cold night. She wasn't ready to die. Not yet. Not like this. If he was going to kill her, then she would make it loud and messy. She'd fight him and maybe lose. But fight him she would.

Thomas was talking. He held a firm grip on her arm and reached for his gun with his free hand. "This is it, Sage," he said. "I'm sorry. It could have ended much better for both of us."

Sage's brain searched wildly for something—anything—that would distract him. "Don't patronize me, you filthy low-life!" she shouted. "All the money in the world won't fix you." She kicked him in the shin as hard as she could. And she screamed. She screamed as loud as she could, loud enough to be heard at the North Pole.

It worked. It distracted him. Thomas's free hand swung around as if to shoot her, but instead he clapped her face hard with the gun. She heard and felt the crunch as metal collided with her cheek bone. She screamed in pain and fell to the ground.

Sage thought he'd grab her, but he didn't. Instead, she heard a scuffling behind her, but not the expected vise grip of his hand on her arm. She scrambled to her knees and crawled as fast as she was able. Still no one grabbed her. Then to her feet. Clumsy. Staggering. What was going on? She couldn't have disabled him. The gun fired, and she heard more noises behind her. A grunt. A thump. *Don't look back! Don't look!* She ran to the edge of the clearing. The gun fired again. She ducked and kept running. It hadn't hit her! She ran into the brush like a wild thing. She crashed through the underbrush. It didn't matter where she went. She only needed to keep going until he couldn't find her.

Deeper and deeper into the darkness she ran. She heard

noises in the brush as animals took flight. Somewhere a bird screamed. She tripped on a tree root, fell flat, and got up again. Branches scratched her face. She kept running, how far she couldn't guess. She only stopped when she felt her lungs might burst. She had no idea how long she had run or where she was. She looked around her. Listened. For a moment nothing stirred. The only sound she heard was her own ragged breathing.

Now it was time to be quiet, to leave the path she'd created in her wild flight. It was time to creep deeper into the woods where she couldn't be found.

Chapter 30

HOW LONG HAD SHE LAIN THERE, covered with fir boughs, brush, and muck, afraid to move? Ground moisture had soaked through Ross's heavy jacket and her clothing. Even her hair was wet, and she shivered with cold. She thought of her grandmother and the man who had killed her, had killed her brother, killed Janice and others by his own admission. She dared not move. He would kill her if he found her.

Sage knew hours had passed. She couldn't stop shaking. She clenched her teeth until her jaw ached, so they wouldn't chatter. He could be near, waiting for her to give herself away. She didn't allow herself to breathe deeply. It was too risky. She heard movement in the forest. Occasionally a branch snapped. Was it an animal or was it Thomas Kitt, the monster, the man who killed people to satisfy his need to feel superior, to fill the hole in his soul, to enrich himself?

How long would she be safe here? When it got light, she'd be easier to find. Maybe he was just waiting for daylight to come, resting in the Land Rover, eating a sandwich, drinking hot coffee. Sage imagined fearful scenarios as she lay very still, body clenched, afraid to move.

And then she heard him. Tentative steps. One, and then another. Soft as a leaf touching the ground. Getting closer. She held her breath. He wouldn't find her. *Please, no.*

She was not on any trail, she'd made certain of that before she took cover. She'd taken care during the last hundred yards or so before she lay down not to break through the brush as she done earlier. She'd picked up fallen boughs from the recent storm. She'd created a bed in the brush that she hoped looked natural. Invisible.

And then she heard his voice. "Sage, where are you? Sage! Answer me." It wasn't Tommy. But who? She didn't respond. The steps came closer. One, a short pause, and then another. Very close. Nearly close enough to touch. She froze, closed her eyes, and willed herself invisible. She waited for the gunshot that would end her life. And still she didn't move.

"Sage. Come out! You're safe now!"

She stirred, grunted. Stinging like nettles shot through her body. Groaned.

"Sage, it's me. It's Andy. You're safe." A light shone down on her, piercing her cover. Game over.

"Are you okay? Come on out. I'll help you."

Andy turned off his spotlight and pulled back the brush that covered her. She could see his outline in the near-darkness. It would be light soon. She moved a little, tried to struggle to her feet, but her legs were numb, too cold. She found she couldn't move them. Andy reached down with both hands and pulled her to her feet. He put his arms around her and held her tightly.

Tears streamed down Sage's face. She buried her face in his chest and smelled his comforting body, felt his warmth. Her body shook.

Andy released his hold, stepped back a little, still holding her upright, and looked her in the eye. "Are you hurt? Did he do this?" He reached out to touch her swollen face.

Sage jumped back in pain, and her feet stung. "Yow!" She'd forgotten being hit with the gun. She was alive. That was what mattered. And the monster wasn't there. She touched her face. The lump on her cheek felt enormous. "You found me," she said. Her voice sounded unfamiliar and far away.

Andy helped her out of the wet jacket, removed his own coat, and helped her struggle into it. She could feel it, warm from his body, against her soggy shirt. "Yes, I did find you," Andy said. "I wish you could see yourself!" He grinned at her. "You're a mess!"

She reached to feel her wet, matted hair. He wiped a streak of dirt off her face, then pulled her against him again and surrounded her with his arms. His warmth went through her. "Kitt is dead," he said.

Sage stiffened and looked up at him.

"What? How?"

Andy rested his chin on her head. "It seems you have a guardian angel," he said. "When we got to the clearing where the Land Rover was parked, we found him on the ground. His neck had been broken."

Sage jerked back and looked at him again. "He shot at me twice. What on earth happened to him? It makes no sense."

Andy nodded soberly. "Well, it makes sense to me," he said. "That man we call Crazy Phil was Army Special Forces in Vietnam. He knows how to eliminate an enemy."

Sage envisioned the gangly man she'd met on the trail that day, with his soft brown eyes and shy manner. It was hard to picture him killing a spider. "What was he doing there? Why would he kill Thomas?"

Andy's sharp eyes searched hers. "He said he keeps an eye on you. He told the feds you're his sister, and that Kitt was going to kill you. They're with him now, trying to sort that one out."

Sage took a deep breath. She told Andy about her past brief meeting in the woods with Phil. "Thomas did intend to kill me," she said. "He saw me going back to talk to Misty after our lunch. He followed me and saw me stop off at the Hoot Owl, then followed me home and watched me loading the car. He let himself in to the hotel with a key Ross gave him ages ago. He was waiting for me in the office when I went to get Granny up so we could leave. He told me he killed her."

She noticed the sad change in Andy's expression. He nodded slightly. "I'm afraid he did, Sage," he said. "I can't tell you how sorry I am. I liked your grandmother."

Sage blinked back tears. She would have to save those for later. Granny was gone. It hit her like a punch in the gut. She couldn't. Not now. More than sad, she felt confused and overwhelmed. She stomped her feet to get feeling back into them and felt electric prickles all the way up to her thighs. She made fists with her hands, wiggled her arms, shrugged her shoulders.

Andy smiled and said, "Do you think you're going to be okay? Come with me."

On the way back to the clearing, Sage asked, "How did he do it?"

"Do what?"

"Kill Granny." Her voice sounded flat.

Andy stuffed his hands into his jeans. "It looks like he smothered her with a pillow. She looked very calm." They walked a few more steps before he added, "I'm just so sorry, Sage."

She couldn't help herself. She started crying. Would there ever be an end to the sadness in her life? "Yeah, me too," she blubbered.

Andy took her arm, and they walked a while without speaking. "How did you find me?" she asked.

Andy snorted. "That wasn't difficult," he said. "I followed what looked like the trail of a bull moose in full charge. When it ran out, I tracked you. It was easy for me, but I don't think Kitt would have been able to find you. You did a good job."

Sage was quiet for a moment. Then she said, "I can't believe he's dead. I've known him almost all my life. He was our best friend."

"And then he wasn't," said Andy.

"And then he wasn't," she echoed.

Chapter 31

THE CLEARING HELD A GATHERING. Men and women in uniforms, important-looking men in suits, and the puffed-up, self-important Sheriff Terry Thompson. They cheered as Sage and Andy walked into the small open space, and someone handed Sage a Styrofoam cup filled with hot coffee. She felt she didn't belong there, as if she had crashed someone's party. And then she saw Phil sitting on a stump with a blanket around his shoulders, holding his own cup of coffee. He looked even more dazed than she felt.

She walked over to him. He glanced at her shyly before he looked away. She knelt in front of him and took his hands in both of hers. He looked nervous, like he wanted to run away into the woods, but he remained sitting. "Phil, thank you for saving my life. Thank you isn't enough, but it's all I've got right now."

He nodded, and she felt his hands relax in hers. "It's no big deal," he said, finally looking at her with his sad brown eyes. He smiled. "It's what brothers do."

And then she was surrounded. People asking questions, fighting for their turf. Sage put her hands over her ears, and two guys in suits whisked her into a large sedan. She sat in the backseat, shivering. She ached all over. The car was warm inside.

One of the men slid into the passenger seat and closed the door. He looked over the seat at her. "How are you doing?" he asked.

Sage looked at him. He was about her age, good looking. He smiled at her. Smiley face. Perfect white teeth—teeth that had seen braces. She liked his haircut. Nothing else registered. "I'm alive," she said. Or was she? It might have been a dream. She tried to shake off the cold, the forest noises, Thomas Kitt's vise grip on her arm as he'd pulled her through the woods, and those long hours on the wet ground. Scenes came back to her like nightmare fragments, flying into her mind, trying to penetrate the fogginess in her brain.

She felt the road beneath her, the gentle vibration of a car speeding down the highway. She must have fallen asleep. She was in a vehicle with no windows, covered in a blanket, strapped onto a cot. A strange man sat beside her. She saw a tube attached to a plastic bag near his head. The bag contained a clear liquid. What were those things called?

Finally, she felt warm enough. Groggy. "Where am I?"

The man looked at her, smiled, and opened his mouth. He moved his lips and garbled sounds came out. She didn't understand what he was trying to say. And then she felt sleepy again.

She woke up in a bed. Not her bed. A nurse took her pulse. "How do you feel, Ms. Blackthorn?" The nurse looked like a younger version of Betty, with grayish hair cropped short. She wore green scrubs. She had an accent. Australian?

"Where am I?"

The nurse released her wrist and began bustling near the end of the bed. "Good Samaritan Hospital in Portland. Your dinner will be here soon. How do you feel?"

"I feel okay."

The door to the room opened, and a younger woman carried in a dinner tray. She set it on a table next to the bed, while the nurse adjusted the bed to a sitting position. She rotated the table's top, so the tray was in front of Sage, and removed the stainless-steel dome that covered a dinner plate. Sage looked at pale orange salmon, soggy green beans, and abnormally white mashed potatoes. She realized that she was ravenous. A foil packet of margarine sat with a round, white roll on a small plate. A bowl of Jell-O dessert glowed a strange electric green. The strangers left the room, and Sage ate everything on the tray.

When she woke again, two men stood at the end of her bed. Neither were dressed like doctors. The younger one looked like the guy who sat in the car with Sage in the clearing after she came out from her night in the forest. She blinked at them. "Hello."

The older of the two was maybe fifty, with short bristly hair and bushy black eyebrows. He wore a dark suit and black raincoat. He spoke first. "Ms. Blackthorn, we're FBI. We want to ask you some questions. Will that be all right?"

Her brain felt furry, separate from the rest of her, as if it wanted to curl up beside her like a cat and go to sleep. She tried to prod it into action. The younger guy smiled at her. Sage liked his haircut. She smiled at them drunkenly. A nurse entered the room and shooed them out before they could say anything more. She dozed.

The door to her room opened. A doctor came in holding a clipboard. He was short, wiry, with a receding hairline and a spry walk. He made eye contact with Sage and smiled. "Hello Sage, I'm Doctor Ellis. We need to talk for a few minutes." He reached out and shook her hand. "I gave you a healthy dose of Librium earlier, so you could relax. You've had a big shock. You also suffered mild hypothermia, but you'll be all right. You might be confused for several days. It's normal with these drugs."

Sage nodded. He talked more, but she couldn't understand what he was saying. She knew something awful had happened. But the edges were fuzzy. She went to sleep again.

In the morning she was poked and prodded some more. She ate breakfast. Andy brought her clothes. Nurses came in and out. The dapper little doctor told her there was nothing wrong with her, and she could go home. Andy picked her up and drove her downtown to the FBI office. Someone there shoved a cup of coffee into her hand and she began to tell them everything she knew. Everything.

The next day, Andy drove her home. Only it wasn't home anymore. It was a shell. Her family was gone. And when she walked inside the Blackthorn, it felt like Evil had taken up residence while she was away.

It was late morning, sunny and cold. Andy set her things on the floor next to the front stairway. "I'm not going up there," Sage said, and walked to the kitchen. It was as she'd left it. The bag with the sandwiches. Dishes in the sink. She stood at the sink and looked out the window. Down by the boathouse, a cluster of men worked around a large, black container about five feet high that sat on the ground twenty feet or so from the boathouse door. A tow truck waited, parked to the side, to haul it away.

She watched the men as they removed packages from the container and placed them in a white panel truck. The container had been dragged from the water, up the riverbank, and onto the firm ground. It must have been heavy. Sage could see where the shoreline was torn up from the dragging. She felt Andy standing behind her. "He told me where they were storing the drugs," she said to him.

"I know. You told the agents yesterday morning," Andy said. "And then there was Ross's diary. That yielded a trove of useful information according to the Feds."

Oh yes, yesterday morning. Yes, the diary. Somehow, an

entire day had escaped her notice. They had interviewed Andy separately, but she had talked with him over dinner last evening before they headed to their respective hotel rooms. She had slept like the dead.

She stood back from the window. Her brain was still foggy—from the drugs, from shock. Who knew? And there was so much to do. A funeral for Granny, and God only knew what else. "I can't stay here," she said. "I need to get all my clothes packed and leave. I never want to set foot in this place again."

"I understand," Andy said. "Just tell me what you need me to do."

And so, she slogged through it. A week that included a short funeral and burial in the family cemetery for Granny, crowded with many neighbors from Stevenson and even more people, media and curiosity seekers, who had never seen Granny in their lives.

She stayed in a motel in Stevenson, and Andy coaxed her out to the property one last time to choose a few things to take away with her—Susan's trophies and the photos in the office, an old family photo album assembled by Susan when Sage and Ross were young, and Ross's poems—plus the clothing and personal items she'd brought with her in September. They filled a large box with mementos, and Sage shipped it to her apartment in New York.

Andy was with her when she chose the headstones for Granny's and Ross's graves. He chased off the reporters who continued to show up during the days following Thomas

Kitt's destruction of her old life, of so many lives. Andy was there when Sage gave Betty the envelope full of cash that she'd found in the office, money she was certain had come from spa customers who paid in cash during the months before Ross was murdered. Betty cried and said she'd never seen so much money, and Sage made a mental note to take care of Betty once the Blackthorn sold, to allow her to retire with dignity.

Andy helped her find a realtor in Portland and prepare to list the property "as is". He kept things moving when she was too confused to process what was going on around her. Law enforcement swarmed over the property and the surrounding area. Donald the Pothead was among the several people hauled into custody. Andy kept her informed. He also reminded her she was in shock and not to overdo it. She needed time, he said. Where was Phil? She wondered one day. "Gone," Andy told her. "Nobody can find him. He cleared out."

Throughout it all, Sage didn't drink alcohol. She wasn't certain why or how. She knew it wouldn't help. Somehow that was enough.

Finally, at the end of October, Sage boarded a plane and flew home to New York.

Chapter 32

New Year's Eve, 1985

SAGE BLACKTHORN'S HAND SHOOK as she lit the fat candle on her coffee table. She blew out the match and ran water over it in the kitchen sink before putting it in the garbage under the sink. She walked through her living room to the window that looked down four floors to the street outside her building. Traffic was light. Gentle snow fell onto the street and dusted parked cars. The lights in the restaurant across the street and the bar on the corner twinkled through the snowflakes.

Sage folded her arms across her chest and watched the snow. She'd prepared a nice dinner. The only thing missing was the dinner guest. He'd called more than an hour ago, so, where was he? Did she even want to see him? She wasn't certain. She felt uncomfortable. Put upon. She'd said yes, he could come. But now she wasn't sure she'd made the right call. Maybe it was too soon to have someone over alone like this. Her friends in the program said don't get into a relationship for a year. But this wasn't a relationship, or anything close to it. She didn't think of relationships these days. She couldn't.

She turned on the 24-hour classical station and adjusted the volume. She'd been sober seventy-two days now. At first, each day had seemed like an endless slog of Diet Coke and coffee and work and AA meetings—at least one a day—until she could fall into bed at night. Now it was better. At least she wasn't obsessing about or craving alcohol every minute of the day. She had a sponsor, a woman in her forties, sober for fifteen years, with a recently opened gallery in Soho. Karen had explained meeting protocol and was coaching her through the steps. Karen was cool. Sage talked with her every day.

She'd made some new friends from the meetings, professional women about her age, women who did exciting things and had fun. She no longer felt she was the only alcoholic in New York City. She'd learned she wasn't unique. She and her new friends had gone together for dinner a few times. They'd hung out on Christmas Day, seen a movie, and eaten wonderful food. One of them worked for a competing magazine, but they didn't talk about work when they were together. So far, she'd only gone to women's meetings. It felt safer that way. She still wasn't certain how she felt about AA, but she felt okay going to meetings; she wasn't drinking. And when she wasn't drinking, she wasn't getting into trouble.

At her job, Sage was restless. They'd just put the February issue to bed. She had made writing assignments for the late spring issues and was planning to cover a couple of features herself. But she wasn't happy at her job. Nor was she comfortable in her apartment. Yes, it was very nice. Great location, but bad memories that refused to leave the premises.

There was an opening at *Vanity Fair* that would be a move up. She'd heard about someone quitting at *Vogue*, but was that really a good fit? She wanted to make a career move, and she felt compelled to find a new place to live. The buzzer jolted her into the present. At last. She walked to the intercom and picked up the receiver. "This is Sage."

"It's me. Happy New Year!"

She pressed the button to let him in, stepped into the bathroom to check her lipstick. There was a mote of lint on her sweater. She picked it off and opened her door.

When Andy stepped off the elevator he looked momentarily confused. Then he saw her standing at her door and his face lit up. He waved at her. "I made it!" he called. Sage smiled at him. He carried a large, flat box and a small carry-all. When he reached the door, he dropped the bag and hugged her briefly. Sage stepped back into the apartment and tripped on the entry rug. Why was she so nervous? There was no reason to feel nervous about Andy. "C'mon in," she said.

He raised his eyebrows and handed her the box, then brought his bag across the threshold and closed the door behind him. "Things are pretty slow out there with the snow and all," he said. "But I finally made it." He seemed nervous too. He looked around the room. "This is nice."

Sage reached behind him and bolted the door, then walked into the living room. "Yeah, I just got it where I wanted it, and that awful thing happened. I'm going to have to move. I can't bear to live here anymore."

"I understand," was all he said.

She looked at the box and took it to the kitchen to open it. She felt a nudge of wariness as she turned it over on the counter, then rummaged in a drawer for a box-cutter. "Have a seat, Andy," she said. "What did you bring me?"

Andy sat on the sofa and smiled. "A salmon. It's frozen so you don't have to do anything with it right away.

Sage's eyes popped. "A fish? You brought me a *fish?*" She started to laugh.

He laughed too. "Hey, lady, I'm just this Injun from the sticks. Isn't a fish what a guy's supposed to bring a woman?"

She opened the box and beheld the frozen, ten-pound Chinook minus head and guts, carefully packed in dry ice. "Thank you so much," she said. "You can cook it for me before you go home."

The ice between them was broken. She slid the box into the refrigerator. "Now, what can I get you to drink?"

Andy looked at her, and she detected a fleeting look of

concern. "Nothing alcoholic," he said. His voice was flat.

"No, there's no alcohol in the place," she said.

"Good," said Andy. His face showed relief. "How long?"

"Seventy-two days and counting."

"That's great news!" he said. "I decided I don't need to drink alcohol either. My family has an unfortunate history. There's no sense taking chances."

Sage furrowed her eyebrows. "But you own a bar," she said. She retrieved a bottle of sparkling water from the refrigerator.

"Not anymore," he said.

Her hands dropped to her sides. "What? What are you talking about?"

Andy's head was tilted, looking at her. A slow smile appeared on his face. "I sold it. The sale closes January 10."

Sage's head was spinning. "But, what's this about? What are you going to do?" She filled two glasses and added wedges of lime.

"That's one reason I wanted to come out and see you," Andy said. "I've sold the Hoot Owl, because I'm going to medical school."

Sage's mouth made an "o". She handed him a glass. "How can you do this?"

Andy grinned like the Cheshire cat. "It's taken a while," he admitted. "I took my prerequisite courses at Clark College, and then moved on to Portland State to finish. I finally earned my degree the end of fall term. Even got an A in Organic Chemistry. So, I'll be moving to Manhattan—or maybe Brooklyn—in the spring and starting classes at Columbia Medical School as soon as they'll let me."

Sage set her glass on the coffee table. "I had no idea," she said. "Why didn't you tell me earlier?"

Andy sipped his drink. "I didn't tell anyone," he said. "I got the bug when I was in Vietnam. I discovered I liked helping people, I liked patching them up, and there's a lot that needs to be done in tribal communities. I didn't know if I was smart enough. Or if I had the discipline. I figure as a doctor, I can make a big difference in peoples' lives—and there's a great need for docs who will practice in rural areas. Columbia gave me a full-ride scholarship."

This was not the Andy Sage thought she knew. Then she thought again. His military experience, his paramedic training. How deftly he'd treated her ankle when she sprained it so badly. "I'm thrilled for you," she said after what seemed like a long pause. "But why New York?"

Andy stood up and looked around the room. "I'll tell you more as soon as you feed me," he said. "It's been a long day. Where's the bathroom?"

Sage removed the lamb shanks from the oven and tossed the salad. Andy returned and entered the kitchen. "Do you want me to slice the bread?" he asked. She handed him a bread knife.

"That smells unbelievable," he said, nodding toward the lamb.

They ate without much talk. Sage was pleased to have cooked something delicious. Then, as his hunger pangs were sated, Andy began to talk—mostly about what was happening back in Stevenson. "I listed the Hoot Owl right after you left," he told Sage. "I was done with it. I was ready to graduate and move on. And then I heard from Columbia. That's why I invited myself out. I need to get the lay of the land."

Sage rested her fork on her plate. "Wouldn't you be better going to school on the West Coast? This will be such an adjustment. It seems like the hard way to go."

Andy grinned at her. "Really? You did it. You survived in this chaotic city, and apparently found your calling."

"Point taken. But it wasn't easy. I almost killed myself drinking in the process," she said.

"I have the advantage of having a friend in the city," said Andy. "Hopefully that friend will show me around, help me learn the local customs."

Sage smiled. She felt more relaxed by the minute. "Yes, I can do that," she said. "We do have a very strange custom here on New Year's Eve that involves Times Square. Do you want to go uptown and watch the ball drop?"

"No thanks. I'm not in the mood for crowds," Andy said. "You can start showing me the city in the morning."

"So, what do you want to do?" she wondered.

Andy looked around him. His eyes rested on the sofa. "I want to sit over there." He gestured with his head. "I want to sit next to my New York friend and drink some of her excellent coffee and talk about life and acceptance and possibilities."

ACKNOWLEDGEMENTS

Writing is a solitary pursuit. Nevertheless, it takes a village to produce a book. I am truly grateful to everyone who helped me bring this book to life.

A big thanks to early readers—Linda Baldwin, Michaele Dunlap, Lynn Greenwood, Margaret Hurle, Toni Morgan, Janet Nedry, and Wynne Peterson-Nedry—who spotted boo-boos, gave plot suggestions, and kept me going. Encouragement is so important to authors, who tend to live in their heads for way too long.

Special thanks to Michaele Dunlap for an extra edit after the book was completed. There will still be errors. We never catch them all. Any errors in the copy are mine and mine alone.

A huge thank you to Aaron C. Yeagle, consultant, designer, web guru, and longtime friend. Aaron designed the cover, designed and formatted the book, and earns extra accolades for the total revamp of my website, **www.judynedry.com**. Aaron may be reached at **www.aaronyeagleconsulting.com**.

Jennifer King, Portland friend and fellow book group member, takes special pleasure in portrait photography. Big thanks to Jennifer for a beautiful author photo!

Jessie Allen and Margaret Hurle joined me at different times for explorations in Skamania County that were almost too much fun to be counted as work. We enjoyed lovely lunches in Stevenson, discovered a small family cemetery that inspired the one in Blackthorn, soaked and were massaged. It's a dirty job, but somebody had to do it!

The people of Skamania County, Washington, deserve an apology. I moved hillsides, inserted fictional businesses, and was inspired by a number of existing sites. Such is the business of creating. The taking of such liberties with your county and the lovely city of Stevenson have only increased my appreciation for the Columbia Gorge and its beautiful, mystical landscape. The Columbia Gorge is, to me, one of the world's most special places! I feel so honored to have found a story here.

Thanks for reading!

Customer reviews are very important to authors. It's one of the most important ways indie authors get the word out about their books.

Please add a short review on Amazon, Goodreads, or Barnes and Noble and tell me about your experience!

I hope you've enjoyed *Blackthorn*!

Please visit my website https://judynedry.com/an-unholy-alliance/ and use coupon code "BLACKTHORN" to receive the digital version of my first novel, *An Unholy Alliance: An Emma Golden Mystery*, absolutely free! Thanks for your support!

Made in the USA
Columbia, SC
11 April 2019